Wonderful. Simply wonderful. There are so many wonderful, amazing truths in this book that I think every teen girl should read. I found myself in several parts wishing my teenage self would have had that advice, and reading things that my adult self still appreciated and needed to hear. I also love how the Christian messages are presented. You get to see the love of God shown through Poppi's life and the people around her, which I think has an especially meaningful impact. I can't wait to read what Tina writes next!

—Hannah Davis, middle-school teacher

I was hooked from the very beginning when, upon arriving at Camp Eden, Poppi immediately feels, "This is home. I am home." This is exactly how those of us who have been lucky enough to find that "BPOE" (Best Place on Earth) feel about our special places—no place on Earth we would rather be! (For me, it also happens to be a summer camp.)

The writer captures the very essence of a Christian (or any) summer camp experience: the sights, the smells, the traditions, the romance, the music, how lives are changed, along with the problems that are also prevalent.

—Marilyn Ogden, cottage owner,
Norman B. Barr Camp in Lake Geneva, WI

Any camper knows that life at a summer camp has plenty of ups and downs. S'mores and stings, campfires and chaos—it's all there! Christina Hergenrader captures the smiles, songs, and smelly socks of outdoor life in her teen book *Last Summer at Eden*. So pack up your sleeping bag, tennis shoes, and bug spray for a fun reading escape.

—Lisa M. Clark, author of The Messengers *series*

Last Summer at Eden by Christina Hergenrader is a beautifully executed book about love, motivation, and a young girl's relationship with Jesus Christ. This remarkable story is about a nineteen-year-old girl named Poppi who recently moved from her home state of Minnesota to sunny California to work as Camp Eden's summer camp director. While working at Camp Eden, she quickly learns about the devastations that are to come to the enchanting camp. Not only does Poppi wrestle with saving Camp Eden, but she also immediately develops a major crush for camp worker Jake, who, to her, seems to be unmotivated in doing the right thing. This story brings you through a vivid journey of hard work, struggle, and fighting for what is right, all while encompassing God's true love.

This book will surely remind you of your days back in summer camp, the strength in fighting for what is right, and God's plan. *Last Summer at Eden* will definitely reside in your heart and teach you to love God in eccentric ways.

—Brooke Goss, teen and avid YA reader

I loved this book! Oftentimes the importance of outdoor ministry is forgotten, but Christina Hergenrader's characters brought back my own cherished memories, summer loves, and horror stories of campers all getting sick or just two counselors having drama. Beyond a magical camp story, *Last Summer at Eden* delicately and intentionally empowers young women and affirms the always difficult aspect of trusting in God's vision. If I could, I would have every young Christian read this, especially if they are considering working at a camp this summer! It's fun, it's uplifting, and it's refreshing! Great read!

—Allison Westerhoff, program director,
Mt. Cross Ministries

Last Summer at Eden

Last Summer at Eden

Christina Hergenrader

CONCORDIA PUBLISHING HOUSE • SAINT LOUIS

DEDICATION

For all the camp counselors who have given their summers to sing, dance, hike, pray, and share Jesus with kids.

For Amy Cavalleri, whose dear friendship proves that ten weeks together at camp translates into a lifetime of love.

For Jen Ward, who insisted teenagers needed a book like this—and then gave me a library card and told me to learn how to write it.

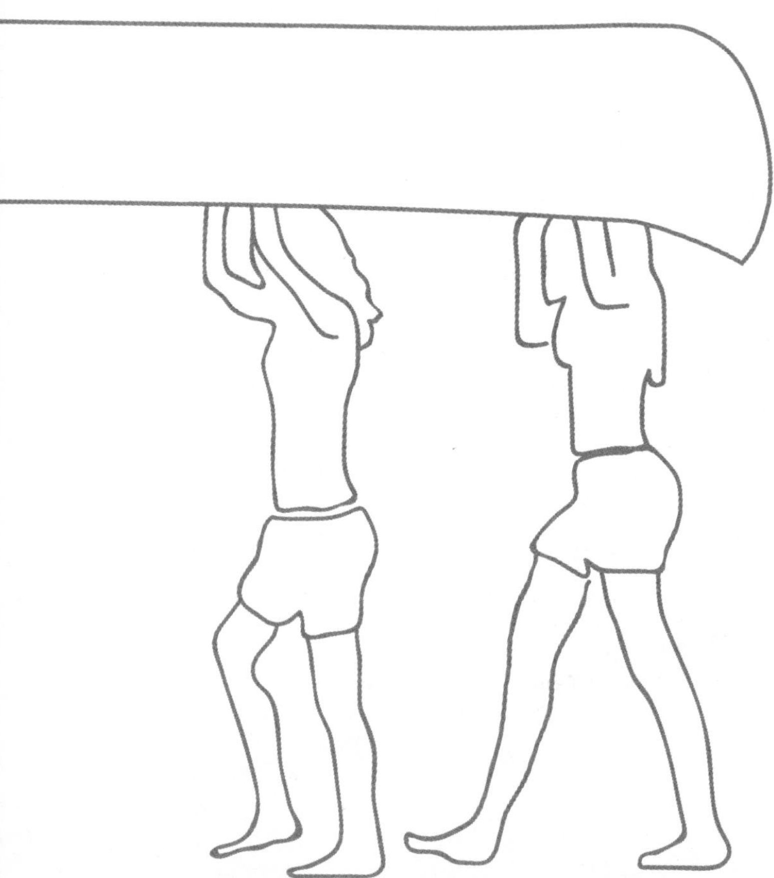

Published 2017 Concordia Publishing House
3558 S. Jefferson Avenue, St. Louis, MO 63118-3968
1-800-325-3040 · www.cph.org

Manufactured in the United States of America

1 2 3 4 5 6 7 8 9 10 26 25 24 23 22 21 20 19 18 17

AUTHOR'S NOTE

Hello, you wonderful reader . . .

Welcome to Camp Eden—a world of sparking campfires, musty cabins, winding trails, goofy skits, singing and dancing counselors, and (of course) a summer crush.

As you read, I hope you can smell the campfire smoke, taste the charred marshmallows, see the rippling lake, feel the sunburn on your cheeks, and hear the guitars playing worship songs.

My favorite part of camp has always been the music. To celebrate the generations of much-loved camp songs, I've named each chapter after a different worship song.

When you read the chapter titles, hum along with their familiar tunes. These songs are surely lodged in your soul from nights around a campfire, and I bet "hearing" them brings back the best memories.

Now you have a little bit of camp playing in your head. The world is a better place.

Wishing you warm campfires, perfectly toasted s'mores, and catchy songs about Jesus.

Christina

BRYAN'S CABIN
ALLELUIA
CAMPFIRE CHAPEL
OFFICE
TO FLOWERHEAD
TRAIL
DIRECTORS' CABIN
& STAFF LOUNGE
PARKING LOT
EDEN
ATHLETIC FIELD

Omega
Alpha
Savior
Truth
Girls' Cabins
Way
Rock
Lord of Life
Light
Boys' Cabins
BBQ
Dining Hall
Crafts Cabin
Patio Tables
Trading Post
Trading Post
North
Lakeside
Canoe Shed
Tire Swing
Lake Eden

CHAPTER 1

"I Love to Tell the Story"

I really want to love Southern California. For four days, I've driven eighty miles an hour toward this tiny camp just outside Los Angeles. I've aimed myself at it like we aim horseshoes at stakes back in Minnesota.

On the map on my phone, I've watched the blinking red dot—Camp Eden—while the blinking blue dot—me, my car, five suitcases—has moved toward it. The carbonation that's bubbled in my stomach sours as I snake my way through the L.A. traffic. It's noon on Tuesday. Where are all these people going? Lunch?

I miss the stoplight turning green because I'm checking the map on my phone. The SUV behind me honks so loud and long that I jump and I feel like I might cry.

I don't like L.A. At all.

In my nineteen years, I have wanted to do so many things right. College was the biggest and most recent one. But my freshman semester at Minnesota State in Mankato did not go well.

That's because last summer, right after graduation and before my first semester of freshman year, my mom died. After that, I couldn't get my thoughts to line up in any order. I really tried. I made deals with myself. "Tomorrow, you have to eat dinner with a friend." "You must read all the history chapters and study for Friday's test." But I couldn't focus—I didn't want to focus.

At Christmas, I told Aunt Lily that college wasn't for me. She tried over and over to get me to go back for spring semester, promising me it would get better. But I stood my ground every time. These conversations felt like scrubbing my skin with an S.O.S. pad.

Aunt Lily was so disappointed and so worried about what I would do with my life. She wanted me to follow through with the plan that Mom and I had laid out for me—Minnesota State, where I would study to become a high school English teacher, like Mom had been. I hated not following through with that plan. I hated the thought I would be letting everyone down. But I had hated college more.

So, a regular four-year school wouldn't be my thing, but I did have something else: eight straight summers at Christ Camp on the Boundary Waters in Minnesota. Those summers had molded me from the inside out. When I no longer had my mom or a college plan, camp was what I was left holding.

I needed more than just a summer job, though. I needed a full-time *career*—with a steady paycheck and insurance and a place to live year-round. I wanted constant sunshine, lots of happy kids, trees that never lost their leaves. Frantically, like you want a blanket when you're shivering, I wanted campfires and Jesus and the steady busyness of camp.

Christ Camp didn't have a job opening for me. But Christ's director, Allen, called his friend Bryan, who was the executive director at Eden Lutheran Camp. I liked the idea of Southern California—far from home and memories and failure. I sent Bryan my résumé and a letter of recommendation from Allen. Immediately he hired me as Eden's summer director.

That was two thousand miles and two months ago. Now, sitting in my old car in horrific L.A. traffic, I have to wonder. Maybe I'm too young to move halfway across the country? Maybe it's too crazy to start a life in a place I've never been, with people I've never met? Maybe I won't be a very good director? Maybe I should have just gotten a job at the Dairy Barn back home?

Wondering about all this—and knowing my whole next life is twenty minutes away—makes me taste the Cheetos I ate for lunch.

CHAPTER 2

"We Believe in God the Father"

Eden's parking lot is pretty much empty, except for a small(ish) Hummer and a black pickup. I turn off my Kia and climb out and into the blinding sun. I collect the four Diet Coke cans from the car floor and toss them into a nearby recycle bin. I need a bathroom.

But right there—on top of the hill overlooking Eden—I have one of the strangest moments of my life.

I have been here before.

I've never been to California—but I feel I have stood right here and looked out at this same scene. When? In a dream? A premonition? Déjà vu? A moment from God?

Standing right here reminds me of what Aunt Lily said about the moment Mom died: "This one second is the one you'll remember forever." In an instant, I recognize that Eden is a place that's buried deep in my consciousness. My soul knows this place in eternal time. The deep part of me that remembers the coolness of peppermint fudge and the dark, earthy smell of trash burning and the soft nubbiness of my favorite quilt. My body remembers this place in these same ways.

Without even turning my head, I know to my left a dozen canoes are stacked near a shed. That shed will be painted bright purple, and the paint will be peeling. This is not a picture of Eden that Bryan put on Instagram. Besides, it's not what I'm seeing so much as what I'm feeling. The sun is hot, but my arms pebble with goose bumps.

My whole body wants to soak up all of this place. L.A. was not for me, but the green stillness of Eden is. It's as if all of it was supposed to happen. This is landing. Horseshoe ringing the pole. I want to crawl inside all of this place and be covered by it.

This. With the perfectly still lake, the quiet forest, the Lincoln Log cabins lined up . . . this is home.

I am home.

CHAPTER 3

"Big, Big House"

My first conversation with Bryan Simes—Eden's executive director—was in late February. It was over the phone, and it was kind of horrible. He called on the coldest night of the year, while I was sitting in our farmhouse's dim kitchen, packing boxes of dishes with Dad and Uncle Ed.

In Minnesota it was only six o'clock, yet it was already as dark as midnight. Because I had been packing all day, because snow had been falling for hours, because I was probably a little depressed, I just wanted to curl up in my warm bed and pull the quilt over my head.

My dad is an alcoholic, which is why my parents divorced. Dad isn't drunk all the time, and he's never loud or violent when he's drinking. That night, while Dad was helping at the farmhouse I had shared with Mom, he was sober and shaky.

The easiest way to explain my dad's drinking—and my parents' divorce—is that Dad is very sensitive. He drinks because it helps him mute his own feelings. Over the years, I've accepted that Dad is sweet, sentimental, quiet, fragile—and completely unreliable. My mom couldn't stand the uncertainty of a life with him. After years of trying to get my dad help, my mom filed for divorce. I was nine.

Dad, my mom's brothers, and Aunt Lily decided to sell the farmhouse so I would have money to pay for school. Then, after I failed, the money was meant to help with my living expenses.

Mom had inherited the house from her parents, so it was full of seventy years of junk and memories. Dad and my uncles came over almost every day that winter and together we cleaned and organized and avoided talking about anything too hard. Now that Mom was gone, all of them—my mom's side of the family and my dad's—were working so hard to make sure I would be okay.

That February night when I answered Bryan's call, my voice was gravelly. Allen had given me such a glowing recommendation that Bryan started the conversation by offering me the job as Eden's summer director.

"Really?" I couldn't believe it. I'd be a boss at a California camp—just like that. I had to be sure. "I would be the summer *director*?"

Bryan explained that Eden was tiny—only forty-six campers and six counselors. Eden's usual summer director was taking college classes and wasn't planning to come back. Bryan said he was excited about bringing me out to be in charge of Eden's ten weeks of summer camp. "Allen has told me about your energy, Poppi, and what a hard worker you are. Eden is struggling to stay alive. I think you could be our shot in the arm."

"What do you mean, 'struggling to stay alive'?" I didn't like this. I wasn't strong enough to keep anything alive. I realized this with a dull ache, like when you have the flu and someone announces you have to go to school.

"This is our smallest group of campers ever," Bryan explained. "And I'm having trouble finding staff to come back to such a small camp. I know you're young, Poppi, but you have a lot of camp experience. And I like that you're not from Eden. We need some cross-pollination from a strong camp like Christ."

"I could help Eden," I said, even as I wondered if I really could. I really *wanted* to. I loved the idea of a small camp. Everything in my life . . . from my tiny town to my even tinier school . . . has been small. "You're sure it's okay I'm only nineteen?"

"Sure. It's different at a small camp," Bryan explained. "Our last summer director was only nineteen too. In fact, the association of churches that owns Eden has thought about bringing on board a winter retreat director, to do family reunions and church groups in the off-season. Is that something you'd be interested in?"

Now I was fully awake, standing in the mudroom of our house. "Yes," I said, excited. "Yes! I would really like to be in California through the winter. I would love to stay out there long term."

Bryan's voice was so smooth, so bright, that I could tell it wasn't dark yet in L.A., that it wasn't twenty degrees below zero there. He was talking loudly and happily, like you do at noon, on the beach, in July. My responses—in my rusty, dark, tired voice—couldn't match his sunny one.

As Bryan told me about Eden, I stared into my childhood kitchen. Dad was sitting at the big oak table I had scratched with a pocketknife when I was six. Uncle Jim peeled magnets from the humming fridge and a list of Mom's medications fluttered to the ground. Every cabinet, drawer, tile, and counter was heavy with history.

Uncle Ed—who at this moment was crouched down, pulling plastic cups from a low shelf—still treats me like I'm about nine years old. He tells me the weather report and reminds me if I need to wear long underwear or rain boots. He tells me it's time to go to bed. He once read an article that girls don't get enough calcium, so he always sets a glass of milk next to any meal I'm eating. Even if it includes broccoli (which has plenty of calcium) and cheese.

But on the other end of the phone—probably sitting outside in shorts—Bryan was talking to me like I was already grown up. He told me how I would be in charge of three other directors. One guy was the cook. The other guy would take care of the trails and the male counselors. And there was a girl, Natalie, who would be the nurse and the boss of the female counselors. They were all my age, but I would be in charge. The boss of the other directors. I would also be responsible for Eden's financials and paying the counselors.

This felt like an invitation to adulthood. California would let me grow up. Leaving home would make me strong enough to be the summer director. I *did* have good ideas about camp. So what if I was only old enough to be a counselor at most camps? If Bryan was willing to make me the leader, then I would prove he was right.

Four years of studying, or start my career now? Living with my Uncle Ed and his family in Minnesota, or hiking and singing at Eden in California?

I wanted to live at a place where my voice could be as loud and friendly as Bryan's, even in February. I wanted to trick the system and start my career now. So, even though I was afraid I wasn't strong enough, I said yes to his job offer. Yes to all of it.

Over the next three months, Bryan emailed me an official application, employee training manuals, and summer calendars. We became friends on Facebook, where he posted about hiring summer counselors and reminders for kids to register for camp.

As Aunt Lily and my uncles sold the house, as men from church picked up our furniture, as I rented a storage unit in the nearby town of Blue Earth and packed the rest of my past in there, I checked my phone constantly for updates from Eden. As I closed down this Minnesota life, the California one was unwinding, waiting for me.

CHAPTER 4

"Sanctuary"

When I find Bryan in the camp office, he shakes my hand, offers me a chair, and says he has important news. He sits behind an enormous desk, left ankle on his right knee, and bounces his foot against the drawer. He's nervous.

"Is it good news?" I collapse into the chair. It's disorienting to be here. After all the packing and planning and driving, my head buzzes with too many what-ifs and Diet Cokes.

"I believe it's very good news." Bryan leans forward. He looks different from his profile picture. On Facebook, he's tan with short blond hair. But under the fluorescent lights of his tiny office, his face looks gray. He mentioned he was twenty-eight and that he had been at Eden six years. He looks more like forty. A tired forty.

"Okay." I'm not really that surprised Bryan has news. Something had changed with him. In April, right around Easter, his Facebook posts ended. He stopped sending me updates about the counselors he had hired. Instead of answering my emails a few hours later, he took days. This sudden communication drop-off had felt weird, but I decided it was just part of the transition. In a month, I would be running Eden's summer program. He was just trying to untangle himself from it and let me take over.

Now I'm not sure. He's not looking me in the eye or asking about my trip. I feel like I'm the only customer in a café that closed three hours ago, like he's impatient to get rid of me.

"Look, Poppi. First, I'm supergrateful you've come. Don't get the impression I'm not appreciative. I remember what you said about your rough year. I know that it took a lot of guts for you to drive out here."

"Thanks. I'm supergrateful to be here." My voice is a little squeaky, but it feels important to get that on the record, before he builds up to his news.

"But things have changed here in the past month. And since we haven't officially started summer yet, there's time for you to head back home." He leans back and looks out the window, like something's caught his eye. I turn too, but the patio is vacant.

My heart is pounding. All I can do for a moment is stare at him. Is he *kidding*? I've left everything I know to take this giant leap into adulthood, and he tells me to turn right around and go *back*? Bryan looks at me, and I finally find my voice, even if it's just a whisper. "You want me to go back to Minnesota?"

"You don't have to, I guess. My other idea is that you could try another camp." He shrugs but seems to be sincere. "I've heard that Camp Lone Star still needs counselors. It's right near Austin, and they run a great summer program."

"Wait. Eden isn't having camp this summer?"

He hesitates, but then says, "We are running camp this summer. But yesterday, my old summer director, Jake, said he would come back. He'll work out better for us, since he knows the ropes. He'll be a sophomore at UCLA, so he can head back there in August after camp."

"But that's the whole point. I'm not here as only the summer director. Remember? I'm staying on through the winter—to host the retreats. Like we talked about?" Could he really have forgotten Eden is my career plan? Maybe Aunt Lily was right about expecting too much from this job.

"Yeah." He frowns and keeps kicking his desk. He looks down, looks up at the ceiling, looks anywhere but at me. "That's our biggest change around here. At the end of the summer, Eden will close. Just last week, I got an offer from a corporation. They're buying the land for five million dollars. And obviously, I couldn't say no to that."

"*What?*" My heart is pounding so hard, I can feel it in my sinuses. Bryan finally looks at me. "Why didn't you tell me the camp was for sale? I wouldn't have taken this job. I wouldn't have come all this way!"

"Eden was never for sale, *exactly*. It's just that we keep getting fewer kids and it's so hard to find counselors. This spring, STUF—this personal storage company—approached me. They love this space for their corporate offices. The CEO digs the lake. He wants an office overlooking it." Bryan studies the trees around the patio again. "Really a cool use for this space, you know?"

"But this space is a camp. It's not so some CEO can have a nice view. It's a place for kids to play outside and get dirty and learn about Jesus—"

"Are you worried about where to go, Poppi?" Bryan's voice makes it clear I'm a problem he has to get rid of. "We'll get you settled someplace else."

Suddenly I'm back in my cold, dark Minnesota kitchen, waiting for Uncle Ed to tell me when to go to bed. Decisions happening to me. Following orders.

"Come on, tell me where you want to work this summer." Bryan leans forward, and I can smell cough drops on his breath. "I can call Camp Lone Star right now. Or if you're set on California, there's also Mount Cross up north."

I'm quiet for a moment, considering his words without really considering them. Because I already know. "I want to stay at Eden. I think I'm supposed to be here." I remember that moment in the parking lot. "Like, I know this sounds insane, but Eden is home already. I can *feel* it."

"Huh," he says, furrowing his brow at me. He's not trying to hide that he totally believes I'm insane. "I wouldn't get too emotional here. Decisions are harder when you complicate them with too many feelings." He stands. I think I'm getting kicked out of his office.

"What about you?" I ask. "You've been here a long time. Don't you need a job? Where will you go?"

"I'm headed to Michigan at the end of the summer. I'm going to sell insurance with my dad. I've always been good at knowing when it's time to move forward."

Maybe that's wise. I shouldn't base my future on one feeling, should I? Maybe I should just hop in my car and start driving to Texas. Or back to Minnesota.

But camp starts at Eden in just a few days. In fact, the counselors will arrive tomorrow. For months, I've thought about coming here, about these kids and counselors and our summer together. This little camp, struggling to stay alive—I want to be *here*. I'm certain of it. "I'll plan where to go next when the summer ends. For now, I can still work as the summer director, right?"

"Okay." Bryan stands and puts his hands on his hips. "Yes. I'll let Jake know you're here for the summer."

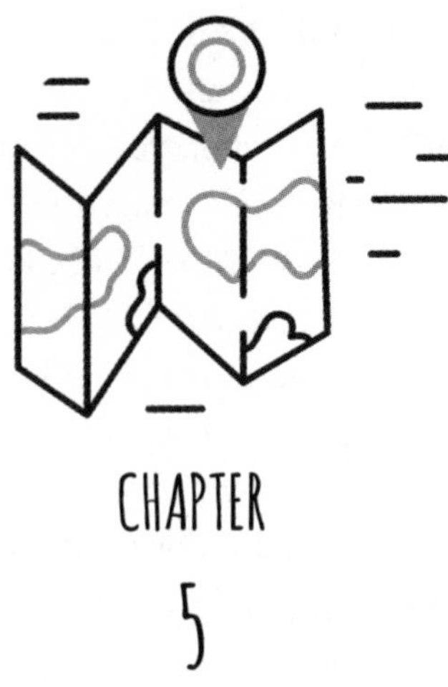

CHAPTER 5

"Everybody Ought to Know"

While I'm pulling my suitcases from the trunk, I hear a voice behind me.

"Hey there. I didn't know you were already here."

I turn to see a tall guy walking across the parking lot. Thick eyebrows, blue eyes, and the kind of nose that would be too big for most faces but instead makes his more interesting.

"Ummm. Yep. About an hour ago, actually." Who is this? "I'm Poppi."

He's wearing a pale blue shirt with an alligator on it and expensive-looking dark-washed jeans. His pants fit so perfectly that he either is the body double of a mannequin or gets his jeans tailored. It's probably his Hummer too.

"I'm Jake." We look at each other. His eyes move down my long, pale hair, past my faded red Minneapolis tank top, linger on my cutoff jean shorts, and finally to my old Chacos. "Straight from Minnesota, right?"

I cross my arms over my chest. Is he checking me out? "Yes. And you?"

"I'm from Dallas. But I go to school at UCLA. So now I'm from here."

The parking lot is hot, and he's standing just a little too close. I want to be by myself, by the lake, back in that moment when I was certain I should be here. Or hiking the trails, with time and space to think about Bryan's news. Anywhere else but here. "So. Um. You're the old summer director? The one who wasn't going to come back?"

"I just decided yesterday. I heard about STUF turning Eden into some kind of corporate campus. I wanted one more summer here."

"Bryan told me about you. You've been here a long time, right? You were the summer director the past couple of years?"

"This is my tenth summer. Six as a camper. Two as a counselor. Two as director of the summer program." Jake pokes his tongue in his cheek and keeps studying me.

"So, I'll be your boss then? That's awkward." Maybe I should just volunteer to let him take over. Technically the job is mine, but it would make more sense to let Jake be the director. Except, what about cross-pollination? What about my plans for Eden?

"I don't think it has to be awkward. It takes a lot of time to be the summer director, and I'll be too busy with summer classes." I can't tell if he's being nice or if he's being superior. His eyes seem to be taking in layers of me, like a microscope that's studying things I don't even know about myself. I back away. I don't want this guy to understand layers of me.

Maybe it's the Hummer looming behind him or the way he's staring me down, but he is not one who wants a boss. About that I am sure.

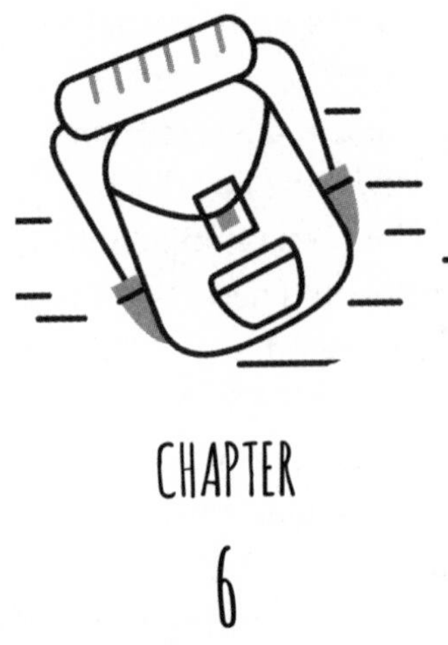

CHAPTER 6

"I've Got Peace Like a River"

"Poppi! I'm Natalie!" A big blonde girl bounds from one of the cabins. Natalie is a good four inches taller than me—about five ten—with a wide, white smile. "Omigosh, I've been *dying* to meet you." She gives me a long, hard hug. "I've been here for two days thinking, *WHERE* IS *SHE?* because it is *so* time to get this summer started!"

Natalie starts shaking her shoulders and swinging her hips. Then she breaks into a full-on dance. Her mouth is open and she's swinging her head from side to side. She doesn't seem to care there's no music.

"You look freaked out. You know the Pink song, right? 'Get this party started'? I've been playing it nonstop. Like, get this summer started!"

"I have no idea what you're talking about." I do sound a little freaked out.

Natalie stares at me. "You are kidding. Don't tell me you aren't a Pink fan. Girls our age *have* to love Pink. She is, absolutely, the strong female role model for us."

"Okay. Maybe so," I laugh. "Tell me about yourself." I slide onto the picnic table sitting outside the cabin. "We're roommates, right?"

"Yes. Oh, sorry! I'm always too friendly too fast. It's my lack of boundaries. Let's start over." She holds out her hand and I shake it. "I'm Natalie from Pasadena. You know? Right outside L.A.? Rose Parade? I'll be a senior next year at South Pasadena High. Go, Tigers!" She makes claw hands and lets out a loud growl. I smile because she is so cute. "I have three older sisters, so I'm the spoiled, whiny baby of the family." She grins. She has chocolate on her front tooth. "That's all me!"

"Is this your first summer at camp?" I ask. Natalie is nothing like my friends at Christ Camp. She's wearing a short denim dress and either false eyelashes or several coats of really good mascara. She has a narrow ridge of black roots, and her perfume smells like a box of vanilla cupcakes.

"Nope. Number nine. Mom and Dad feel like I watch too much TV so they send me here every summer. Since third grade. After a while, this crazy place just kind of grew on me, you know? It's my first summer as a director, though. I'm in charge of the girl counselors. And I'm the nurse. I mean, obviously I'll have help. Eva—her husband, Mike, is on the Association board—lives close. She can come out if we have an emergency."

"I'm so glad we're working together," I say. And I mean it. I don't know how anyone could not like Natalie. Already, in the first few minutes of meeting her, I feel like I can trust her. "So, I've talked to Bryan and I've talked to Jake, and now I'm trying to make sense of what's going on around here."

"Well, you've come to the right person because I will tell you exactly what. Bryan is thrilled because he's sold Eden to STUF, and they just want the land for their Our-CEO-Likes-to-Hear-Birds-While-He-Works corporate offices."

"Why would Bryan do that? He's the executive director. Who sells their house and their job right out from under themselves?"

"Bryan does. He's been here too long. Like year after year, his own loneliness has frozen him into this bitter person." She grins. "Sorry, that's psychoanalyzing. My sisters hate when I do that."

"And the association of churches agrees? Bryan says there's six people that are voting. All of them are okay with selling the camp they created and have supported for decades?"

"Yes? No?" She holds up her hands. "Who knows? Eva says they're all freaking out. They can't decide if they should take STUF's offer or not. From what she told me the other day, two of the churches are done with Eden, two aren't sure, and two don't want to sell."

"Wait. The Association might not sell? Eden might stay open after August? Bryan didn't say that. He made it sound as if he'd already accepted their offer."

"The Association has been having all these meetings to decide what to do." Natalie shakes her head. "I don't think anyone really knows right now. Eva said we might not know until the end of this weird summer."

"Yeah. It'll be a weird summer. What about Jake? Do you think it'll be awkward that, technically, I'm his boss?"

"Oh, he'll be busy with his summer classes. But he knows everything about Eden. Having him here will be a huge help to you." She wraps her arm around my shoulder. "Okay! Enough about Jake. I have an entire Jake Warning Speech to give you, but it can wait until later. Give me your story. Minnesota, right? College dropout?" She's grinning, so I don't think she's being mean. I smile back.

"Right. I'm from a little farm town. Pretty much the opposite of L.A."

"I can totally see that. You've got the willowy, scrubbed-up thing going on." She squints at me. "I'm calling you Gwyneth Paltrow."

"Gwyneth Paltrow? The pretty actress? The one whose mom died?"

"You're thinking of her dad. And that was years ago. Although you're right. She has been very fragile since then—" Natalie covers her mouth. "Wait. Did your dad just die? I feel totally weird asking you that, but you're fragile too. I can, like, *feel* your fragility."

"My mom. Last summer. From cancer. I actually didn't go to camp last summer because I was helping take care of her."

"Awww, Poppi." Natalie hugs me for the third time in ten minutes. "How are you doing? I mean, *really*? We're living about four feet apart all summer so you have to be totally honest with me. Are you doing therapy? antidepressants? both?"

"Therapy, actually. Or I was. Back in Minnesota, with my aunt. She's a school counselor. But being here might be exactly what I need. I love being outside and active. It's guaranteed healing."

"I know you're totally like, 'Stop with the Gwyneth stuff!' but you must know that's *exactly* what she did after her dad died. She started Goop and turned to all this really natural stuff. Oh, wait. Don't tell me you're a vegan. Vegans have, like, nothing to eat at camp."

"Natalie, I grew up next to a feedlot. Vegans are arrested in my hometown."

"In L.A. you're arrested for not being on a diet. I'm Paleo right now. And I know you're wondering why I'm so fat then, but it's because I just started. You'll see. By August, I'll be as skinny as you."

"You're not fat."

"I love you already." She kisses my cheek. "Okay. And now I will give you the Natalie Hatfield tour of Eden and tell you absolutely everything you never wanted to know about this crazy place."

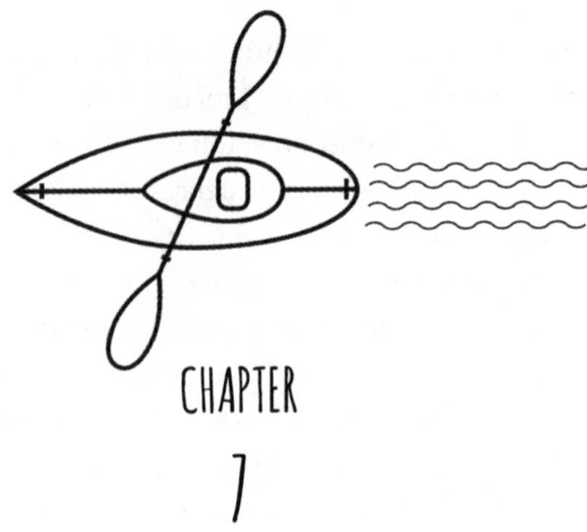

CHAPTER

7

"Hip, Hip, Hip Hippopotamus"

Natalie's tour is three hours long, and she talks the whole time. Here's what I learned: Eden is different from Christ Camp in almost every way. At Christ, there are lots of lakes and rivers, and every camper becomes an expert kayaker.

Eden has only one lake—it's not huge and feels more like a movie backdrop than a place to actually canoe. The camp is almost a hundred acres, and the lake itself is just one whole acre.

The room I'll share with Natalie is in the directors' cabin, and it only holds two beds, with a tiny closet between them. Outside our door is the staff lounge, where the counselors will meet every morning for meetings and devotions. On the other side of the lounge, Jake and Pete, the camp cook, share a little room exactly like ours.

Another difference is that oak trees grow everywhere at Christ. They're like the camp itself, with deep roots and gigantic branches that stretch wide and give shade. But the trees at Eden are pines—straight up with shallow roots. Instead of giving shade, they drop big cones and millions of little needles. The needles are everywhere—heaped in piles along the trails, floating in the lake, and covering the roofs.

Three summers ago at Christ, we updated the cabins with air conditioning, new bunk beds, and huge bathrooms. But Eden's cabins are right out of the 1970s. The beds smell like thousands of wet towels have dried on them. There is only one community girl bathroom and one community boy bathroom. And they both stink like old sewage.

Even with the smells and maintenance problems, Eden wins the prize for the prettiest. It's the mountains in the distance. It's the thousands of trees so green they look like they've been Photoshopped. It's the sky that's cerulean blue and so clear. And I love how small and rustic Eden is. It's like my hometown, not trying to prove anything. But with so much potential.

Eden is so charming that I find it hard to remember that L.A.'s skyscrapers and strip malls and crowded highways are only twenty minutes away. The air feels and smells clean at Eden—like the oxygen is scrubbing out my lungs.

Actually, Eden is just like its namesake. It's beautiful in that way you never get over—and yet it feels abandoned. Maybe it's because the campers aren't here yet. That's part of it. But Eden is neglected. Signs are falling down. The door to the arts and crafts cabin is hanging by one hinge. The trail markers are so sun-faded they're unreadable.

I keep asking Natalie what's going on here. Why don't more kids come? How did Eden get to this point? Why neglect such a beautiful place?

Natalie says it's because Southern California is too cynical to appreciate Eden. The culture is too fast-paced, too glossy. A quaint camp like Eden doesn't fit with that.

But that isn't true. I have met cynical kids. At Christ Camp we had really, really messed-up kids who deserved to be sarcastic and suspicious. But they all loved camp. By the end of the summer, camp had changed them.

Why can't that happen at Eden too?

CHAPTER 8

"Here I Am to Worship"

After Natalie helps me unpack, we walk through the late-afternoon sunshine pouring through the trees and up The Hill to the dining hall. Natalie named The Hill "capital T, capital H" because it's so steep, I'm a little out of breath when we reach the top. Climbing this to get to meals will be a workout for my unused muscles.

The dining hall is very old but striking. Dark wooden beams run the length of the A-frame room. Big windows provide an overlook of the lake and mountains. Six tables (one for each cabin) are pushed against the wall.

At Christ Camp, we had sixteen cabins and lots of staff—both directors and junior counselors. But at Eden, there are only three girl cabins and three boy cabins. The kids stay the whole ten weeks, which is also different from most camps. I wonder if more kids would come to Eden if they didn't have to commit to the whole summer.

Natalie pushes the swinging doors open into the big kitchen. There's an island in the middle, and pots as big as tubs and pans that could be weapons hang from the ceiling. "We're on our own for dinner," she tells me.

In a pantry off to the side, rows of spaghetti sauce, canned corn, and big sacks of flour rest on the floor. Four old refrigerators hum on one side, and a stove with sixteen burners takes up the entire length of the other wall.

Natalie disappears into the pantry and comes out with a package of hamburger buns and huge white bucket of peanut butter. "This is all I can find. And I know the bread isn't Paleo, but the peanut butter totally is." She pops the lid off the bucket and sticks in a knife. "Wait. Peanut butter is Paleo, right?"

"I have no idea. Want me to cook something? I could make spaghetti for us."

"Nah. Pete is a grumpy cook. Sometimes he just goes on strike. Over the next two and a half months, you'll have plenty of chances to step in with spaghetti. Besides, I don't feel like cleaning up tonight."

Just then, a short guy pushes open the door and comes into the kitchen and asks, "Want the good news or bad news?" He has longish, sandy-blond hair and a blue T-shirt that says, "Eden—2016." He stops in front of me and salutes. "I'm Pete. Second summer as cook. Freshman at Humboldt State. Welcome."

"Poppi," I say, but he's already in the pantry, and I don't think he hears me.

"Both," Natalie says. "But give us the bad news first." She licks the knife and then smashes the bun together. Pete steps out of the pantry, and she holds the sandwich out to him. "Want one?"

"No. That looks disgusting." He glances inside the bucket. "Don't eat all that. We don't have another delivery until Tuesday." Then he goes back into the pantry.

Pete's bad news is that Savannah, Jake's younger sister, isn't coming back this summer. Everyone loved Savannah, but she's interning with the Dallas Ballet Company.

The good news is that Beth, another counselor, is coming at the last minute. She's the daughter of Mike and Eva Browne. She's only sixteen, which seems crazy young to be in charge of a cabin of kids. But Natalie says Beth has grown up around Eden and will be just fine as a counselor.

Pete kicks out a huge crate filled with potatoes. "Counselors arrive tomorrow midmorning. We'll have a fancy lunch of real baked potatoes. I need to get those ready today. Can someone grill burgers tomorrow afternoon? We'll eat at five."

"I'm happy to help," I say.

"Glad to hear it." Pete grabs the hamburger buns and twists the bag closed. "When you're this short-staffed, we have to all pitch in."

Earlier, Natalie had told me that she had a crush on Pete last summer, but he had told her that she was the kind of girl he found interesting but not attractive. Which seems a little mean. Or like a guy who's not paying a lot of attention to how sensitive girls are.

"So, there's Beth," I say. "And the other counselors? They're a little older, right?"

"The other two female counselors are Emmy and Ellie. They're both seventeen. My age," Natalie says. "I think the counselors for the boys are all seventeen this summer too."

"Seventeen? You had to be out of high school to be a counselor at Christ Camp."

"Like I said, things are different at Eden," Pete says. "Think of us as every underdog sports team in history. It doesn't seem like we should be able to make this work, but somehow we always do." He uses a paring knife to cut an *X* in each of the potatoes. "But to make it work, all of us pitch in together. And we don't follow the rules other camps follow."

"And Bryan?" I ask. "He helps with cooking and stuff?"

"Some," Pete says, but Natalie is shaking her head. He looks at her. "Yeah, I guess he was pretty worthless last summer."

Natalie finishes her sandwich. "He will be so checked out this summer. You can give up on him already."

"Okay." I feel equally excited and terrified about this. For so many years, I've lived under all these layers of protection—a protective mom, my uncles living so close, our small town, tiny school. Then, suddenly, life peeled all those layers away. But I'm ready for the front lines of whatever this summer hands us.

"So, the counselors will be here in twenty-four hours," I say and look down at the list I made earlier. "Pete, you obviously have the meals covered?"

"Always. And the trails. I've cleared most of them. I'll finish the last two after we're done here."

Natalie raises her hand. "I've cleaned the cabins and bathrooms. Which, by the way, were *waaaay* nasty. We still need wood for the fire pits, but Jake can take care of that."

"Jake can take care of what?"

We all turn to see him coming through the door, crunching on an apple. The screen door slams behind him, and his eyes dart around the kitchen before landing on me.

"We're making a list of what needs to get done before summer starts." I glance toward him, then immediately back to my list. Jake's tallness, his attractiveness, and his general confidence make him look like a leader. And when he walks over to look at my list, I feel like a substitute teacher. But who cares? I got this job legitimately. I am the boss. "We'll all meet the counselors in the parking lot and help them get moved in—"

"Are we just going to act like Eden isn't closing?" He takes a bite of his apple. Then, *while* he's chewing, he says, "If I were you, I'd start with a meeting. Tell the counselors about STUF."

"I will tell them about STUF. I just thought we should get them moved in first."

"Do you understand that Eden will be bulldozed?" He bites into the apple again. It feels too intimate to watch him eat that apple. "We're just going to pretend like it's business as usual? Just run summer camp like normal?"

"I totally am," Natalie says. "Absolutely. I will give the kids one last, good summer. Or—and don't forget this, cynical Jake Bass—maybe it won't be. Maybe the Association will decide to say no to five million bucks."

The look Jake gives Natalie is so condescending, I step in front of her to protect her.

"What else can we do, man?" Pete stabs another potato. "Spend the summer crying? Don't you see? For the kids and the counselors, everything has to be totally normal."

"Not totally normal! Not camp as usual!" I screech. "We will make this the best summer of their lives. Maybe if everything goes really well, we can be the ones who save Eden."

"How do you figure that, Minnesota?" Jake is squinting at me and chewing.

"I don't know," I say, ignoring the "Minnesota." "By running a really good summer program. By raising money. By spreading the word so more campers enroll next year." I'm just getting warmed up here, and I like the way my ideas sound. "Eden might be on life support, but I am not calling in hospice. We can resurrect it."

"Five million dollars," Jake says, very slowly. "Or keeping this place open for forty-six campers. If you had the choice, which would you pick?"

"I'm picking the campers. I *have* picked them. I stayed here instead of driving back to Minnesota." My voice sounds venomous now. "Of course I stayed here. Because where I'm from, camp is not about making money. You don't close it and call it progress. You don't sell it so a CEO can have a nice view. You fight for the kids."

"Whoa." Natalie stands up, and her fake-eyelashed eyes are even huger. "Poppi, we all want to fight with you. Seriously. We love this place. Something will work before August. We are your Team Eden."

"All of you?" I'm drill-sergeant yelling. I look at them. "Do you really believe we can save Eden? Are you going to do what it takes? Are all of you on Team Eden?" I don't have to wonder where this passion is coming from. That moment by the lake—I want Eden to be my home. I want to *know* like that. I want to hold on to this. Fight for this.

"Yes ma'am," Pete says, nodding. "I believe that good will prevail here." He looks at Jake. "You think we can do this, right? Team Eden?"

"Do *what,* exactly?" Jake takes another bite of his apple. "This isn't some movie where we all fight and then magically overcome the bad guys in the name of Jesus and nature. This is real life."

"I am *aware* of real life." My voice is sticky with tears. From the corner of my eye, I see Natalie shaking her head at Jake. "I'm the one who predicted you didn't want a boss. I can see I'm right."

"This isn't about me wanting a boss." Jake lowers his voice. He's trying to soothe me now. "This is about being fair to the counselors and campers who are coming. About being fair to the Association. Just because *you* want something to work doesn't mean it will. I'm just suggesting that if we want to make this summer different, we should probably have a plan for that."

"I don't know what my plan is yet." Hot tears blur my vision. "I mean, I do know. My plan is to make this the very best summer we can." I stomp over to the screen door.

Before I step outside, I turn back to Jake. I say the only thing I can think of. "And for the record, *you* are not invited to be on Team Eden."

CHAPTER 9

"Happiness Is the Lord"

The next morning, the counselors come to Eden. Beth arrives first. She's the sixteen-year-old daughter of Mike and Eva, and right away I like her very much. She wears a Patagonia backpack, her blonde hair in two French braids, black athletic shorts, and Chacos.

As I help her lug her trunk and duffel bag to her cabin, she tells me everything she'll do with her girls this summer. "As soon as I found out I got to work as a counselor, I started making these Care Crosses." Beth opens one of the boxes we just carried into her cabin, which is called Alpha. "I raided the recycling at school until I found enough egg cartons." She sets out eight bright crosses. Each is made from a cardboard carton, but she has painted them bright colors and added bent wire and yarn so they look like something a boutique would sell. "Before bed, the girls will write letters to God about what's bothering them. They can set the letters by their bunks. During the night, I'll put a Care Cross there instead. When they wake up, the cross will be in place of the letter."

"I love it." I toss her sleeping bag onto the bed. "You are going to be a phenomenal counselor. The girls in your cabin will love you."

"Thanks. And I have hundreds more ideas like that one." She points to her guitar. "I've been practicing this year. Like constantly. You know my dad, right? Mike with the Association? He's like, 'Get through your sophomore year of high school first. Then worry about camp!'"

"I was the same way." Looking at Beth is like looking in a mirror. All of it—her decoupaged trunk (with pictures of her every summer at camp, she explained), her construction-paper-and-marker signs to welcome the campers, her tattered book of camp songs.

"We've been talking about STUF constantly at our house. My mom is so upset about this. My dad is *obsessed* with convincing the rest of the Association members to say no." She turns from hanging a butcher-paper sign from the bunk that says, "The Best Summer of Your Life!" and looks at me. "The other churches are tired of losing money, though. Too many special offerings. Those Association members think it's better to get out."

"I know. I get that. But it's just so tragic. I mean, corporate offices for a storage company? *Yuck.*"

She makes a face. "I can already picture it. Eden will be all metal and glass and shiny buildings. It hurts my stomach."

When I look at her standing there, with her braided pigtails and purple marker on her cheek, she looks very young. And then I realize she's trying to impress me with the Care Crosses. She wants very much for her boss to think she'll do a good job. She thinks I have answers.

So, I act like I do. "I think your dad is right. I think we can convince the Association to say no. And I think this will be the best summer of all of our lives."

CHAPTER 10

"As the Deer"

Emmy and Ellie get here next. They are best friends from the same small L.A. suburb. Their moms help them move their luggage into their cabins. Emmy and Ellie match in almost every way. Their trunks are pink and green and monogrammed. They both wear black, oversize sunglasses, and their brown hair is in messy, perfect updos.

Unlike Beth, Ellie and Emmy don't know about STUF. As we drag their trunks up The Hill, I explain what's going on. They interrupt us with outrage.

"It's a *storage* company?" Ellie asks. "They want to turn Eden into an overcrowded attic of other people's stuff?"

"Not quite. They want the land for the view of the lake. I guess the CEO lives nearby," I explain. "He doesn't like driving into L.A. and going to the headquarters."

Emmy giggles. "Probably because it's full of capsules of other people's junk."

"Yeah. I wouldn't blame him for that." I'm already kind of sick of talking about STUF. It's like that feeling you've eaten too much soup—waterlogged with it all sloshing around in your stomach. It's only Day One and STUF already feels like that.

As Ellie and Emmy are saying good-bye to their moms and I'm coming down The Hill, I stop to really look at the scene of Eden's summer unfolding. Jake is talking to a guy in the parking lot—a counselor who just arrived. Wolfgang, I think. A white truck with two guys in it just pulled up. That's probably Aaron and Kenny, the last two counselors.

Natalie and Beth have started making nametags on the patio, and Pete is sitting on the little porch outside the camp kitchen. He's wearing earbuds and grating cheese.

If I still prayed, I might do that now. Because this summer might work. Our little staff—this random bunch of teenagers—might be able to pull this off.

CHAPTER 11

"If I Were a Butterfly"

When I get to the parking lot, I meet Wolfgang, a German foreign exchange student. His host parents—a Korean couple from Santa Barbara with silver hair and a new Mercedes—hug him a dozen times and promise to send him packages and letters. Wolfgang is seventeen and just finished his senior year of high school. He applied at Eden because he wants to meet kids from all over California.

When his host parents drive away, he turns to me with a wide smile. "So, this is where my summer adventure begins! Camp Eden and its parking lot!" He's radiating tourist excitement, like he can't wait to strap a camera around his neck and capture Eden. He's wearing a "USA" T-shirt, and his denim cutoffs are shorter than mine.

I try to grab some of his luggage, but he insists on carrying it all himself. "Have you worked at a camp before?" I ask.

"I have never even been to camp before! My dad is a university teacher in Munich, and we are living in a very small apartment. We never travel into the country. I am here at Camp Eden for my chance to eat campfire marshmallows. And to swat all the bugs. Are there a lot of bugs at this camp? The only bugs in Munich are roaches. You have banana slugs in Eden? We have zero slugs in Munich."

I laugh. "I'm sure there are slugs. I'm actually new to Eden too. Your cabin is The Rock. All the cabins are other names for Jesus." I point toward the cluster of boys' cabins on the east side of the lake. Jake is not far away, spraying off the orange life preservers in front of the purple shed.

"The cabins are named after Jesus?" He's nodding so hard his whole body is rocking. "Yes. This is exactly the thing I like about America. It's all very creative, right?"

"Right," I say.

Kenny and Aaron arrive next. They're football players from Altadena and juniors at a Christian high school. Aaron's back for his third summer, but this is Kenny's first.

"What made you come to Eden?" I ask. Kenny is a linebacker and weighs about double what I do. Probably even double what Aaron weighs. He's looking at his phone and breathing heavily from lugging his trunk up The Hill.

"Hold up a second." He stops at the water spigot and gulps some. He keeps his eyes on his phone the whole time. "We get service credits at our school for working with kids. I don't have time during the season, so I'm trying to get hours in this summer. Plus, my coach says I need to chill out."

"Chill out by spending the summer with kids?" I take the shoebox Kenny is juggling and peek under the lid to see that it's filled with gooey, crumbly brownies.

"Uh-huh." His face is red as he lugs his trunk into his cabin. "That's what I'm hoping. Coach thinks I'm too intense."

"Dude, it's because you *are* too intense." Aaron stops and turns around. "He's been getting in fights. But don't worry, Poppi. Jake will know how to make him chill out."

I look at these boys—these football players—who are athletic, cute, and, really, just about my age. They kind of scare me. Even though they're not aggressive, just their *boyness* is intimidating.

For the first time, I'm glad that Jake is in charge of the male counselors. Maybe—just maybe—it will be good that he's here this summer.

CHAPTER 12

"Mighty to Save"

Right before Mom died last summer, my Aunt Lily came to our house and stayed for three months. She's Mom's sister and has lived in Minneapolis for thirty years. Aunt Lily has short, gray hair like Mom did, and she works at the elementary school three blocks away from her apartment. All you need to know about Aunt Lily is that she has walked to work every single day of her life. In Minnesota. In the winter. I come from tough stock, and Aunt Lily is the toughest.

Aunt Lily had been temporarily sleeping on the couch during hospice with Mom, but she moved in for good after Mom died. She bought boxes of chamomile tea, tins of shortbread cookies, and already-made Tater Tot casseroles. Whether I was ready or not, Aunt Lily got busy on some heavy-duty healing.

Even though I'm ten years older than the kids she usually helps, she gave me all these ways of working through the really awful parts of Mom's breast cancer.

Thinking about last summer with Aunt Lily makes me happy. Aunt Lily is sarcastic and very funny. Even though we had hard work to do, we laughed almost constantly.

This afternoon, as I help Pete out by cooking the hamburgers on Eden's huge outdoor grill, I think about her and everything we talked about. As we tried to figure out how to take care of Mom's garden and met with real estate agents, Aunt Lily gave me Orphan Lessons. This was the joking term we used for learning how to figure out life without a mother.

According to Aunt Lily, my most important job is to always take radical care of myself because now I have no mom to do that. Lots of water. Snacks with protein. Don't hold on to hate. Long walks. Lots of time outside. Keep a gratitude journal. Forgive, forgive, forgive. Go to church. Always be in a Bible study. Pray all the time.

I think about those Orphan Lessons a lot, especially now that I'm far from my family. I do remember to take care of myself. Physically at least. But the God stuff I haven't been doing. Aunt Lily says I'm mad at Him, but I don't know if that's it. Not exactly.

More accurately, I feel about God the way I feel about my own dad. He seems unreliable. I like the idea of a God who would take care of me, but it's not reality. When I really needed God—when I begged Him to not let the cancer spread, to keep Mom alive—He didn't come through for me.

Believing God is unreliable feels like a betrayal of Mom, of Aunt Lily, and certainly of my job here. But I can't see Him as my personal God. Yes, we can sing about Him and talk about Him, but I'm not interested in any of that for myself.

As I grill the burgers for dinner, the big barbecue grill sputtering flames, I inhale Eden's piney smell. California is cooler than I expected. It's like an invisible air conditioner hovers right over the foothills. Except for the wasps that swarm around me, this is the most peaceful I've felt since I got to Eden twenty-four hours ago.

I've just finished grilling the first batch of burgers when Jake comes over from the kitchen. He starts talking to me like we're still in the middle of our fight, which must mean he's been thinking about Team Eden all afternoon.

"Don't get me wrong, I want this place to stay open. Eden is my childhood. But I can see the problems with camps—in general they're not worth the trouble they take to run. If we don't close this summer, it'll be next."

I flatten a patty with my spatula and watch the fire spark under the hot grease. "Okay. I'm not sure why you feel the need to convince me of that. Because I obviously don't agree. But really . . ."—I make my voice sound very tired—"why is camp not worth the trouble?"

"Easy. You have constant staff turnover, a facility with more maintenance issues than any ministry can afford, you're dependent on variable income, and you have an emotional and erratic fan base." He's ticking the evidence off on his fingers. "And the legal issues are a nightmare."

"I've been at camp for eight years, and I never worried about legal issues," I spit back. Maybe Jake isn't really aggressive. Maybe it's just that his confidence makes him seem this way. Maybe if I passed Jake—in an airport or something—I'd be vaguely impressed with him as a hot guy who looked like he had it all together. But the idea of living and working so close together, it's too much proximity. He zaps my confidence.

"The liabilities of kids *living* at your facility?" He swats away a wasp hovering by his nose. "The risks that come with sixteen-year-olds staying alone in cabins full of kids? We've been safe at Eden so far, but who knows?"

"If you really believe this camp isn't worth the risk, then what are you doing here? Why keep coming back if you're so against every part of it? Go live at UCLA for the summer. Or go home to Texas with your family."

He studies me and I look away to slide another batch of burgers onto the grill. The silence between us is tangible, like an awkward third person standing here. Finally, when I'm just about to tell him to forget my question, he sighs. "If I tell you, will you let me be on Team Eden?"

I look at him. "You're serious?"

He's grinning his wide, winning smile. "Of course I'm serious."

Of course he's not. He's flirting. Or harassing me. "I probably won't ever let you on Team Eden. But you could try me."

"Okay. I don't really know why I came back here." Two wasps buzz around his face and he dodges them in a quick motion that is so athletic, there's no doubt he plays rugby or lacrosse or some other preppy sport.

"What?" I accidentally drop my spatula and have to bend over to pick it up. I inspect it for dirt and decide it's okay. Jake is all quick-talking confidence. I can't believe he doesn't have an answer for the simple question of why he's spending his summer here.

"I told you. Up until two days ago, I wasn't even going to come back. I really do need to study this summer. But I just had a nagging feeling that this was exactly where I needed to be. Maybe because this might be Eden's last summer?" He shrugs. "I don't know. But I have learned not to ignore those kinds of feelings."

The glimmer of vulnerability in his eyes takes me by surprise, just like his answer. I can't help but grin at him. "I like that. Very much, I like that."

"And what about you?"

"Well, you know, I don't have many other options." I use the spatula to chase away a wasp. My tone is light and I hope Jake thinks I'm kidding.

"You have other options." He pauses. "Don't you?"

If I'm honest right now about how much I need this job, we will both have shown a bit of vulnerability. That will have pushed us into a new realm. No longer enemies or strangers, but something like friends. "Really. I am as hard up as you might be guessing. The whole deal—an unemployed, orphaned college dropout."

He looks at me for a couple of seconds, and it feels like he's registering this about me. "Wow. You're in a tough spot." He picks up the hamburger platter. "So, what will you do if Eden closes? Where will you go?"

"I can take care of myself, Jake. Look, I come from a tough bunch of women and we figure things out."

"If you went to another camp right now, you might get a full-time job at the end of summer. Then you would have a real plan."

"But I like Eden a lot. If I have to leave in August, I will."

"You're being stupid." He drops the platter on the brick barbecue with a clank.

"I'm not being stupid. I'm being realistic. I don't mind taking risks. I'm not a wimp."

A wasp hovers right in front of me. Before I think about it, I drop the spatula and clap my hands over it. The slap is like a crack of lightning between us. Immediately I realize I just killed an actual wasp, with my bare hands.

"Oh. My. Gosh." Jake steps back, his eyes wide.

I open my hands, which are now on fire. Both of my palms are covered with smears of black, smooshed wasp. "Oh, ouch. Oh! I think my hand is swelling."

Jake pokes the black sludge in my cupped hand. Then he looks up at me, cringing. "Did you mean to do that? I mean, you really meant to kill a wasp with your bare hands?"

"No. Or yes, I guess I meant to do it. But it's not like my *thing* that I kill wasps. I've never done anything like that in my whole life."

"You're not allergic, are you?"

"Nope. Just a very good shot." My giggle is high-pitched and annoying and I despise the person I am around Jake Bass. He makes me so nervous that I end up fighting or giggling or looking like some kind of a backwoods orphan who kills poisonous insects.

He holds my hand up to the sunlight. A long red welt—sort of the shape of California itself—is rising on my palm. "You need to get the stinger out of there. I'll get the tweezers from the nurse's station."

"I don't want to wait to go all the way over to the office. I can just use my fingernail. It's really starting to hurt."

"Let me see." His fingers wrap around mine as he inspects the furry wasp leg on my hand. I have to take a gigantic breath because my hand is throbbing with pain and because his hands on mine must be what it feels like to live inside a kiss.

Then, just when I think I will melt—either from pain or from the awkwardness of this moment—Jake blows on my palm. His breath tickling my hand makes me gasp. "What are you doing?"

He looks me right in the eye. Either he doesn't understand the effect he's having on me—or he understands exactly the effect he's having on me. "I'm getting the wasp guts off your hand so I can get the stinger out."

I don't like his hot breath on my palm or his fingers wrapped around mine. I yank my hand out of his. And in one quick motion, I pick out the stinger with my fingernail. "There. It's out."

"Wow." A slow smile spreads across his face. "Ten years at camp and I've never seen anyone do that. Definitely never a girl."

"I guess I'm different from the girls at UCLA, huh?" I mean this to sound like a fact, like I'm giving him information about myself. But it comes out as defensive.

A breeze blows and on it is the smell of burning hamburger, but also the green and brown smells of Eden. It's like sensory overload, and suddenly I want badly to be away from all of this.

I shove the platter at him with my good hand. "Get half ready for dinner and freeze the other half." I stomp away to my cabin, where it's quiet and where Jake Bass is not.

"Does this mean I'm on Team Eden?" he calls, laughing.

CHAPTER 13

"We Are One in the Spirit"

Campers will be here in only twenty hours and Team Eden is coming together. Pete, Aaron, Wolfgang, and Kenny are splitting wood for the campfires we'll have this week.

Kenny is tackling the task like he probably tackles quarterbacks during football season. (If that's what linebackers do. I really have no idea.) His earbuds are plugged into his ears, like he's cramming in as much music as he can before the kids get here and he has to leave his phone in his cabin all day. Kenny was outraged when I explained counselors aren't allowed to use cell phones. He argued it wasn't fair that the directors got walkie-talkies. I reminded him that during his hour off every day, he could text or call whomever he wanted. "One hour a day?" he asked, looking like I had suggested he eat wood chips for dinner.

Wolfgang is picking up cords of wood in his skinny arms and heaving them into the back of the camp truck. Every time he throws the wood, his shirt lifts to show his pale stomach. I think he's skinnier than I am, but he's still lifting twice his weight in wood.

Aaron is zipping branches through a wood chipper so the counselors can use the chips for campfire kindling. When he started this job, I asked why we can't just use pine needles, and

Aaron looked at me like I had never built a fire in my life. "Pine needles smoke like crazy. You didn't know that?"

Jake and Beth are mowing the ball field, where we'll play soccer and other all-camp games. Jake cleans the grass from the mower while Beth weed-eats around the patio. It's a funny scene—tiny Beth wielding the awkward Weed Eater while rugged Jake bends to carefully wipe the blades.

The sun, which had us sweating all day, has disappeared below the clouds, leaving behind a chilly evening. I found a can of white spray paint in the office, and I'm painting all the trail markers before worship tonight. As I watch the staff working, I feel like I did when I opened every one of the cards after Mom's funeral. Completely overwhelmed by other people's kindness. Totally undeserving.

Kenny's face is bright red, and Beth has pit stains from working in the heat. *I promise,* I say silently to these hard workers, *I will not let you down.*

Their effort, their *dedication* feels like their silent deal with me. They're doing all this because they believe camp is worth it. Isn't it my job to make sure that's true?

Later in the day, Eva Browne, Beth's mom, stops by to see if we need anything. She seems young, even though she's old enough to have a sixteen-year-old daughter. Her hair is a faded red and she has freckles all over her cheeks and arms. She wears hiking boots and one of those fishing shirts with vents in the back.

She's as determined for Eden to succeed as I am—more so, actually, since she's been part of this place for three decades. She gave me her phone number and Mike's number and told me to call or text anytime I needed anything.

"What do you think about you and me having a weekly prayer time?" she asks.

I nod. I really want her to like me, but praying with her sounds horrible. "Sure," I say, hoping she'll forget.

CHAPTER 14

"Awesome God"

An hour later, as we're all walking to Alleluia for evening worship, I still don't know what to say to the staff tonight. After the kids get here, different cabins will take turns doing the nightly skit, but campfire tonight is my chance to inspire the staff.

Above us, the sky is filled with billions of white stars. As we sing worship songs, shoulder to shoulder on old logs, there is no place I would rather be than staring at this glowing, sparking fire.

As Natalie strums her guitar, we sing "Awesome God" together, our voices gathering in the cold night air and hovering around the fire, like smoke. I close my eyes and listen. This reminds me of being a little girl and Mom and Dad singing together.

My mom was competent in all kinds of weird hobbies—growing veggies, knitting, playing the ukulele, and even darning socks. But she was the best at singing. She had a tenor voice and Dad's was a strong bass. Music was the background noise of my childhood—worship songs, classical ones, and even hymns. Up until the day Mom packed Dad's things, the two of them sang a constant duet.

But tonight, even with the pretty music, I can't relax. First, I don't know where Jake is. I'm guessing he's somewhere with Kenny, who isn't here either. Second, the staff is still fragmented. Even though they're singing along with Natalie's guitar, their voices sound stringy. They sound separated, like they need a conductor to unify them. They sound afraid.

Natalie sets her guitar on the pine needles and nudges me. The flames crackle and spark. Everyone stares at the blowing fire. Pete clears his throat. "Poppi, you're on."

My mouth is stuck, like a marshmallow is melting between my teeth. Emmy giggles and Beth shushes her. Finally, I find my voice. "The last time I sang that was at my mother's funeral," I say, even though I didn't plan on saying anything about Mom tonight. I didn't even realize that was the last time until I opened my mouth.

Immediately I realize this was the wrong thing to say. The people around this fire might be dealing with dozens of possible issues: homesickness, worry about being a good counselor, hormones, making friends, fear Eden will close, excitement about living away from home. But I'm the only one with a dead mother.

Then, from the shadows of the forest, Jake and Kenny appear. Jake takes the only space at the fire, right next to me on the log I'm already sharing with Natalie. I close my eyes. Why did he have to come back right *now,* just when I found the courage to start talking?

I focus on the orange flames. "It's hard for me to say that," I continue. "I don't like to talk about everything that happened last year." My throat tightens. "It was hell."

I can hear people shuffling. Oh, great, I'm making them uncomfortable. I need to get to my point before this becomes a group therapy session where I'm the only sharer.

I turn to the glowing faces around the fire. Courage. Total honesty. "I'm scared for this summer. Maybe some of you feel afraid right now too." Beth and Kenny nod. Jake and Natalie are on either side of me, so I can't see their faces.

"I'm afraid about STUF, about why kids don't come to Eden anymore, about trying to save something that's dying."

I can feel Jake's gaze, and it's hotter than the flames just a few inches from my feet. "But I cannot let myself be scared of all that.

I believe that kids need camp. I think you believe that too. All of you are willing to make this summer happen. That's enough of an inspiration for me."

Even though I know what I'm saying is pretty stupid, it's something. Beth and Wolfgang are grinning, and I love them for that. Emmy and Ellie are staring at me, like they're not sure what to think of me. Aaron and Kenny are poking the fire.

The flames hiss and sputter, and we all watch them silently.

"I'm scared too," Natalie says into the darkness.

Without even realizing it, I was holding my breath, worried no one else would say anything.

"I'm afraid I won't have passion for this. I'm afraid that I don't have any fresh ideas for these kids," she says.

"Oh, I wouldn't worry about that." The fire lights up Beth's smiling face. "Because *I'm* afraid I won't have as many crazy ideas as you always do."

Everyone laughs. Probably I laugh the hardest because this is exactly what I needed.

A burning log drops away from the roaring flames and sizzles by itself. A bird calls out in the distance, and Wolfgang clears his throat.

"I am afraid that I will miss my Germany too much while I am here at Camp Eden." I think his voice might break a little at the end. His life must seem strange right now. Germany. Santa Barbara. Eden. So many different realities for a seventeen-year-old.

"I'm worried I should've gotten a real job this summer," Emmy says quietly.

"My mom's worried about that too." Aaron shoves his stick into the fire and a shower of sparks ascend into the night sky. "I mean, that *I* should have gotten a job. Not you, Emmy." He glances at her. More giggles.

Out of the corner of my eye, I look at Jake. I'd like to hear what he's afraid of. But he's staring at the fire, his lips in a tight line.

Natalie pats my hand and picks up her guitar. Instead of starting the last song, she hands the guitar to Jake, and he begins to strum. In the firelight, I stare at his hands as his fingertips skate over the strings. The rich, deep melody of "Beloved" fills the air. His fingers reach different positions on the strings. The muscles in his forearms cord as he plucks the strings. Then he begins to hum.

I close my eyes. Because, oh my. He's good. Really good. Natalie played the background melody to the songs, but Jake is a musician. He is leading us, taking us along with him like a needle guides thread. Our voices can only follow the notes he's giving us. Even the flames bounce around to the rhythm of Jake's voice.

I'm not actually breathing; I'm just staring at his hands. Natalie said his dad is a country music singer. Which must be the answer. Because this is not the talent of a kid who took weekly lessons.

Suddenly the fire is too hot, I'm too hot, and I can't look away from his hands. This is really bad news. I don't even like Jake, but his guitar playing makes me melt, like I'm an ice sculpture in front of the fire.

"Beloved, let us love one another. For love is of God," Jake sings, leading the rest of us with his clear baritone voice.

Everyone else has joined Jake in the song, but I can't. All that I'm aware of is the hot fire and his singing. I watch him—and try to convince myself it would be completely inappropriate to grab him by the collar of his hoodie and kiss him.

15

"Jacob's Ladder"

Natalie!" I hiss in our dark room. "Are you awake?"

She keeps snoring. My best friend back home, Leah, snored too. Whispering in a dark room and listening to the wheezing a few feet away feels like I'm back in our farmhouse and ten years old.

Thump! Again I hear the weird banging. At night, the woods are filled with owls calling to one another and possums hunting for trash. But this sounds like something human. It's coming from the picnic tables on the slab, right outside our window.

I sit up in my bed. "Natalie! Did you hear that?" I ask loudly. "Wake up! Someone's out there." Or some*thing*. Yesterday she told me about a skunk that bit Jake when he was eleven. Maybe it's that. Or a bear.

I step out of our room and into the staff lounge. On the table, next to the counselors' mailboxes, there's an open bag of Doritos and two black bananas that I can smell from over here. Jake and Pete's door—on the other side of the couch—is wide open. Their room is tiny too, and I can see a male arm slung over the side of one of the beds. I pivot on my bare foot and creep out the front door and onto the slab.

Bryan is standing by the picnic tables, sliding earbuds in and stretching his leg on the picnic table. He's wearing hiking boots and a navy fleece. "Hey there," he calls.

I check my watch. It's 5:03. "What are you doing?"

"Doing a five-miler today." He's filling his CamelBak with water from the yellow water cooler. The bladder part of the CamelBak clunks to the ground, and he picks it up, looking at me. "Oh. Uhhh . . . you were still asleep, weren't you?" He looks around. "Oh, sorry. I guess I'm used to having the place to myself."

I hear the door shut behind me and then a low male groan. Without even turning around, I know it's Jake. I close my eyes. I really hate that I'm wearing this Snoopy nightgown.

"Hey, Bryan." He yawns really loudly, right behind me. "You said you're doing five miles today? Is that how far you're going up? Or that's how far you're going total?"

"I'm tackling Flowerhead, so it'll be five up and five down." He chuckles. "You know, hopefully five back down. Some of those trails are so steep, I might end up sliding down on my butt."

"But you'll be back in time for breakfast, right?" I ask.

"I hope so." Bryan is fiddling with his watch. A Gambitt. When I noticed it yesterday, he told me it's completely water and crash resistant. He said they make them for skydivers and stuntmen. And that they're only sold in Switzerland. "If I'm not here by then, I'll definitely be back before lunch." He bounces on his toes in a calf stretch and nods to the trails. "If I can get up there soon, I'll make it to see the sunrise."

"You've got to be back by nine, man. You know that campers start coming then." Jake's voice is gravelly with sleep. I move my head half a turn and see he's only wearing pj pants.

Oh my. Turning my head any more is out of the question. I can't look at him full on because I will never be able to unsee shirtless Jake. Forever—at every campfire and dinner and soccer game and staff meeting—I will only be able to see what he looks like right here, wearing only pj pants

"Yep. Really hope I'm back by then." Bryan turns toward the trail. "But if I'm not, I'll be back shortly after. Jake, you can handle the welcome speech, right?"

"Sure." Jake has moved so he's right next to me. Standing next to Jake feels like standing next to a bull—and I really wish there was a fence between us.

"The parents will already be nervous that the camp might be torn down the day after their kids leave," I say to Bryan's back. He has already turned toward the freshly painted trail marker. "We really need your help answering questions and bolstering confidence."

Jake nudges me, and when I look at him, he whispers, "Let it go."

"Sure!" Bryan adjusts his fanny pack and gives a little wave. "I will absolutely be back by nine."

Jake leans against the picnic table. Right here in front of me. As if he has completely forgotten about being shirtless.

"Bryan isn't going to be back by nine, is he?" I ask.

"Nope. He's given up. Do yourself a favor and stop counting on him."

"Probably good advice." I look over at the moon, which is fading in the dawn. Jake's face is hidden in the shadows, but the soft light reflects off his chest in a way that makes it look like a carved statue.

"Look," he says, "what you said last night at campfire was really good. The staff already likes you a lot. Just because I'm telling you the summer will be hard doesn't mean I don't see how much you're trying."

I hear a noise and turn back toward the staff cabin, so relieved I don't have to think of words to say back to Jake. Pete steps outside and a sleepy-looking Natalie is right behind him. "What. Is. Going. On? Seriously. Why are you two out here?" she asks.

Last night she gave me the Jake Speech—which detailed all the reasons I cannot fall in love with Jake. He always dates girls at camp. . . . He "pathologically" (Nat's word) breaks their hearts. . . . It's a disaster every summer. I told her not to worry. I had no plans to fall for Jake. Yet Natalie is glaring at me like I've been caught kissing him out here.

I roll my eyes. "Bryan was up. He forgot other people could hear him."

Pete is just wearing athletic shorts, but I can look right at his skinny chest without any trouble. He stretches. "I'm starting coffee." Then he looks at us. "It's going to be a long day."

"It already is," Jake says, walking back into the directors' cabin.

CHAPTER 16

"Morning Has Broken"

At eight thirty, I stop by the office. I have about two minutes before families start arriving to drop off campers. Pete is down at the driveway with a camp walkie-talkie. He'll call when the first car turns off the highway and onto Eden's property.

Jake is sitting at the desk with Eden's old laptop open. Because he knows the computer system, he's helping take care of tuition payments and payroll this summer.

He looks different today. Maybe he couldn't get back to sleep, because he still has bed head and his eyes are puffy. The good news is that he is wearing a Camp Eden "I'm a Happy Camper!" T-shirt over his muscular chest. So now, at least, I can look directly at him.

"All the counselors are in their cabins and ready for the campers." This comes across as too much of an official report, so I relax my tone. "Nat will check medical forms with parents, and I'll send anyone who hasn't paid all their fees up to you. Is that good?"

"It's only two campers who still need to pay—Jacob Gordon and Finley Mertins." Jake is bent over Eden's laptop, which is black, and heavy, and old. The Mac I saw him using Thursday during our downtime is silver and sleek. "Bryan said Eden's computer crashed this winter. I've been trying to piece together the financials from what's left."

"Find anything interesting?"

"That even after these two campers pay, we still don't have enough income to pay our bills."

He looks up at me. I stare at him. "Which bills can't we pay?"

"The biggest one is payroll." He turns the laptop toward me. "Bryan said he had to use all the tuition for repairs. With the money left, we have just enough to pay the staff through the end of June."

"And then?" I glance past Jake, back to the other part of the office. Right over his shoulder is a large storage room, and it's like an episode of *Hoarders* in there. Boxes as tall as the cabinets threaten to fall over onto the floor. Old tarps are stacked against the windows so no sun can come through. On the other side are props from a musical—about mice, I think Natalie said—that the counselors did one summer. This whole camp—the office, the trails, the cabins, the finances—is such a mess.

"If we can't get paid, we can't stay and work here. Unless we get a surge of income, we'll have to wrap up the summer early." Jake studies me and pokes his tongue in his cheek.

We stare at each other, and I don't know what he wants me to say. I mean, he's the one with money. Jake is rich. And Bryan is wearing a two-thousand-dollar watch. I have the savings account from the sale of my mom's house, but that has to last me for years. "What have you done all the other summers?"

"The Association churches came up with more money before. They've done special offerings. But I don't think we've ever been this short before."

"Which is why now is a fantastic time to accept that five million dollars," I point out. I sound bitter, even though this is actually the truth.

"I am not your enemy on this, Poppi. When I tried to tell you that Eden was struggling, this is what I meant. I really want to be the one with the solution here. But I have no ideas."

The camp walkie-talkie crackles in my pocket. “First car! First car!” Pete’s voice whines. “They just turned in the parking lot. They’ll be to you in just a couple of minutes.”

“Well, do you want to hear *my* ideas?” I stare at him for one more moment—realize I don’t have time to be coy—and then I say it. “If I had the money, I would give it to Eden. I do not have the money. If you really want to solve this, make a big fat donation.”

Jake looks at me like I’ve just burped or something. “My parents have money. But I’m a college student. I work at a camp that can barely pay its employees. So, as you can see, I do not actually have money either.”

I don’t care that I’m treading on really awkward ground here. I have about thirty more seconds for this conversation. “Then ask your mom and dad for a donation. Or I will. Or Bryan can. Or maybe Mike and Eva will. This is Eden’s last chance, Jake. If we don’t do *everything* we can, Eden will become some executives’ cush office space.”

“How is it even your business that my parents have money?” He leans back against the ripped leather desk chair. “Or what they do with their money?”

I could say fifteen snarky comebacks: It’s my business because if your parents don’t give a donation, I’ll be unemployed next month. . . . I would ask my parents for help, but they’re busy being dead and drunk. . . . It’s my business because you are the richest person I know right now and you’re telling me you don’t have any money. . . .

But Natalie is yelling my name from the parking lot. So, I say the only thing that comes to my mind. Which we both know is a dumb lie. “Whatever, Jake. I really don’t even care.”

CHAPTER 17

"Praise God from Whom All Blessings Flow"

Forty-six kids, (mostly) ten-year-olds, show up in minivans and SUVs, wearing an entire mall of Under Armour shirts, Justice shorts, and Nike tennis shoes. Their clothes look so new I'm surprised I don't see price tags hanging from them. The girls' ponytails are tight and straight and the boys' haircuts look like they were done yesterday. They step away from their parents, toss them their iPads and phones, and walk breathlessly toward Eden.

In ten weeks—by the time they leave this place—grass, ketchup, and mud will have stained all those new shirts. Their baseball caps, watches, and earrings will be lost at the bottom of the lake. They will have forgotten their passwords for Instagram. They will be expert hikers and even better singers.

This change will come one campfire and hot-dog roast at a time. For now, though, these kids are scared and checking one another out. Even the veteran campers—as they hug each other and screech their hellos—cast sideways glances at the newcomers. Who got boobs during the school year? Who grew two inches? Who isn't back? Why not?

Without talking to the Association, or me, Bryan had emailed the parents yesterday and told them all about Eden's financial crisis. Natalie says he does things like this because he's the most passive-aggressive human ever. And he's bitter. He's the kind of jerk who unceremoniously announces he's sold the camp that the kids love. Then he isn't here to give answers when the parents come at us with a million questions.

As the parents slowly leave and the kids go to their cabins to start to bond, I sort wristbands for the swim test: green for the kids who can swim in the lake's deep end, red for those who need to stay in the shallow. Jake and Natalie will run the swim tests tomorrow morning while Pete and I train KP groups about the proper way to load the dishwasher.

"I need to talk to you."

I look up into the bright sunlight where Jake is standing. "Okay. I can talk to you now. Have a seat."

He does not take a seat. "My mom and dad will be here tomorrow morning. To give Eden a donation."

"Wait. What?" I jump up. "Really? They're flying in from Texas?" I want to hug him. "*Seriously?* Just like that? They're coming with money for us?"

"They were in L.A. anyway, at his recording studio. They're just driving down for a couple of hours."

"Jake, thank you. This is fantastic news. This is the best news ever. This is—"

"Calm down. The donation won't be enough, and it will take a bunch of time and energy that we don't have on the first day of camp. And he'll want a bunch of press for it."

I stare at him. Eden's staff polos this summer are peacock blue—and the exact shade of Jake's eyes. Of course they are. I wish we had bright pink polos that would make Jake look like a flamingo. "Who cares if he wants press? Who cares how much time and energy this takes? He's giving us money!"

"He'll give us ten thousand dollars!" Jake barks. "That's not enough to get us through the summer. And the press needs a lot of attention."

"We want press! More press is good!" I hear the excitement in my own voice, but I don't care. "Thank you. Asking your parents for help was very sweet."

"This has nothing to do with being sweet, and it's a bad idea. But it's the only idea either of us had."

"Eden is getting money and publicity. Trust me. This is all crazy good."

"Poppi, the story will be about how George Jackson Bass supports his son, who works at a quaint little camp. My dad's publicist doesn't mess around. He'll spin it so my dad looks like a fantastic family man and so Eden looks like a pathetic charity case."

"Okay. But we'll also put Eden's website in the article, and I can set up a page on the YouCanShare crowdfunding site. We'll ask them to put that in the article too. We can use this as momentum." I squeeze his shoulder. "Seriously. Thank you. I could hug you right now."

His shoulder shifts away from me. "I'll handle my dad!" Jake barks. "You just focus on the kids."

CHAPTER 18

"Sons of God"

"When we were campers, George Jackson Bass came every year to give a big donation," Natalie explains to me as we head toward Beth's cabin to drop off the last of the first-aid kits for the girls' cabins. "And it was sooooo awkward for Jake and Savannah. The whole reason they spent their summers at Eden was to get away from Dallas where their dad is like the president of the city or whatever."

"Jake and Savannah told their dad to stop visiting Eden?"

"I guess. Jake and his dad don't really get along. You'll see. GJB will show up with this whole entourage, and he's just a big jerk. He's Lord Farquaad, but bossier and taller."

Inside Cabin Alpha, the girls are spread out on each other's bunks, painting nails and doing hair. When Beth answers my quizzical look, she says, "We're getting ready for dinner. You know how it goes on the first night. We have to primp." She shrugs in a What-can-you-do? way. But she's wearing glossy pink lipstick and her hair is piled on top of her head in a big, fancy bun.

Jamie Grace is blaring from Beth's alarm clock and two girls—Catie and Jilly—are choreographing a dance by the bathroom. Makeup cases are open on the floor and a cloud of hair spray hangs in the air. Over the music are the sounds of the other campers shrieking and laughing. The continuous summer sleepover has begun, and the girls' excitement is as obvious as the smell of peach body spray.

A short camper with olive skin and thick eyebrows appears next to me. "I can do your makeup," she says.

"Really? Then we have come to the right place." I shake my hair out of its ponytail. "I need a total makeover. And a new hairstyle. Especially for the first dinner. Can anyone French-braid?"

"Me! I can!" Harriet, a girl with very curly black hair, jumps from her bunk. "Sit down!" she commands. "I'm the best French-braider at my school."

"Hold on five minutes. I need to help Nat finish delivering these first-aid kits." I pat Harriet's head because she is very serious and very cute. "But I will be back."

Beth walks us to the door. "I love these girls." She wraps one arm around me and one around Natalie. "I love being a counselor! I can't believe this is my actual life. My friends back home are going to summer school—and I am here!"

"You've been preparing for this since birth." Natalie leans her head onto Beth's and squeezes her in a side hug.

Outside, Natalie drops her voice. "I have to show you something. And it's really awful." She pulls a piece of folded construction paper from her pocket. On the outside is her name, written in small, messy, boy handwriting.

As I open the orange paper, a daisy—the type that grows wild around camp—falls out. "'A flour for my flour.'" I look at her. "Who's it from?"

"I don't know. Emmy gave it to me this morning at breakfast. She said she found it in the kitchen."

"Whoever he is, he can't spell."

"I noticed." She sounds disgusted. "Who can't spell *flower*? And who picks wildflowers as a gift?" Natalie's tone lets me know this note and the potential of a secret admirer are a really big deal to her. She wants this—but not *this*, exactly.

"So, who do you hope it is? I mean, who on staff would you want to write you notes?"

"Anyone, kind of. I mean, I haven't ever had a real boyfriend, Poppi. I'm just excited someone likes me." We pass Kenny's cabin, and they're already on their way to dinner, even though they're thirty minutes early.

"Maybe it's from Aaron? But he's pretty focused on Ellie," I say. The two of them have been together since they got here. When Ellie had dishes duty last night, Aaron was in there helping. When he built the fire for night worship, Ellie carried the kindling. "Or Jake, maybe?" But dead daisies and hidden notes don't seem like Jake's style.

"Right. Not Aaron. He's crushed on Ellie every summer. Now that he's grown six inches, she's finally noticed him." She crosses her eyes. "And Jake is *so* out of the question, it's like the possibility of me and Prince Harry. Plus, I told you. Jake has issues with girls." I slip into another cabin and drop off a kit.

When I come out, Natalie tosses the note into a trash can. "Anyway, I'm announcing at the staff meeting that whoever he is, he can cut it out. I'm not interested."

"Aw, come on. Have fun with it, Nat. Secret admirers are as old as camps are. There's something about a bunch of people living in the woods that brings out romance. What's the worst that can happen?"

At Christ Camp, a quiet, skinny guy named Gus had liked me. For two summers, before he had the courage to tell me face-to-face, he snuck into my cabin and slipped poems under my pillow. He wrote them in a yellow spiral notebook and added one every day. A couple of summers ago, we started to hang out, but then I stayed home with Mom last year.

"I'm afraid it's Kenny." Natalie slips into Aaron's cabin, Omega. She drops off the kit, then we continue. "He seems like a big, lost teddy bear. And he's always staring at me."

"Yeah?" Kenny's always staring at me too, but I think he's trying to understand what he's supposed to be doing. "Are you interested in Kenny?"

She makes a face as we reach Wolfgang's cabin, The Rock. "Are you kidding? Of course not. Look, Poppi, I know I'm not beautiful, but I can't see myself with *Kenny*."

"Natalie! You are beautiful. You have got to stop the negative self talk. And Kenny is really trying. He's nice."

"Well, I'll just have to be beautiful alone, and Kenny will have to be nice alone because nothing is going to happen between us."

"We'll see. You never know what can happen during a summer at camp."

CHAPTER 19

"Now Let Us Sing!"

Look, Jake. Thanks for doing this. I can tell you're nervous."

"You don't have to thank me." Jake's pacing so much that he's worn down the patch of grass at the edge of the parking lot. He's squinting out at the road like he's watching for a military invasion.

I'm yawning—already tired from a long first night with campers. Kenny woke me up at three this morning because Wyatt, a red-haired boy in his cabin, was hysterical to go home. Once I was awake and outside on the patio with them, Kenny explained he'd let Wyatt use his cell phone to call his mom.

Even though I had told all the counselors the first night they arrived that Homesickness Rule Number One is to never, ever let a kid call home. So, Kenny and I were up past four, trying to distract Wyatt with absolutely everything he would get to do this summer. "Canoe trips! Rumble Ball! Hiking! Dodgeball tournaments! S'mores every night! New friends!"

When Kenny finally ushered Wyatt back to his cabin at five, they were both yawning, but I was wide awake. I strapped on my running shoes and headed out to the trails. Because it was o'dark thirty and because I had heaved and struggled to the top of one of

Eden's highest hills, I was rewarded with the best sunrise of my life. Life Lesson Number 1,483: More suffering = more rewards. Always.

Now, six hours later, Jake and I can't agree if I should meet his parents in the parking lot or if he should. I think it would make a much more professional impression if *I* accept the donation. That way, it's more like George Jackson Bass is giving it to Eden and not to his son.

Jake is so tense about his dad's visit that he's trying to ignore me. But that's impossible since we're sharing the only three feet of shade out here. He drinks two long swallows from his can of Red Bull, and his eyes dart in a frantic way. This is not his first energy drink of the day.

"I'm too tired for you to be this agitated, Jake. I really am sorry if this is awkward for you. But pleasepleaseplease, relax about your parents."

"I'm not agitated. Why do you think I'm agitated?"

"Okay, Omega, I guess you're not *late* either." I grin at him, hoping he gets the joke. Last night, Jake had to tell Aaron to get his Cabin Omega guys where they need to be on time. They'd already been late to dinner, all-camp kickball, worship, and breakfast. When Jake told Aaron to work on getting his guys there on time, his whole cabin was offended. "But we're not *that* late!" Aaron and the boys all whined.

Jake stares at me—and then he laughs. "But I'm not *that* nervous," he says in Omega's exact tone. For one tiny moment, I like him again.

Then a glossy black Escalade is crunching gravel in Eden's parking lot and the moment is lost to Jake guzzling more Red Bull, tossing the can into the recycle bin, and striding toward the SUV. His shoulders sag, and he looks way less like a prelaw sophomore from UCLA and more like one of the nervous new campers.

A uniformed driver steps from the front and then opens the back door for a tiny woman. Her heart-shaped face looks like the picture Natalie showed me of Jake's sister, Savannah. The woman is in her midfifties, her white shirt is military crisp, and her denim skirt hangs straight from her narrow hips. She has teased-and-sprayed platinum-blonde hair and is wearing lots of turquoise jewelry.

"It's really good to see you, Mom." Jake meets Mrs. Bass in the middle of the parking lot and kisses her cheek. "Thanks for coming up with Dad." His voice is so sweet that out of nowhere, my own grief stabs me. Which is so ridiculous because my mom was nothing like Mrs. Bass. She never wore makeup or jewelry or even skirts. Mom wore jeans and flannel shirts and tennis shoes. It's Jake's tenderness that reminds me of what I don't have.

Grief is like nausea—it's sneaky and unpredictable. Suddenly I want to write down absolutely everything I can remember about my mom. The powdery smell of her cheeks. The little red calluses on her palms. They were always there. Why didn't they ever heal? Should I have known this as some kind of sign her body wasn't healthy? I bite my cheek until the tears pass.

A short, pudgy man climbs out of the Escalade. He's wearing a white cowboy hat that shades his ruddy face. The logo on his polo says, "George Jackson Bass Inc."

After shaking Jake's hand and complaining how the mountain roads always make him sick, he turns to me. "Well, hello. Aren't you a pretty little thing? I'm Buddy. I help GJB out with publicity and things. You new to Eden?"

"Yes sir. I'm Poppi, the summer director." My cheeks are probably red from his "pretty little thing" comment. Yet, I can't help but check to see if Jake heard it. I feel like I've received a five-star review and he needs to know. His face says nothing.

Buddy has a wide, helpful face, like my Uncle Ed, who helped Mom and me slaughter chickens, sat next to us in church, and, at the end, during The Last Horrible Winter, shoveled the driveway after every snow. Uncle Ed would do anything to help. I hope Buddy will too—that he'll cooperate with the ideas I've come up with for the donation.

"I'm Honey Bass, and I'm so happy to meet you." Mrs. Bass smells wonderful, like almonds and cocoa butter. She takes my hand. "When Jakey called and said y'all could use a little help, I climbed right in the car and told GJB we need to get down here."

Honey Bass is still holding my hands, and I don't mind because she is just so nice, like one of the sweet women at cosmetic counters who rub cream on your face.

"Thank you for taking this job," she continues. "Really. Eden is Jake and Sissy's childhood home. GJB always toured in the summer, and they just grew up here." She squeezes my hand. "And you, poor sweet girl! Here you are, just starting at Eden. Then you find out they're closing this place. That is just not *fair* to you."

"I'm not giving up on Eden yet. Jakey and I are doing what we can to save it." I wink at Jake. He looks at me with absolutely zero amusement.

George Jackson Bass steps out of the Escalade, a cell phone to his ear. He's very tall, even taller than Jake, but with the same broad shoulders, Roman nose, and piercing blue eyes as his son. He's also barking into the phone, the same way Jake does. GJB is wearing his own George Jackson Bass Inc. polo shirt. Later, I'll realize that all I needed to know about GJB is that he is a guy who wears a polo shirt with his own name on it.

"Well, you let us know what we can do to help you." Honey is still stroking my hand. "We owe you the world for helping Jake out as the summer director." She drops my hand to grab Jake's, and now we're standing in a weird triangle. "Aren't you so glad for Poppi, sweetheart? You could not have taken those classes if she hadn't come to help you out."

"She's not helping him out," George Jackson says, joining our group. "She took his job." He's grinning. "Poppi, congratulations on becoming Jake's boss."

"Hi, Dad." Jake's teeth are clenched as he steps forward and shakes his dad's hand. They stand like that, toe to toe, running shoe to cowboy boot. GJB nods to Jake and then asks him about his classes.

Before Jake can answer, GJB starts to climb The Hill. Over his shoulder, he calls, "Where do you call home, Poppi? And don't try to tell me it's this Left Coast of California because I can tell by looking at you that you're a good southern girl."

"Minnesota," I call to him, but George Jackson is back on his phone and leading us over to the shaded patio outside the dining hall.

Wolfgang's cabin comes around the corner, wearing trunks and carrying towels. George Jackson stops to ask them what they think of camp. Two of the boys have heard of him and they want his autograph. Suddenly, Buddy is handing out T-shirts to the whole group. They're so excited for the T-shirts that hang down to their knees, you'd think he was handing out Pokémon cards.

Lance Hanks from the *L.A. Times* arrives, and we all sit down at one of the long picnic tables. Here, GJB tells us exactly how the donation is going to happen. He's giving the usual ten thousand dollars and he wants the write-up to be about how he supports the camp his own kids have been a part of for a decade.

Lance Hanks starts to ask questions about Eden. Somehow, the reporter already knows about STUF. When he asks why GJB doesn't just fund Eden for the long term so the camp can stay open, Buddy interrupts to list *all* the nonprofits that George Jackson Bass Inc. supports. Lance writes it all down, and Eden is at the bottom of the list of GJB's charities.

I'm guessing Eden is the only one of those charities that's on life support. Without a bigger gift from GJB, it's Eden's funeral. This is my only chance. "Can we talk about that donation amount?" I ask Buddy. "Eden had several unexpected expenses this spring. Without a bigger donation—at least thirty thousand—we'll have to send all these campers home next month." I dig my nails into my palm to keep my hands from shaking. The worst that can happen is that GJB will say no. Still, I can't move my eyes even one millimeter toward Jake.

George Jackson squints at me and explains that ten thousand is the amount he has given Eden every single year—and the amount he will continue to give. Then he tells me about all the other worthy charities he supports—including children's hospitals, music programs in schools, and the Farmers Union.

"I understand. But we really need the money to make payroll." I feel the toe of Jake's running shoe digging into my calf. I don't look at him because I know he'll be glaring. I glance at Honey instead. "Even if Eden is sold in August, these kids should get to finish their last summer."

Everyone at the table stares at me. Lance Hanks stops writing. Jake's breathing is so thick, he's panting.

"Excuse us for a minute," Buddy says. He takes George Jackson aside and Honey follows. While they're gone, Jake doesn't say one word to me. Lance looks from me to him. He clears his throat. "You two known each other long?"

"Less than a week," I say. When I glance at Jake, I almost laugh. He's grabbing his hair like I give him an actual headache.

When the entourage returns to our table, Jake's dad hands me a GJB Inc. check for thirty thousand dollars. "This is going to take care of that payroll," he says. "No kids are going home early. Not if I can help it."

"Wow." I hear the tears in my own voice. "Thank you so much." There. Just like that. One morning I find out we have to close Eden before the end of the summer. And the next, we have *thirty thousand dollars*. I feel like I could run very far, very fast. Like my blood is pumping through my body at twice the normal speed. Anything is possible.

I'm sure it was Honey who made the gift happen. As the men were walking away to talk privately, I saw her pull her husband aside and whisper to him.

The only awkward moment was when the reporter asked me which of GJB's songs I liked the most. I could not remember even one of his songs. Natalie has told me, but no actual song titles came to mind. Lance Hanks *loved* this. And so did Jake.

I told Lance Hanks I was a new convert to country music, and Buddy took that very seriously. While Jake's dad took another call, Buddy filled me in on all GJB's greatest hits. Jake, I noticed warily, watched this with his hand over his mouth, laughing at me.

I'm walking back toward the office with the check when Jake calls my name. My body sizzles. I wish I could unzip myself out of my skin because it's too hot. "Yeah?"

He crosses the courtyard to where I'm standing. "I just wanted to tell you good job. You handled my dad well. And"—here, he smiles a little bit at me—"you were right."

I look up into his blue eyes. Giddy from my success with G. J. Bass, I have the courage to give Jake my widest, brightest, best smile. "No problem, *Jakey*."

<u>Los Angeles Times</u> B-10

Preaching to the Converted

Country Great Evangelizes about His Music

By Lance Hanks

Poppi Savot, summer director at Eden Lutheran Camp, is no stranger to conversion stories. She's witnessed how the lost will dramatically repent of their sins. But Savot never expected to be the one promising to change her heart.

That is, until she met George Jackson Bass, country music legend and also evangelist about his genre of music. Today he showed her the error in her ways.

After listening to the album *Heaven's for Hillbillies*, Savot left behind her days of shunning country music and walked into the honky-tonk light.

Bass has shared more than just his music. He has given Eden $30,000 to help fund their summer program. With the help of Bass's donation, kids across California will be able to spend their summer canoeing, camping, and getting converted at Eden.

"Nothing's more important than God and family," Bass said. "Eden gives kids the chance to learn about the Lord. It lets them enjoy being kids—not just being babysat by a screen."

"This will help Eden offer kids an affordable summer at our beautiful facility," Savot said. "Children will learn about God right in His creation. Camp changes lives. Try it and you'll never be the same."

Both Savot and Bass mentioned Camp Eden is still accepting donations at the crowdfunding website YouCanShare.org.

CHAPTER 20

"I'm in the Lord's Army"

It's two weeks into camp, and the cabins really have become little families. The six counselors act as the parents. Just like in real families, their campers have inherited the parent's DNA. Wolfgang wants to learn all the camp customs all the time, and his boys have become like German tourists in their enthusiasm to do this too.

Their latest obsession is to improve the basic American s'more. So every night after worship, The Rock stays around the campfire to roast all their crazy creations. They use chocolate chip cookies instead of graham crackers, sub Reese's Peanut Butter Cups for Hershey bars, and—this was everyone's favorite—add the leftover bacon from breakfast.

The problem with these adventures is that Wolfgang is a pretty terrible counselor when it comes to safety and common sense. He lets his boys leave the marshmallow sticks on the ground and ants find them; they build a huge bonfire, even though it's only for a few marshmallows; and they always, *always* forget to put the fire all the way out.

So, every night I stay for s'mores with Wolfgang's cabin to act as their very own Smokey the Bear (and because chocolate and marshmallows taste so good with bacon). Last night we made Hawaiian s'mores with ham and pineapple and the boys tried to convince me to teach them how to hula. Then we all stayed up way too late talking about all the dances that are uniquely American.

Wolfgang loved the idea of square dancing and pretty soon his boys did too. I told him that I brought my mom's call book from when she was a kid in Minnesota. The boys decided they *had* to learn how to do all these complicated formations. By the time I put out the fire, they were more excited about square dancing than the s'mores—and that's saying something.

They needed partners so they asked Beth's cabin to square-dance with them. This is mostly because Hector has a crush on Harriet. Every arts-and-crafts project Hector makes, he gives to Harriet. This Wednesday, he painted an incredibly detailed picture of her playing soccer (and he included himself cheering in the stands). The painting stood on an easel outside the arts-and-crafts cabin, like a one-man art show.

Wolfgang had never even been on a hike before he came to Eden. He tried one with his cabin last week, and the group got so lost they missed dinner. When I finally found them, sweet Wolfgang had tears in his eyes. He was so frustrated with himself, he declared he was going back to Santa Barbara to live with his host family.

But we came up with a solution: I'll go on every hike with them until he feels more comfortable on the trails. Wolfgang is so German—so tenacious about learning how to hike better—that he wants to try a new trail every day. So, every morning at ten, we take off together. While we hike, the boys have two topics of conversation: how Hector loves Harriet, and what new s'mores recipes they should try.

Despite my challenges with the boys in The Rock, Jake has the harder job: supervising Kenny's cabin. Kenny has decided that camp is dumb, and true to the cabins-become-like-their-counselors phenomenon, his boys agree. So, Jake has become the enthusiastic opposite to Kenny's cynicism.

Yesterday we passed them on a hike and Jake was trying to start a chant with "I don't know but I've been told!" but instead of repeating, Kenny's boys answered with everything obnoxious: "Singing makes me wish for a cold!" Then, "Walking with no Gatorade makes me feel old!" And my favorite, "If this hike was poker, I would fold!"

But Jake wasn't discouraged. He started enthusiastic versions of cheers: "The Way has the fiercest Nine-Ball players, HOW ABOUT YOU?" . . . "The Way can fry superdelicious breakfast ham, HOW ABOUT YOU?" . . . "The Way has incredible bathroom cleaners, HOW ABOUT YOU?" The boys tried to stay cynical even as they tripped over each other's shoes to hear what Jake would yell next. I led Wolfgang's cabin down a longer route so I could hear too.

The cocoon of the summer has draped over all of us, like we're huddled together under a blanket fort, only breathing one another's air and only seeing one another's faces. We've settled deeply into one another and into the comfort of the little kingdom we've created here at Eden.

Our camp kingdom is enchanted and as big as our imaginations. The counselors decided Friday was Blue Day, and Pete went along with it and used food coloring to dye the oatmeal, mashed potatoes, and sugar cookies blue. Also, every sentence we spoke to each other had to include the word *blue*. I've lost count of the number of times Nat has declared, "I love camp!"

We shout a different funny prayer for every meal. We've memorized one another's moods, and most kids have teared up during Bible study. The campers fight and cry and forgive and learn about Christian love in the most important way ever—by living shoulder to shoulder.

But when I crawl into my sleeping bag each night, it's not the peace of this cocoon I think about. It's a much sadder thought: How can this beautiful, safe place—full of decades of history—be taken away so easily?

CHAPTER 21

"Hootananny, Hootananny, Hootananny, Who?"

"Get off the ground, now your partner should be found! Grab that girl and swing her around!" I call into the microphone I found in the spare room of Eden's office. It's very old—as big as my face—and kind of horrible. Every few minutes, it just stops working for no reason. But even this ancient mic is better than calling square dancing by yelling over the crowd of kids on the patio.

Today is the hottest afternoon we've had. The lake is like bathwater and even the shadiest trails feel like stepping into a dryer. But even the brutal heat hasn't stopped Wolfgang's and Beth's cabins from a rowdy afternoon of square dancing.

Just as their cabins are getting into the do-si-do-ing, Aaron's and Ellie's cabins come back from a hike. As the kids refill their water bottles at the cooler, they stare at the other kids promenading.

Suddenly, Christoph throws down his Star Wars water bottle, grabs Jenna's hand, and joins the group. Christoph is always the first to jump into Rumble Ball or to volunteer to do the motions for worship songs. Square dancing is no different.

Then Aaron grabs Ellie's hand and pulls her around the patio. The girls giggle and the boys make kissing sounds. But pretty soon all of them are on the patio, finding partners and joining squares.

"Promenade around the square," I call. I have to look in my book because I really only know about three square dances. "Now, let's try a Star by the Right."

The kids stop shuffling. "What's that?" Bonnie yells.

"That's where everyone puts in their right hand to create kind of a giant star," I explain.

After some confusion, the cabins form a really big star. "Wow! This looks great!" I yell. "You're all naturals."

Then Kenny's cabin shows up. They were with Jake, doing his Quiet Critters Adventure. He hikes the kids high up to Flowerhead and introduces them to banana slugs, spiders, scorpions, and all kinds of beetles.

"Hey there!" I call. "Want to learn how to square-dance?"

They guys look back at me like I've asked them if they want to sing opera. Alpha, Omega, The Rock, and The Truth swarm Kenny's cabin. "Come on! It sounds dumb, but it's really fun," Christoph says. "I promise, you'll like it. It's kind of like line dancing."

"Y'all can go ahead. We'll watch," Luke, a quiet kid with a buzz cut, says. "I think it looks pretty stupid."

"Okay! Promenade back to your spot. Then . . . uhhhh . . . fruit upset on the partners!" I don't think "fruit upset" is really the term to get everyone to change partners, but Hector's arms are around Harriet, and they need to mix back into the group.

"Are you sure you don't want to join?" I call to Kenny. He's looking at me with the same horrified look as his boys. I want to tell him he's being a terrible example, that his fear is just as infectious as the ringworm we were dealing with earlier in the week.

Kenny shakes his head while the boys shuffle their feet in the dirt. "Hey! Stop kicking dust!" he yells at them. "I'm sick of having black boogers!"

Just then, Concorde, from Ellie's cabin, marches over to Camron in Kenny's cabin and pulls him up by the arm. They're twins—even though they never talk to each other here at camp. They're also distant cousins to Buddy (of George Jackson Bass Inc. fame).

"Get up!" She sounds like an old wife actually, just the way my grandma yelled at my grandpa when he started to lose his hearing. "Quit acting like you don't know about square dancing!"

"Stay away from me!" Camron sounds just like Grandpa did. "It's hot. I don't feel like it."

"He knows how to square dance!" Concorde calls to me. "We go to this school where we have to learn all kinds of cultures, and they teach us real square dancing for an entire year. We even have a big square dancing festival, and Camron won a trophy because he was so good at it." She pulls on her brother's arm. "Stop acting so cool. Because you know you like square dancing!"

"It's okay, Concorde," I call back. "No one has to dance."

But Camron stands up and takes her hand. "All right." He grins at the group. "Stand back and watch. Because I really do know what I'm doing."

Then the afternoon takes a weird turn. Everyone gets really into square dancing. Even Kenny's cabin wants to learn every dance in my book. The guys—who compete over everything from who can eat the most French toast to who can run up The Hill the fastest—fight about who can square-dance the best. It's because Camron really is good and the other boys want to learn how to swing their partner like he does. When he struts around the patio, he looks like he should be on *Dancing With the Stars*.

We're all laughing because, when you take square dancing seriously, it's ridiculous fun. It helps that Charlie, a short guy with crazy curly hair who has become Eden's comedian, does a running commentary of the scene. "Hey, Hector! You dance like my grandpa—the one in a wheelchair! Look, everyone! Camron is out there like he is straight-up Kanye, like he *knooows* how good he looks doing the do-si-do. Poppi, after you finish calling, you've got to Lady-Gaga-style drop the mic."

"Come on, Poppi. Give us more!" Wolfgang yells. "We need more square dancing!"

But just then I spot Bryan leaving the office. "Hold on just a second, everyone. I need to catch Bryan."

At the sound of his name, he looks up. "Hey, Poppi. You've got them square-dancing!" He shakes his head as if to say, "Isn't camp so crazy?"

"Umm . . . Bryan? Staff Night Off starts today at four. I'm just checking to make sure you'll be around for dinner. The counselors need the time off, so it'll just be the directors with the kids. We really need another set of eyes."

"Is Staff Night Off *tonight*?" He shakes his head again, like he just can't keep up with everything because it's so busy around here. How odd that I'm the one telling him what's going on at his own camp. "Sure. I can lend a hand."

"Also, and this is maybe a little random, but there's something I wanted to talk to you about—" I start but stop.

Bryan's glancing at his fancy watch like he's already done with this conversation.

I surge ahead. "I've noticed the office is a little bit cluttered and I'm concerned about what might happen if Eden does get sold. I think there might be important mementos in there for people. Have you thought who will clear out all that stuff?"

"Oh yeah. Hilary—she's the lady we're working with at STUF—said not to worry about all that junk. She said to just leave it. I mean, they *are* a personal storage company!" His tone is crowing, like this is just so convenient. "The plan right now is that she'll just use their equipment to haul the stuff away. You know, before they tear down the office. Same with the cabins. They've found a great company to handle the demolition."

"Oh." I stare at him because who talks like this about a camp getting torn down? *His* own camp? "Okay."

Bryan walks away, calling over his shoulder, "Have fun square-dancing!"

CHAPTER 22

"Father Abraham"

Now, tell me everything that's going on." Jake's voice floats in from right outside Eden's office. "I'll hear the story anyway—but I'd rather hear it from you than someone else."

I look out the open window. He's talking to Hector. I've been so absorbed in trying to figure out Eden's finances, I haven't paid much attention to what Jake's been doing. Right after the article ran in the *Times*, several little donations came in—all less than fifty dollars, and mostly from past Eden staff.

YouCanShare's policy is to collect money and then deposit it into Eden's account at the end of the every month, but I've been emailing back and forth with the director of accounts at YouCanShare, insisting we need immediate access to the money.

The same glitch happened last year with Mom's medical bills. I had to call the YouCanShare people back then, too, and explain I needed the money right away. I also remember when Aunt Lily and I realized that the crowdfunding wasn't enough. We decided to sell Uncle Ed's smoked ribs at Eagle Little League games to help pay for Mom's at-home nurses.

Same here. We're going to have to rally Eden's fans to give more—something to show the Association we have enough support to keep Eden open. But what? How can we make the Eden alumni realize this could be the end? No sending their own kids to Eden one day. No more visiting the place they first learned to canoe.

"Come on, Hector," I hear Jake say. "It's eleven thirty. I can't believe you were up because you wanted to see the moon. Why are you sneaking around out here?"

"I was supposed to meet someone." I can't see Hector's face, but he sounds scared. And maybe a little ashamed.

"Who?"

Hector doesn't answer.

"One of the girls?" Jake asks.

"I don't want to get anyone in trouble," he mumbles.

"I need to know if there's a girl wandering around these woods like you were. Who and where?"

"Not in the woods. Outside her cabin. She's in Alpha. Harriet."

"I'll go and check for her in a minute. First, you. Tell me why it's against the rules to meet a girl after lights-out."

"Bears?"

"What?"

"In the woods," Hector answers. "The other guys said they're all over the place. I put Airheads in my pocket. If they come after me, I'll throw the candy to distract them."

Jake doesn't say anything for a moment, and I imagine he's trying not to laugh. "Okay, bears. Why else would there be a rule against it?"

Silence. Then he mutters, "Jake." Heavy sigh. "We weren't going to *do* anything."

"Hector, listen to me, I can remember being eleven. If you're anything like I was, you don't believe that."

Hector's quiet. He's probably staring at his feet—or praying for the apocalypse.

"Hector, I'm going to be superhonest with you. Then you be superhonest with me. If your friends are like mine were, they say they're doing everything with girls. I wanted to keep up with them. I remember thinking that meeting a girl after lights-out and doing *something* was the best idea."

"You did that when you were eleven? You snuck out to meet a girl?"

I lean way over the cluttered desk to hear exactly what Jake says. "When I was your age, I didn't know what I was doing." Jake laughs a little. "But I've learned a lot since then. I've learned not to rush the good stuff."

"Seriously, dude. I was just meeting her. We weren't going to do any—good stuff."

"I'm glad to hear it. Because you'll have the rest of your life for the good stuff. Do you know when that is?"

"We're being superhonest?" Hector sounds unsure. "Are we talking about sex?"

"We are."

"When I'm married?" Hector asks. "I'm trying for the superhonesty here. Really. But I don't know what you're trying to say."

"Yep. Here's the thing. God created sex to be powerful stuff—think of it as marriage glue."

"Jake." Hector sounds flustered. "I'm telling you. I haven't even, like, hit puberty. I know I'm not ready for any of that."

"And I'm telling you, I've been eleven. I know what meeting in the woods after dark leads to. It gets you too close to the good stuff. Understand?"

"Yep," Hector answers quickly.

"Glad to hear it." Their voices fade as they walk away. "You've lost Trading Post this week for breaking the rules."

"What? Noooooo! I need snacks! Jake! I am a Nerds *addict.*"

I yawn and get back to work, staring at the smudged screen of the camp laptop as I try to figure out the bookkeeping from this past winter. I can see deposits from the Association congregations, and they gave a lot of money. But what I'm really looking for is some huge expense that set Eden way back. New mattresses? A termite infestation? But there's nothing here.

It's like we're leaking money. Maybe it's Bryan's salary? I check the payroll again. His salary isn't here. And every other deduction looks fine—automatic drafts for the electric bill, for water, for insurance. Because we own the land, we don't even have a mortgage payment.

Maybe if I can find the leak, I can solve Eden's problems. I can keep my job. I can give Natalie and Jake and all the others back their favorite place. It's somewhere here—in the middle of these numbers.

My phone buzzes with a text from my dad. It's a picture of his black Lab, Nina, wearing a tiara. The text under it says, "Missing my Princess."

I text back a smiley face and "I miss you too."

My dad also liked numbers and spreadsheets. He does the books for a seed company. Back when he still lived with us, he would shut his office door, crunch the numbers, and sip his Jack and Coke.

I shut the heavy laptop and go to the door. Outside, the patio is quiet after the ruckus from this evening. Jake had organized a Nine Ball tournament before dinner, and the boys fought like feral animals to win.

Bryan did not, in fact, show up at dinner. The kids held a little revolution, running around the tables, yelling across the dining hall, and flinging Tater Tots at one another.

I yawn as I lock the office door and then turn to the patio. It feels deserted out here. Maybe that's why Hector had planned his woods rendezvous for tonight.

Then I turn and see who's standing there.

CHAPTER 23

"Breathe"

Long day?" Jake steps toward me.

He's wearing a long-sleeved shirt against the cool evening. It's worn white cotton with red writing down one sleeve that reads, "ROGUE." That's a sunglasses brand, I think. Even in the dim moonlight, I can see that his eyes are so bloodshot, they coordinate with the script on his shirt. He's as tired as I am.

"Long day." I smile. I feel underdressed. Tonight I'm in pseudo-pajamas: the huge yellow fleece I saved from Mom's closet and cutoff sweatpants. "It wouldn't be a Staff Night Off without a few food fights and rendezvous in the woods."

He comes closer. "You heard me talking to Hector?"

I nod. "Good job. Teachable moment. Camp is full of them." I can't quite meet his eyes, so I look down and watch a trail of ants disappearing into a crack in the concrete. Even this late, they're hauling white specks. Do all ants work this hard, or is it only camp ants?

"I had to set him and Harriet straight. They were headed down the wrong path."

"Literally." I smile. "I hope he takes your message back to his cabin."

"I hope he takes the message back home." Jake slides onto a picnic bench. He scoots way over to make room for me, but I stay exactly where I am. "I met Hector's dad on the first day. His girlfriend was with them. She lives with them. And is pregnant."

"Oh, wow. That's a confusing message for a kid."

"Yeah." Jake shrugs. "So, who knows how much of what I said makes a difference. If that's what he sees the other three hundred days."

"We can still give them the message, though."

Jake doesn't say anything else. I watch the ants. But when it becomes clear we have nothing else to say to each other, I turn toward my cabin. "Well, good night."

"Hey, Poppi. One more thing. Just wanted to let you know I put Kenny on probation."

I turn back to him. "You did what?"

His eyes are blue steel. "I told him he has one week to get his act together. If he's not able to change his attitude and handle his cabin by Saturday, he needs to go home."

"Go home? Like, just leave camp? As in fired?" My voice is steel too. "You can't do that."

Jake's lips disappear in a thin line. "I'm the director of the male counselors. Kenny is a male counselor. And I consider him a liability."

"Oh my gosh with your *liability* talk. I don't even know what you mean about 'liability.' How is a heavily supervised counselor at risk to do anything that wrong? He's playing dodgeball with kids, not performing brain surgery."

"It's Week Three, and he still takes his kids swimming without really lifeguarding them. I talked to his campers and found out he hasn't been doing Bible studies. I can't go on every single hike with them. But if I don't go, he forgets water and lets his boys hike in flip-flops. I would rather send kids home than have to call 9-1-1."

"We won't have to call 9-1-1. You read too many law textbooks. This is camp, not a courtroom."

Jake leans away from me like I'm in his face, even though I'm totally not.

"More importantly, this is *my* staff, Jake. You do not threaten to send one of them home unless you've talked to me."

"Then do something about Kenny. He's got a bad attitude, and it's infecting the whole camp."

"I will. But I will *not* send a cabin of kids—eight boys—home. I'm no math genius, but subtracting kids seems like the very stupidest thing we could do for a camp we're trying to add to."

"No, the very stupidest thing we could do is keep Kenny in charge of kids when he's negligent. Look, I'm afraid—"

I cover my ears. "I am so tired of being afraid!"

Jake's whiskered jaw sags. "Hey. Okay, Poppi—"

"I have been afraid so much. And it's awful." Warm tears burn my eyes. Full-on ugly crying is just a few seconds away. I need to hurry here. "You have no idea how many hours I wasted being so scared that I would lose my mom."

"I'm sorry." His voice is even, the way you speak to someone very old or very young.

"But guess what? Fear doesn't solve *anything*. She still died."

"Poppi." Jake reaches for my hand. He fumbles with my fingers until he's holding my index finger and my thumb. Then he squeezes them hard. This little act—his big, rough hand wrapped around mine—feels very nice.

"I'm so mad at myself for being afraid." I inhale. "If I could do it over again, I would do it differently. We wouldn't spend so many hours worrying."

He squeezes my fingers again, and I want to collapse against him and cry until I'm empty. But I don't. Instead I watch those stupid ants while the hot tears slip down my face. I hate myself for being too afraid to lean forward onto Jake's soft white T-shirt.

"I'm sorry," he whispers, like six times. Maybe he hopes that saying it a bunch of times will calm me down. But there are too many tears.

Then he raises his other hand and wipes my cheeks. "Nothing you could have done," he murmurs. And this time, when he pulls me close, I do sag against his chest.

I sniffle and gasp for a long time. After a while, I don't want to stop crying because then it will be awkward. Then I'll have to say something, and it's a million times easier to have Jake's arms around me than it is to try actual words.

"Poppi, Eden is not your mom," he whispers. I can smell his certain Jake smell—something like trees, so earthy and nice. We're in each other's personal space, breathing the same air. My breaths are ragged and his are calm.

He raises our intertwined hands and taps my collarbone, near my heart. "Your mom—that was a big deal. Eden is something separate. You were right. It was on life support when you got here. But that's my fault. Or Bryan's. Or just the way God wants this one to go."

I try to suck the tears back into my nose and eyes. The noise I make is the same Grandpa made when he had emphysema.

"Look, let's be superhonest with each other right now, okay?" Jake whispers. "The Kenny situation really is my fault. I shouldn't have let Bryan do all the hiring this year." Jake dips his head to look into my eyes. "So, there. I take all the blame off your shoulders. You've got to understand that there's nothing you could have done."

"There's something I can do now, though."

He runs his fingers through my hair. "Poppi, I'm talking about something bigger than both of us. Maybe God is closing Eden. Have you thought about that? Don't you agree that He can end good things? Don't you believe that can be totally okay?"

I look at him. "No. And I don't like this kind of talk. 'God's will' talk."

"Really?" He leans back and looks at me. Again, I can feel his gaze is calculating, like he's understanding new parts of me. "Let me ask you a superhonest question. Okay?"

"No," I say. But then I give up. "Okay."

"Isn't everything up to God? It could be up to Him to close this place, right? I mean, that's what trust is all about."

"Jake. I know what you're saying here. And I don't want to—"

"Come on, Poppi. Superhonest. What do you believe?"

"About trusting God?"

"Yeah." He spreads his arms to the trees. "We're at a Christian camp. We sing fifteen songs a day about how God is good and we trust Him. Isn't this what we're singing about? *Exactly* what we're singing about?"

I shrug. I watch the ants and think about crushing them with the toe of my running shoe.

Then, I turn toward my cabin. "I don't think I want to be superhonest anymore."

CHAPTER 24

"Jesus Savior Wash Away"

For the next few days, Jake and I are extra-polite to each other. It's because he thinks I'm unstable. When I sit next to him at dinner or campfire, I can almost hear what he's thinking: *Don't say anything to upset Poppi or she will slobber-cry all over you.* Or he's seeing me as the fraud I am. *She leads all these prayers about trusting God, but deep down, she doesn't mean any of it.*

Every morning, Jake and Pete are the first ones up. Pete starts breakfast, and Jake fries bacon because he has some kind of crush on crispy bacon. After this summer, no matter where I end up, the smell of slightly charred bacon and very strong coffee will remind me of Eden.

Every morning I eat with the campers, then grab a cup of black coffee and a couple of slices of the (really delicious) bacon. Then I head to the staff lounge for the meeting we have with the counselors. Pete supervises KP duty and then takes the campers up to the cabins for clean-out.

Natalie is always the last one up, and she's notorious for barely making it to staff meeting in time for the morning bell. This morning, Natalie is wearing a red T-shirt dress I've never seen before with big brown hiking boots. She flops down next to me on the orange faux velvet couch. A splash of coffee sloshes from her cup onto the upholstery. "Oh, oops-oops-oops." She swipes at the stain with the hem of her dress. "That wasn't supposed to happen."

"I wouldn't worry too much about the couch," I say. The nubby orange material is so stained, it's become a pattern of chocolate smears, green and red marker, and weird grunge.

"The natives are restless today, huh?" Natalie yawns with her mouth wide open, and I can see her fillings. "I'm going to need more hot liquid crack for this meeting." This is what Nat calls camp coffee, and she drinks it all morning, filling up her silver travel mug every time she passes the kitchen.

Wolfgang and Kenny are stretched out on the floor, repeating some German phrase. I think it includes swear words because they both laugh every time they say it.

Beth and Emmy sit criss-cross applesauce together, planning a tea party. I promised high tea to any cabin that won the Golden Broom three days in a row. Their girls have been so focused on winning that Ellie's cabin has started leaving breakfast ten minutes early so they can sweep the dirt area around their cabin's porch. The boys don't even care anymore because the girls always win the Golden Broom.

Aaron and Ellie are snuggled under a ratty brown-and-green afghan. She rests her head on his shoulder. I think they've officially progressed to boyfriend and girlfriend. For the past two days, their cabins have met up for picnics, Bible studies, and an epic kickball game. Aaron constantly teases Ellie. Every time I see them, he's laughing and she's yelling, "Aaron! Stop!" Usually with a big grin on her face.

When I see Ellie and Aaron snuggled like this, or when I watch the cabins scuttling all over the camp to their activities, or when we all stand shoulder to shoulder to sing, I kind of can't believe we are pulling this off. Bryan is nowhere to be found. It's just us, a bunch of kids. How are we doing this?

Natalie yawns again. "It's definitely Week Four. It's the point in the summer when people stop being polite and they start getting real." She drops her voice. "The Real World—Camp Eden."

"Okay, everyone," I say. "First, announcements! Pastor Sean wants me to remind you that when he's here on Sunday to lead worship, he can pray with anyone who wants to. Sign up in the office." Even as I'm saying this, I think about what it would be like to pray with Pastor Sean. What's that even like? Do I talk? Does he? What's the point?

"Testimony here!" Nat raises her hand. "We prayed last week that the camp truck wouldn't punish me. And hallelujah! It actually got me to the store and back. When you're enjoying your cherry Jell-O tonight, you can thank me for braving the camp truck to get you supplies."

A few people clap. Natalie hates driving the camp truck. Usually it ends with some epic story about how she had to bang the hood to get it to start. But the staff is obsessed with cherry Jell-O, so when we run out, someone has to run to town for it.

"Let's sign up for activities." I look at my clipboard. "Girls first. Get over to the board and decide what your kids are doing today."

"Who's in charge of arts and crafts this week?" Ellie asks me. She's standing at the whiteboard, a green marker hovering over the A&C spot.

I glance at my list. "Jake."

"We're making God's Eyes." He holds up a picture in an ancient arts-and-crafts book from the dusty camp bookshelf. It's called *God's Nature Crafts*.

The counselors all groan. "Oh, come on, Jake. We stopped doing those dreamcatcher things years ago. They're weird." Ellie makes a face like she's smelled something bad. "My girls will hate that."

"God's Eyes take too long and never turn out right." Natalie holds a pillow over her face. "I haven't made one since that one summer when we were kids and Bryan wanted us to do a bunch to give to the Association churches. Do you remember that?"

"I do." He pats Nat's hand. "And I have good news for you. You can make one this week. I need to supervise Wolfgang's and Kenny's cabins on their campout Wednesday night. I won't be back in time for Thursday morning arts and crafts." He nods to the whiteboard. "Beth's cabin is signed up for eight o'clock that morning."

"Sorry, Nat," Beth calls. "My girls won't want to make God's Eyes either."

"You are coming on our campout with us?" Wolfgang asks Jake.

He nods. "That's policy. A director always chaperones campouts."

"But I'll be there," Kenny says. "We'll have two counselors to watch the kids. We don't need a *director*." He spits out the last word. Kenny definitely has issues with authority.

"You actually need *two* directors to help you supervise fifteen kids. Poppi and I will both go," Jake volunteers.

"What?" I look at him.

He smiles at me. "You do agree that we need an extra set of eyes on this campout, right?"

"Of course I agree," I say. "But maybe Natalie or Pete could chaperone?" I can't go on a campout with Jake. Alone. In the woods. All night. It would be like sleeping in a fire.

"Pete's already with us," Emily says. "My girls want to find a turtle to be our cabin pet. Pete's taking us on a canoe trip."

"I'll go with you, Jake." Natalie elbows him. She's afraid I'll fall in love with him, so she insists on supervising us.

"Poppi will go." Jake is staring at me, like he's proving something. If I won't fire Kenny, then I can spend the night policing him.

Natalie kicks him. "Jake! I said I would go."

"Nonsense. You're covering Thursday morning arts and crafts." He moves his eyes from me to smile at her. "I wouldn't want you to miss the magic of making another God's Eye."

CHAPTER 25

"Blind Man"

The best time of day is dusk. I love the hours right after dinner—when the heat of the day, and the to-do lists, and the big struggles—are all over. This is also the campers' favorite time of day. After we eat dinner—but before it's dark enough for campfire worship—we play an all-camp game. Week One the kids were obsessed with Capture the Flag, Rumble Ball during Week Two, and sometime during Week Three, Hide-and-Seek became the clear favorite for just about every camper.

Now, Week Four, Hide-and-Seek is still all the campers want to play. We've had to add more rules: (1) You have to hide with a group. This came about after we discovered Charlie had hiked a mile up toward Lakeside. (2) You have to hide with a counselor. This rule began when Beth's girls stretched out right next to a patch of poison oak. (3) No running. This one became necessary when Concorde tripped over a root and sprained her ankle and then—not twenty minutes later—Hector tumbled down The Hill and bloodied his knees. Even though the boys argued about the stupidity of Hide-and-Seek with no running, they finally agreed that, really, they loved the hiding part best.

Tonight, Natalie and I are hiding behind the trash corral, which smells like rotting fruit and is so unimaginative that Wolfgang's cabin will find us in about five minutes. Besides, Natalie is terrible at Hide-and-Seek, so we never last long anyway. Being quiet, subtle, and isolated is the opposite of everything Natalie. Usually I hide with the kids, so I have a chance, but I'm with her tonight because I need to tell her my plan.

"Okay. Now listen to what I want to do tomorrow." I stretch out on the slope. "I'm going to the Association meeting they're having in the afternoon. There are some budget things I want to clarify."

"You guys are caught." Jake is suddenly right next to us. He taps each of our heads and then drops to the ground, stretching out right next to me.

"You're not even It." I scoot over a tiny bit. "I thought you were helping with KP tonight."

"We finished fast." He is so close to me, I can smell his tree scent above the rotting fruit. "And you're safe. Most of the kids are hiding in the Trading Post, but the guys are searching down by the lake."

"So, our spot is actually pretty good then." Natalie scoots closer to me and eyes Jake. I want to tell her I can protect myself from his charms. I'm not going to fall for cynical, future-lawyer Jake.

"I'm going to the Association meeting tomorrow," I repeat. I don't look at Jake because I don't want to hear his advice on this. "I'm going to see what Bryan includes in his financial report. The budget doesn't add up. There's a leak somewhere in Eden's finances."

"Wait. Hold on." Natalie sits up. "You think *Bryan* is hiding money? Wow. Really? No way. Bryan seems—I don't know—too *done* with Eden to embezzle. Wouldn't he have to be paying closer attention to pull that off?"

"You don't have to care about a place to steal from it." I glance, just a tiny bit, toward Jake. "Don't you think?"

"What proof do you have that anyone is stealing? Or that it's Bryan?" I can tell by Jake's tone that he's considering the idea of this. "Why not an Association member?"

"They're turning over the money from the congregations. Plus, they don't have access to the accounts. Bryan is the more likely candidate. He doesn't realize I've been tracking online donations that have come in since the *Times* article. I'm going to slip in to their monthly meeting and see if all those donations are in his income report."

"Who's being paranoid now?" Jake's voice is combative. "Bryan isn't that stupid. He's not going to just hide the money. Of course he'll report the donations."

"I say go to the meeting and check it out." Natalie pulls up handfuls of grass. "What do you have to lose?"

"You have everything to lose." Jake sits up, and he's suddenly looming over me. My stomach clenches around the ham pizza we had for dinner.

"What 'everything' do I have to lose?"

"Bryan will hate you. Maybe at the end of the summer, you will be able to convince the Association members to not sell the property. But you're going to need Bryan to like you. You need him on your side."

"But I don't trust him. I think he's slimy."

Natalie points to Wolfgang's boys, chasing after Emmy's girls. "Watch out!"

I lean back again so Wolfie's guys can't see me. "And you know what else I'm going to do? I'm going to ask him how much he gets paid. Everyone's salaries are in the budget, except his. Why is that? How can he afford that watch? Or those signed baseballs? Or that truck he drives?"

"I don't know," Jake answers, and his voice is too loud for a game of Hide-and-Seek. "He doesn't get paid much, though. I think that's part of his problem. He told me once he hasn't gotten a raise in years."

"But if he has cash for that fancy coffee machine in his office, Eden is paying him too much—"

"You're walking into the Association meeting and saying all that?" Jake groans. "Look, Bryan is a terrible executive director. The Association knows he's never around the kids. I mean, obviously, he is *selling* the camp—"

"Be quiet!" Natalie hisses. "They're going to find us."

"But you're not thinking strategically here, Poppi. You might be able to win the war and save Eden. But you can't win every battle with Bryan. Make sure he still likes you."

"I'm not following your logic," I say to Jake, even though I totally am.

"Besides you won't even be here for that meeting. You and I are chaperoning the campout tomorrow night. We are leaving at four."

"The meeting is at three. I'll be done in plenty of time for the campout."

Jake stands up, committing Hide-and-Seek suicide. "I'm telling you . . . going to that meeting is a really bad idea."

CHAPTER 26

"Heavenly Sunshine"

Jake was so very right about the meeting. Twice he was right: I shouldn't have gone. And it did make me late for the campout. Four thousand times over he was right because the meeting was awful.

I don't get to the dining hall until 4:47. Walking through the door is like walking into after-school detention. Jake, Wolfgang, Kenny, and the boys announce they've been waiting—backpacks strapped on and ready to hike—for almost an hour.

"Here she is! *Finally!"* Johnny scrambles up from where they're playing UNO on the floor. "Can we go now? I've been sitting here for hours."

"Not hours." Jake and a boy with floppy hair, Gideon, are having a guitar lesson. "Hey, Poppi," he calls. "How did it go?"

"I don't want to talk about it right now." Or ever.

"Okay." He's smiling at me. We're going to get along tonight. I can tell by that smile—it's a generous, peacemaking smile. I try to return it, but my face feels like it did during the two years I had braces, like I'm trying to hide my teeth.

"Grab your backpacks, everyone!" Jake lifts the guitar over his head and rests it on the table. "Let's hustle so we can get camp set up and the fire going."

Everyone starts to move toward the door—except a big circle of boys who are stretched out on the floor battling with their Pokémon cards. The parents mail the cards in care packages, creating a black market for the Mega EX ones.

Hector looks up at me. "We'll be done in two minutes, Poppi. Seriously. Let me steal Hoopa from Carter. Then it's all nature, all night. I promise."

Jake laughs next to me. Both of his backpack straps are over his broad shoulders. He pulls the straps and cinches the pack tight across his chest. The whole action is so cute. He is so cute.

When I'm around him, it feels like a spotlight is on me. In middle school, I played soccer, and every time I ran onto the field, I felt like everyone was watching me. Every time I straightened my ponytail or tried to block a kick, it felt like an invisible commentator was reporting my every move. When I'm around Jake, I have this same feeling. He is the spotlight on me, and I bloom in his light.

Jake leads the sixteen boys out onto the patio and up The Hill, singing, "I'm in the Lord's Army" and not turning around to see who's following.

I bring up the rear with Kenny, who is a terrible hiker. He's barrel-chested and top-heavy and breathing really heavily for a guy who will be playing football in a couple of months.

"Are you okay?" I ask as we round the first bend. He's already polished off his bottle of Gatorade. I hand him my water and he guzzles that down too.

"Fine," Kenny says gruffly, glaring. "I am *fine.*"

At this part of the hike, there's a winding stream with a log bridge we have to cross to get to the second part of the trail. Kids love the bridge because it's exactly long enough to be scary. When you're halfway across, if you look down to the flowing water, it feels like your feet could slip. Natalie said that's never happened, but to be safe, we position a counselor on either end of the log to help guide the kids across.

Wolfgang stations himself on the far end and Jake stays on this one until each of us is safely across the brook. The bad news—which I don't realize until Wolfgang and the snaking line of campers are climbing the next hill—is that Jake is now walking alongside me. I try to double my pace, but it doesn't work.

"Hey!" he calls. "Wait up. Talk to me. What happened at the meeting?"

I pretend not to hear him. The meeting was very bad on so many levels. Mostly, I feel like a traitor, like everyone had all been following these rules (don't ask how much Bryan makes, don't go to Association meetings, don't question the accounting) and I broke them all. And it turned out the rules were there for a reason.

"Come on, Poppi!" He pulls my ponytail. "Tell me what you found out. Did you ask Bryan his salary? Was he reporting the donations?"

"How about I admit that you were exactly right and I was stupidly wrong? I'm sorry I doubted you." The guys are already at Lakeside, and we hear Kenny yell, "Put those down! You're going to poke someone's eye!" I sprint to catch up to them.

"Cheater!" Jake pulls my backpack. "Come back here!"

"Cheater? How is saying that 'Jake is right' cheating?"

Is there anything more fun than flirting with a boy you like? anything more exciting than finding ways to tease each other? anything more thrilling than what he'll say next? I wish I could preserve this effervescence forever, like what Mom and I used to do with tomatoes.

"I will get the story out of you. I have my ways." He grabs my waist to pull himself up the last hill and runs past me.

"Hey!" I call.

Then he turns around and winks at me.

CHAPTER 27

"Have You Seen Jesus My Lord?"

Lakeside is my favorite place at Eden—and the campsite at dusk is gorgeous. It's built on a cliff that juts over the lake. From this elevation, the blue water is a sharp contrast to the dense, green forest around it. The whole scene is shadows of gray, indigo, and ivy green. From here, Eden looks peaceful. Pretty much the opposite of this campout.

Jake is right—again. Kenny and Wolfgang are dangerously bad at camping. Wolfgang helps the boys set up their sleeping bags near the ravine, while Kenny sends them out into the forest to find hot-dog sticks. Immediately the boys sword-fight with their sticks. While I pull them in from the woods, Jake takes Wolfie aside and points out that the kids will be sleeping way too close to the edge of the cliff.

I catch Wolfgang pantomiming shoving Jake off the ravine. Kenny mutters, "No kidding." They are so sick of us babysitting them.

"Hey." I put my hand on Kenny's shoulder. "I'm sorry. I'm not trying to be a control freak here."

"Well, you're failing at that," Kenny says, stalking off into the woods.

Jake jumps up to follow him, but I shake my head. "Let him pout. He's tired of feeling like he's doing everything wrong. He needs some distance."

We gaze at each other for a few moments. "You're probably right." Then he flashes me the Number One Cutest Grin in History.

I smile back, my stomach bursting with Christmas-morning excitement. I get to spend the whole night with Jake.

But then we hear, "Hey! Adam's shoe is on fire! Check it out!" and we have to rush back to the fire.

Dinner and devotions go okay. Jake leads worship and I dedicate every brain cell to smelling the burning pine logs, listening to the song lyrics, watching the boys yawn and start to droop—anything to *not* watch Jake playing the guitar.

After worship the campers use their hot-dog sticks to roast marshmallows. When they start shoving each other off the logs, Jake looks at Wolfgang and Kenny. "We've got an hour before we should be in our sleeping bags. What else did you guys have planned?"

They exchange a blank look. "We could play a game?" Kenny looks at me.

"Great idea!" I pat his back.

"How about Assassin?" Wolfgang says. "That winking game that Natalie likes."

A handful of boys groan. "Assassin is for babies," Carter says.

"Yeah." Hector rolls his eyes. "We played that when we were, like, *five*. I feel stupid winking at other guys."

"What about Hide-and-Seek?" Kenny suggests.

The boys like that idea, but Jake points out that it's pitch-black. The last thing we need is fifteen boys scattering in the woods and hiding so well that we can't find them for hours.

"What about something by the fire?" I say. "We'll have to put it out in a little bit. Let's enjoy it while we can."

"We could play Truth or Dare," Sam suggests.

The boys like that idea, and even Jake is nodding.

"Truth or Dare is a terrible game," I say, alarmed. "What about something else?"

"What's wrong with Truth or Dare?" There's an edge to Kenny's voice.

"The truth questions are embarrassing, and the dares are bullying. Isn't there a more positive game we could play?" I ask.

"Yeah, Hide-and-Seek," Kenny grumbles. Wolfgang laughs.

"We could just play Dare." Jake glances around at the campers. "And the dares have to be safe for everyone. Deal, guys?"

"Okay," Sam says, licking his lips. "I'll go first. Ryan, I dare you to walk through the fire."

I clear my throat in Jake's direction. Even Kenny looks startled.

"Can I leave my shoes on?" Ryan asks.

"All right, all right," Jake says to Sam. "C'mon. Safe dares, or we're playing Rhythm Master."

The game doesn't turn out to be a disaster. The boys keep the dares to food stuff—eat a completely charred marshmallow, eat a hot-dog bun with melted chocolate. Then Sam dares Wolfgang to do his Jake impersonation, and the boys immediately start laughing.

Wolfgang stands. He's wearing big black cargo shorts and an orange Eden shirt he bought from the Trading Post. He crosses his arms and sticks his chin out, like Jake does. Then he says, "Guys! Gather up!" in the exact tone Jake uses—but in his German accent. And then, when he copies Jake's stride, we all lose it giggling. The boys cover their mouths and laugh so hard, they fall off their logs.

By then it's after midnight and time for the boys to get to sleep. Like every kid campout in history, it takes forever to get them snuggled into their sleeping bags. It's cold up here, so the boys beg Wolfgang to let the fire burn all night, and he agrees. Jake raises his eyebrows at me, our colleague shorthand for "WHAT?!"

"I'll stay up," I whisper back.

As Jake, Wolfie, and Kenny stretch out with the boys at the tarp, I sit on the other side of the campsite and poke the coals.

The orange and red flames throw off so much heat, my face feels sunburned and my legs sweat under my jeans.

Now, just like every time I find myself solo at a fire, my mind zooms out to take inventory of my current life. My dad has called twice this week to say that he wants to visit me here. Which is sweet but totally unrealistic. Part of being the daughter of an alcoholic is recognizing the fine line of what an alcoholic is actually capable of. Does Dad want to come? Of course. Could Dad get one of his buddies to drive him all the way here? Maybe.

But then something upsetting would happen. He would see me here and realize I'm growing up, and his guilt about the divorce would be too much. Or he would have to socialize too much. That's when he would start sneaking drinks from the vodka he'd bring in his suitcase. You can never totally trust alcoholics because their need to escape—their selfishness—will always be at the center of who they are.

This fire will eat every bit of wood until there are only ashes left. My dad's alcoholism will gnaw at every part of his life until there's nothing left. So, even though my dad loves me, as far as parenting goes, he's about as good as an ostrich. He seems interesting—until you get close.

Then he sticks his head in the sand.

CHAPTER 28

"Pass It On"

"Truth or Dare?"

I jump and almost fall over into the fire.

Jake sits next to me. Right next to me. Six logs surround the fire, and he plops down so close to me, our arms are touching.

Maybe he sits this close because it's cold. Maybe because we have to whisper. Maybe because he knows how much I like touching him. I peek up at him. "What did you just say?"

He looks down at me, and in the flickering flames, I can see he's smiling. "Truth or Dare?"

"That's a dangerous game. It's probably outlawed at every other camp in the country. Talk about liabilities."

Jake laughs, and I feel it rumble through his chest. "I won't make you walk through the fire."

"Maybe I could do my Jake impression then?" I smirk.

"Does everyone have a Jake impression? That's really what I sound like, isn't it?"

"That is exactly what you sound like."

"Wow." He shakes his head. "Does it seem like Kenny and Wolfgang kind of hate me?" But he's smiling and not really asking.

We sit for a few moments and watch the fire. Then he nudges me. "Come on. Quit stalling. Truth or Dare."

I can't take a deep breath. The air is too sharp with cold, too thick with smoke. Where is he going with this? But who cares? I like semisnuggling with him here in the dark. Very much. "Okay. Truth. Just to be safe."

"Perfect. Tell me what happened at the Association meeting."

"I should've taken the dare." I try to take another breath, but my lungs feel at capacity. "The meeting was a disaster. You were totally right."

"Wait. What did you say?" Jake is grinning. He wraps his arm around me and casually leaves his elbow snug against my waist.

"Ha ha. You were right that I made Bryan really mad. I suggested he forfeit some of his salary to help Eden. The Association informed me he already gets paid very little. Like not much more than I do."

"Maybe that's why no one challenges the ridiculous job he's doing this summer."

"Maybe." Then, to change the subject, I say, "Truth or dare?"

"Dare," Jake says meaningfully, so it sounds like it has three syllables. Something has shifted between us at this fire. For the first month of the summer, I felt like marshmallow goo on the bottom of his shoe. This is different. He licks his lips, like I'm some delicious thing he can't wait to taste.

The fire blows and crackles while I think. "Let me take Kenny off probation."

"What? That's cheating." He withdraws his elbow from my waist. "That's not even a dare—that's just a bad idea."

"So, you don't take the dare? You're a wimp?" I ask, using the boys' favorite word. "You're afraid to let me do what I know the staff needs?"

"Like you did at that meeting today?"

"Ouch. Be nice." I glance over my shoulder and then I whisper, "Kenny needs a vote of confidence. He is making progress. Now it's time for us to give him freedom. Let him lead without us hovering."

"Absolutely not. Kenny needs constant supervision. Wolfgang too, actually."

"Let's leave them alone tomorrow. No help. They can do whatever they want. We've been with them constantly for four weeks. They've learned something."

He studies me. "All right. I accept your dare. You're on your own though. Whatever happens when Kenny is unsupervised is on your conscience."

"Good. Because I have even more good ideas. In that twenty-four hours, I'm also going to have a heart-to-heart with Bryan."

"With Bryan?" He laughs. "Are you serious? You said it yourself. Bryan doesn't even like you."

"C'mon, Jake. I dare you to trust my female intuition and stay out of it. First, I'm telling him that I'm sorry about today. Then I'm going to ask him what exactly he thinks I can do to help Eden. I get that *he's* done with this place. But he knows stuff the rest of us don't. He could give me some insight."

"All right." He crosses his arms over his chest. "My turn. Truth or dare?"

I love his jaw when it's speckled with whiskers like this. Obviously I have developed an enormous crush on Jake because imagining him shaving is the cutest thing I can think of. This is The Magic of the Campfire. The flickering light is mesmerizing. Only half my brain is working. "Truth."

"Here goes." He swallows hard. If I didn't know better, it would seem Jake Bass is nervous. He squints at me. "Why don't you like me?"

"*What?*" This time, I actually slip off the log and Jake has to help me back up. "What are you talking about?"

"You avoid me. You argue with me. When I tease you, you're stone-faced." He shakes his head. "I don't get you. You were so nice to my dad. And to Buddy. You're really fun with Pete and Wolfgang and Kenny. Why are you so nice to everyone but me?"

"I'm nice to you." I'm panicky to get back to The Magic of the Campfire.

He wraps his fingers around mine and squeezes. Suddenly the magic is back. "On Saturday night when you cried, I thought everything tense between us would change. But then you didn't listen to me about going to the meeting." He squints at me. "You confuse me. And intimidate me."

"Me?" I lean over to look at him, and my long hair hangs all the way to the forest floor. "I intimidate you?"

"You *surprise* me, that's a better word. You're different from any other girl I've met." He studies me. "You seem so delicate that I want to help you with everything. But then . . ." A smile crosses his lips. "But then you kill a wasp with your bare hands. You march into a really hard meeting. You have this grit."

There's a tickle in my throat. Oh no. This amazing person gives me the nicest compliment—about having grit, no less—and I cry. I sniff loudly, trying to suck the tears back into my face.

"Thanks, Jake." I squeeze his hand and then let go, scooting down the log just a bit to put some space between us. "I do like you. Very much. But my first month here, I was trying to figure out so much. I was scared about making a mistake. I was scared about being your boss. I am very scared about Eden closing. Fear makes people act crazy."

"I dare you to sit right here." He pats the space right next to him.

He's right. I am a hot mess around him. I've scooted to the absolute opposite end of our log. "But it's my turn. Truth or dare."

He doesn't hold my hand or put his arm around me again, but that's probably good. I'm already feverish with all the sparks flying between us. "No question." He leans closer. "Dare."

I want to bask in the warmth of this moment—my shoulder wedged under his arm, his hand on the log next to my thigh.

I think about Natalie warning me that Jake doesn't date girls like me. I turn to him. Oh, wow. He's right there. "Truth. What kind of girls do you usually date?"

"I said dare."

"Okay, I *dare* you to tell me what kind of girls you usually date." I'm actually fluttering my eyelashes at him. *Geesh, Poppi!*

"Cheater. You're really terrible at this game."

"Maybe I'm really good at it."

"Okay. You win." He pushes my hair from my forehead and tucks it behind my ear. "Well, I always fall for blondes." His fingers trail down my shoulder, lighting a path of sparks through my yellow fleece. "I love blue eyes." His fingers leave my shoulder and skim down my nose. "Button noses." He cradles my chin in his hand. I could scream. His thumb rubs my mouth. "And soft, full lips." He leans even closer. "Are your lips soft?"

"Umm . . ."

"I dare you to let me find out," he whispers.

"Yes. Find out."

Jake presses his lips to mine. The world goes completely still. Seriously, I'm so focused on how Jake's mouth feels touching mine that I can't see or hear anything else.

Except one of the boys giggling from the sleeping bags.

We pull away. Jake glances toward the kids and then grins back at me. He looks so casual. I just experienced the most amazing kiss of my life. Maybe the most amazing kiss I'll ever have. But Jake looks like this is just another night—just chatting around the campfire.

"You definitely have the kind of lips I like." He smoothes my hair. "Do you dare me to do that again?"

There's more giggling from the sleeping bags. Jake stands up and cranes his neck toward the meadow.

"Are they, um, watching?" I ask.

"No, but we don't need an audience. How about someplace more appropriate? Can I take you on a date, Poppi?"

"I would love a date with you. A lot. We could go this weekend."

He smiles. The cocky look is back in his eyes. I think of Uncle Ed when he's caught a big bass. "Sure. I'll let you know."

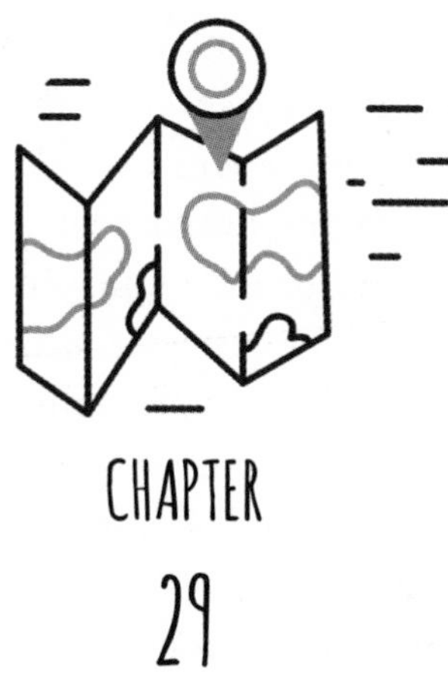

CHAPTER 29

"Better Is One Day in Your Courts"

This all sounds too familiar, doesn't it, Poppi?" Natalie looms behind me in the mirror we're sharing, so she's lecturing my reflection. "What I really mean is that all this sounds *disastrous*, doesn't it?"

There's nothing Natalie enjoys as much as drama. I feel like I'm doing her a favor by going on a date with Jake tonight. It's like when Dad's dog, Nina, has a ball to throw in the air.

Natalie chews on her drama bone, ranting at my reflection. "Eden. A snake. A tree. A warning to stay away from that tree." She's listing these on her fingers. Then she points at me. "The girl who won't listen and then makes a catastrophic choice."

"Tonight will not be a catastrophe." I spread blue eye shadow over my lids. "I'm going out with Jake fully warned. Your job is done."

"Don't you get it, Poppi? This is like watching a movie I've seen a million times. First, it'll be the Incredible-Date-Poppi-Falls-for-Jake scene. Then comes the Jake-Has-Lost-Interest scene." Natalie pulls a big brush from her cosmetic bag and tugs it through my hair. "Then, we'll have several scenes where Jake keeps dating and dumping other girls. Followed by a scene where Poppi cries as Jake dates girls who are pretty and not that interesting—"

"Okay. So, we're all familiar with that part of the movie. Give me a different outcome. How can I be the girl who *does* keep his interest?" I duck away from her brush. "I really like him."

"Don't you get it, Poppi? Everyone likes Jake. He is always the smartest, strongest, most superimpressive guy around."

"But not always," I point out. "I mean, he's here, at this random, tiny camp. He's playing the guitar for campfire worship, not trying to make an album of his own. He's *here*, organizing dodgeball tournaments, not trying to become the next rugby superstar. You've seen him. He can be the very *nicest* guy too."

"Yes. He's complex. I'll give you that. As long as you realize the Teaching-Kids-Hacky-Sack Jake is not the whole package. Promise me you'll remember the snake part too." She's backcombing my hair so it's fuller at the crown. Even though it does look more Hollywood that way, it's a little too Dolly Parton to be me.

I shake out my hair. "What if I go out with him but I have really low expectations? I could treat tonight like a field trip, a chance to get dressed up and get out?"

"Yes. Maybe you can do that." She sits on her bed, smiling a little. "Because you do deserve a nice night—more than anyone else I know." She taps the brush on the back of my head. "But disastrous scenes are coming."

"Natalie. You don't have to protect me. Believe me, I can handle disappointment. I know disastrous scenes. For the past couple of years, I've been on a reality show where the very worst thing keeps happening. Mom dying, dropping out of college. It's like one of those shows where someone creates problems to mess with the poor schmucks."

"Like, God?"

"What?"

"I mean, we're talking about your real life. I think that means you're saying that God has been the one messing with you."

"Yeah, maybe so." Do I really believe that? Does believing God doesn't take good care of me also mean I'm not really a Christian?

"You're changing, though." She leans back against her Miss Piggy pillowcase and looks at me like she's really critiquing an actual character on a reality show. "Camp is wearing you down. When you got here, you had, like, this shell around you. You were kind of like a turtle, like you were pulling your head in all the time."

"This is your predate pep talk?"

"It absolutely is because you're not a turtle anymore. Like, all these campfires and s'mores and worship songs and hiking and Bible studies and praying and laughing have, you know, thawed you out. Like what's happening to those ice caps in Norway."

"You mean the ice caps that are ruining the earth because they're melting?" I smile. "This is *seriously* your pep talk?"

"Seriously. When you first got here, you hardly ever led prayers. You were so fragile that you didn't say much during devotions. You kind of frowned whenever Jake or I talked about God. But you're changing. Melting." She smoothes my dress—actually, it's her dress. It's short but not too short, black, and simple, and directly from her garbage-bag-suitcase collection. "Now, you're thawing and gorgeous and strong and ready." She tucks my hair behind my ears.

There's a noise outside our window. Jake clearing his throat. I widen my eyes.

She pushes me toward our door. "Okay. Remember. Snake in the garden. Too close and you'll get bit."

"Thanks, Nat." I kiss her forehead. "I'll keep you posted."

CHAPTER 30

"Love, Love, Love"

Tonight is the coolest of the summer and I immediately wish I had my yellow fleece. I wear it every night to campfire and it couldn't smell any more like smoke if it was on fire. But it's so cozy and exactly the right weight against California's cool nights.

Then I see the way Jake is looking at me, and I know this is not a night for my yellow fleece. Or to smell like campfire smoke. This is a night for red toenails, curled hair, and glittery blue eye shadow.

"You look beautiful." He takes my hand, and I look at him in his green dress shirt and dark-washed jeans.

"Thanks. You too. I mean. You look really, really nice too."

We hold hands as we walk toward the parking lot. From the campfire back over at Alleluia, we can hear the worship skit unfolding. "Take that, Satan!" Then machine gun noises. Aaron's cabin has the skit tonight, and they're very big on graphic spiritual warfare.

Jake opens the Hummer door for me and then climbs into his side. I swing in my legs, careful to not wrinkle my dress. "Where are we headed?"

He turns from Eden's driveway to smile at me. "I'm taking you out. I get to surprise you."

"You're not telling me?"

"When you plan our date, you can surprise me. Tonight I'm in control."

"Deal." I settle back against the soft leather as Jake merges onto the highway, toward the hazy glow of the L.A. lights.

His car is an interesting mixture of polish and clutter. The Hummer itself is new. Or maybe it's just that I'm used to my old Kia or the really ancient pickup Mom and I drove around the farm.

The chrome encircling the AC vents catches the early-evening sun and glimmers. I settle deeper into my seat because I think it actually has its own cooler. My best friend, Leah, had seat heaters in her old Honda Pilot. I've never heard of seat coolers though. I scoot my bottom to the very back of the seat, even though it feels a bit like I wet my pants.

Not everything in Jake's Hummer is cush, though. A rusty red toolbox rattles in the back. An In-and-Out Burger bag and about six empty water bottles litter the floorboard. Two of those space-age silver mugs—Yetis, maybe?—rest in the cup holders. The dashboard wears a fine coat of camp dust that is smudged with fingerprints.

The fingerprints and Yetis and In-and-Out Burger bag are so much more interesting than the sparkling chrome. As we drive in silence, I notice that the red berries that grow around camp are smeared into the light gray carpet. A Butterfinger wrapper is balled into the driver's-side cup holder. These are little clues to who he is.

The most interesting part of the Hummer, of course, is Jake himself. Tendons cord in his forearm from his tight grip on the steering wheel. He's nervous, and I like that. I also like his imperfections. I like the tuft of hair that sticks up at the crown of his head, even more than the shininess of the rest of it. Jake is cute and strong and a little damaged about his dad and sarcastic and determined. I guess Nat is right. Somehow all of this makes him the whole package.

At the end of the summer, I'll keep doing camp—at Eden or someplace else. He'll go back to UCLA and then eventually to law school. Then, he'll flourish in a life so different from mine, we might not even be Facebook friends.

And yet, I really know him—how silly he gets when he's tired, what he looks like when he first wakes up, how he's scared of getting bit by another skunk. In these ways, I know Jake better than I knew our neighbors back home who had lived next door to us for two generations. I bet I know him better than some girls he's dated.

Jake exits the freeway and stops short behind a dark green Jaguar. He looks at me and sees I'm staring at him. "What?"

"I meant what I said at Lakeside. I like you."

He pokes his tongue into his cheek—the thing he does when he's considering something—and glances at me. "Okaaaaaay." He noses the front of the Hummer close to an Impala blasting rap music.

"I was just thinking about how strange it is to go on a date with a person I know as well as you. This is a weird thing about camp, right? We eat three meals a day together. We work together twenty-three hours a day. We are practically the same person."

"I would say there are some definite differences between us." He grins at me. "You like my camp self—but what about my other self? My real self."

"What if your camp self is your real self?"

He shakes his head.

"What if it is? What if guitar playing and skit leading and dodgeball refereeing is who you really are? What if you're just confused that you should be a lawyer?"

"Nope. I'm not confused." He honks at the Impala. "Come on, man. Let me in."

"I'm sure of it. Your camp self is your real self. If it wasn't, you wouldn't tolerate the evil coffee and cheap, greasy bacon and so many nights of patrolling cabins and so many days of teaching kids how to canoe. You just wouldn't."

"Don't call camp bacon 'evil.' That's profane."

"I called the camp coffee 'evil.' But listen to my point. You would spend your summers as a caddy at some country club. Or doing an internship at a law firm."

"Internships are for after your sophomore and junior years." He flashes me a smile as he turns onto a side road. "That's why I'm taking classes this summer."

"Just watch. You'll hate interning next summer. You'll see that your heart beats for camp, not working in some office."

"You are absolutely wrong." He turns down a narrow street, quieter than the others, with small bungalows and big front porches. Then he pulls into a dark parking lot. As he switches off the ignition, he grins at me.

"We're here? Natalie had me expecting a steak place." This is a converted house with a neon sign that reads, "Jax."

"Best hamburgers in California," he says, opening my door.

"See, I knew you defied expectations."

He laughs. "Go inside. I'm starving for some nonevil bacon."

CHAPTER 31

"Hungry"

Only after we're seated do I realize Jax is a really cool little bistro. This is not a chain restaurant—did I really think Jake would take me to a chain?—but a locals' place. A candle flickers on the white tablecloth and a cluster of daisies rests in a bud vase. Although the menu is only burgers, it's four pages. It has everything from a "burger" made entirely of mushrooms to one marbled with six different kinds of cheese.

The second I look up from my menu, a waiter appears. Jake asks me if I'd like cheese straws. I say I would, and he orders them. He calls the waiter by name.

"So, is this one of your favorites?" I sip my water.

"For L.A., it's pretty relaxed. It's a good place if you want to talk."

"You want to talk?" I grin at him. "Is that your usual date protocol?"

He rolls his eyes. "You've been talking to Natalie too much." He snaps shut his menu. "You're getting the cheeseburger by the way. It's a nonissue."

"What if I don't like cheeseburgers?"

"On Monday night you ate two cheeseburgers. And I will admit that the *cheeseburgers* at camp are evil."

"You noticed I ate two cheeseburgers?" I smile. "What else have you noticed?"

He pauses to talk to the waiter, Scott, an older guy with wispy blond hair. Scott calls Jake "Bud" and congratulates him on ordering well. He must know Jake is a good tipper because "two cheeseburgers" isn't really a complicated order.

"Let's see . . . I've also noticed that you broke up with a boyfriend back home. Just before you got here, right?"

"Me?" I laugh. "Before I got here, I was clinically depressed. Not even close to a boyfriend. What gave you that idea?"

The waiter sets down the cheese straws and Jake grabs a handful. "Just the vibe you were sending off. Something was bothering you. Now I understand the whole timeline of your mom and everything. So, no boyfriend? Ever? And you're nineteen?"

"Yep. I skipped kindergarten, so I graduated from high school early. And don't forget that there are, like, five thousand people in my hometown. And I'm related to a bunch of them. So, no boyfriend isn't really that weird."

"You could've dated a farm boy from another town."

"Before last year, before everything with my mom, I was very sheltered. I had friends that were boys, but I don't even know how a boyfriend would have fit into the life I had with my mom. She and I became this very close team—even before she got sick."

He stops chewing and looks alarmed. "The other night. At Lakeside. Was that your first kiss?"

I shake my head no, a little awkward to be casually discussing our amazing kiss. "Prom night was. I know, I'm a cliché." I bite into a cheese straw. "Why are you looking at me like that? Does all this sound kind of ridiculous to Jake Bass, professional dater?"

"Okay, that's it. You're not allowed to talk to Natalie anymore. I'm not a professional dater."

"Oh, please." I tilt my head. "I don't believe you. Not one little bit. Even without Natalie's warnings, I wouldn't believe you. You have the slickness of a guy who has had lots of girlfriends."

"Maybe at Eden. But in Dallas, I had a famous dad and no friends. I think you get to pick one or the other. Celebrity dad or popularity. Plus, I was kind of a punk kid. A know-it-all."

"You? A know-it-all? *Never.*"

"Ha ha. Watch your sass. It's why I got beat up on a regular basis."

"So, you waited for summer to be Big Man of Camp?"

"I mean, I eventually found my way in Dallas too. I played in our church praise band, was on the club's tennis team for ten years, was in Boy Scouts."

"Really? You were a Boy Scout?" I hold up my hand. "High five. I was a Girl Scout."

"A Girl Scout, huh?" Instead of slapping my hand, he grabs it over our appetizer and squeezes it. "How many years?"

"Too many if you ask the other girls in Eagle. I stuck with it to get my Gold Award—that's like an Eagle for Girl Scouts."

"I know. I'm an Eagle Scout." Scott appears with platters for us. He sets a cheeseburger, still sizzling under a puffy bun, in front of me. The French fries smell so different from Eden's frozen ones, it's surprising these are the same basic food.

We talk about our final projects. I built lifeguard stands for the two lakes by Eagle. Jake rebuilt the banks around Lake Eden.

"Really? That's your work? Nice shore."

"Thanks. I got special permission from the council to do a project in California instead of Texas. I came out here for Thanksgiving break my junior year and stayed with Bryan. That's when I realized how lonely he must be. I mean, you cannot imagine how depressing this place is in the winter. There's no one to talk to. You have to make friends with the raccoons so you don't lose your mind."

"Ahhhh," I exhale. "That sounds so peaceful."

"Are you kidding me? It's a mental health nightmare, like solitary confinement. Do you really think you could live like that?"

I consider his question while I nibble on a soft, salty fry. "I could make it work. With the Internet, life in the woods isn't so lonely. So, yeah. Hopefully I'll have the chance to try it."

"If Eden stays open?"

"*When* Eden stays open. Call me next summer when you're hating your internship. I'll let you know if it's tolerable. Or if I've turned bitter, like Bryan."

"When I was a kid, I wanted to be Bryan." Jake looks down at his own fries.

"You're kidding."

"No, really. My dad was hard to live with, but Bryan cared about me. He was like you, actually. Totally passionate about Eden. He was going to raise money to build a whole retreat center."

"But that never happened."

"When you're a kid, you care about how people treat you, not whether they're good at fund-raising."

I think about that. "True."

"When I got a little older, I would come out early to stay with him before camp started. Harvey—he was the executive director before Bryan—would come up here too. So would Mike Browne and a couple of other guys who don't work at Eden anymore. We would hike all the trails. We would build campfires every night and sleep outside. Total guy trip. Best time of my life."

"I feel like you're making this up. Bryan is seriously the cancer killing Eden."

"Maybe now. But for a few years, he was the superhero saving it. This might be what happens to anyone who works at camp long term." Jake shrugs. "I hate to sound like a lawyer, but the evidence is there. There's a music camp in Dallas that Dad supports and it's the same trend there. If you make the wilderness your permanent career, you burn out. Apparently we weren't created to live alone in the woods."

"I absolutely think we were, literally, created to live alone in the woods. Like, Eden? The original creation? God created one person to live alone with the animals and beautiful trees and go for walks in the cool of the evening. It was like camp. It was paradise."

“Ha!” Jake leans forward and points. “And then what happened? He created woman because it wasn’t good for man to be alone in the woods.” He is smiling a know-it-all smile, and I can see why he got beat up as a kid. “I mean, right?”

“Maybe. But I’m not going to live alone. If Eden does stay open, they’ll have to find an executive director to take Bryan’s place. So, I’ll live with whoever that is. But yeah, it will be kind of me and the raccoons.”

Suddenly Jake looks around for our waiter. “Finish up. I just realized where I’m taking you next.”

“Okay.” I push away the plate, with just a few fries on it. “I’m good.” I swallow. “Thanks for this cheeseburger. You’re right. Even better than the camp ones.”

He laughs. “You think?”

CHAPTER 32

"Oceans"

After Jake finishes with the check, we walk outside. When I step in front of him, he rests his hand, lightly, on the small of my back. Maybe it's the delicious cheeseburger in my belly or the good conversation or the rest of the night stretching in front of us, but when Jake opens my door this time, my tension has softened into rivers of adrenaline.

I want to see all of L.A. With him. Right now. I want to stay up all night and tell each other inside jokes about camp and hear about everything he ever did in L.A. and Texas and what he thinks and feels about absolutely every bit of it—from his childhood to his future.

We don't do all of that, but we do go to Cove, a tiny little coffee shop that's run by a guy who knows Jake's dad. The little coffee bar is built right into a cliff that's on the shore of the Pacific Ocean. In one corner of the enclave, two musicians are performing. Between us and the ocean is a roaring bonfire that throws off welcome heat against the cool night.

All around the stage are these little stone tables that look just like the canyon wall. It's like someone carved tables and benches right from the same gray and purple granite.

On the stage a guy named Tate plays his guitar. His Adele-looking girlfriend, Bethany, sings and strums her own guitar. They play worship music and rock songs and even some George Jackson Bass. It's very casual, like we're sitting around a campfire, and everyone calling out requests. Jake calls out "Have You Seen Jesus My Lord?" because he knows I'm so sick of it. Omega loves that song, and they request to sing it at every worship. But the version Tate and Bethany perform is so different—more anger and passion—and it sounds like a completely different song.

As the crowd builds, the waves and wind and fire are too loud for Tate to hear the requests. Finally he just writes his cell number on a whiteboard and tells people to text him requests. The whole thing is very L.A.—and I love it all.

Jake gets us lattes and muffins as big as my hands. He sets the coffee and plates on this rock chaise lounge away from the rest of the crowd. We sit sideways together on the long edge and balance our plates on our knees.

For both of us to fit, I practically have to sit in Jake's lap. And why not? This whole scene seems like a picture out of someone else's life. The crashing white waves, the wild fire, the too-loud music—everything is exciting tonight. Of course I also have a hot guy right here to lean on.

"I've never heard anyone sing like her before," I say into Jake's ear when Bethany takes over the mic. "She's kind of angry, but her words are so true." It's not like most Christian songs, with vague references to struggles and trusting God. She is just laying it all out there: "I think I might outlive my faith; Then where will I be? Still clawing for a bit of Your face."

"I know her. And Tate. They go to UCLA. Incredible people."

I look at Jake. "Why are they playing at some random coffee shop instead of with a record deal?"

"They have a record deal. This is L.A., so it's not a random coffee shop. They are exactly where they need to be." He stretches his arm out so it's hugging my hip close to him. My stomach feels bottomless and prickly.

I snuggle into Jake. I will stay right here for the rest of my life. Because what else is there—really? In the foam of my latte, the barista drew a heart. I stare at it and feel the heat from Jake and hear the beautiful, angry music and smell my coffee and something else vaguely fishy—either from the ocean or a nearby grill.

I don't even want to sip my coffee because that will mess up the foam and maybe this very good moment.

Because right here is inspiration, and warmth, and happiness, and security. Because I realize that this—*right here*—is everything I've wanted for so long.

Thank you. I want to say it out loud. I want to thank *someone* for this. The barista for the heart? Bethany for her music that resonates in my soul? Jake for knowing me—and liking me?

God for the ocean and the fire and the stars?

And for this sudden peace?

CHAPTER 33

"Lord of the Dance"

It's well after midnight—after we help Bethany and Tate load their sound equipment and instruments into the back of their van—when we finally walk back to Jake's Hummer. By the time we're merging onto Highway 1 back to Eden, it feels like we've been gone six months.

Everything at camp seems so far away—the petition Aaron's guys created about not having corn dogs again; the faucet by the dining hall that trickles all day, making a mud pie we all step through as we walk to meals; how I'm so sick of hearing "The Squirrel Song" that I want to stick my fingers in my ears when it's time for mail call. Everything from camp seems dusty and ancient and removed.

Jake is thinking the same thing because when we pull into Eden's parking lot, he turns off the ignition, leans against the seat, and sighs. "Back to the real world."

"I'm not ready." I study his aristocratic profile and the shadowed trees looming behind him. "Is the parking lot always this dark—or is this just what it looks like after the lights in L.A.?"

"Always this dark. By tomorrow night, you won't even need a flashlight."

"Jake?" I take his hand. "Thank you for everything tonight. I needed every minute of it. Like I—*really*—needed it. The conversation and laughing and the cheeseburgers and Cove and everything. You made me very happy."

"You're welcome." He pulls my hand to his lips. Once there, his warm, whiskered mouth breathes on my fingers. With those breaths, something slow and lazy unfolds inside me.

I hear a long, low sigh. I'm not even embarrassed when I realize it's from me. He pulls on my hand until we're both leaning on the center console. Then he kisses me. Jake tastes like sugar and a little like something darker—coffee, maybe?

He reaches over, opens his door, and climbs out. Then he comes around to my side and pulls me out. Bethany's and Tate's voices sing out from the Hummer's speakers.

"Dance with me," he murmurs.

"Here? Really?"

"Here." He wraps his arms around me and I fall against his chest. "I want to see you relax like you did tonight. You can smile like that all the time." He gently rubs his thumb down my face. "Saving a camp doesn't have to mean forehead creases."

Then we dance. We dance until Jake's phone shuffles through all the songs on Bethany and Tate's album. And when the song "Rage & Creation" repeats, we don't stop dancing.

His hand is on the back of my head. At one point, he pulls away for a second to say, "Tonight has been my favorite part of the whole summer."

I say, "This has been my favorite part of my whole *life*."

Jake stops moving, and then he looks at me for a long time. His eyes are wide.

But he does not say anything to that.

CHAPTER 34

"Dance with Me"

Since the start of camp, Beth's cabin has been asking me to help them build a fort at Lakeside. I've been with Wolfgang's cabin so much that I haven't had a free morning to help them.

But last night, everything changed. I wake up this morning, and the world is full of bright, glistening brilliance. Anything is possible. The loop in my mind keeps replaying last night's dancing: Jake's hands on my back, his real voice harmonizing with Bethany's recorded one, the weight of his chin on top of my head, the peppery tree smell of his shirt. It was one night, but it changed everything.

Now I'm living inside this kind of rain cloud, right before it explodes into a storm. Electricity is buzzing down my skin, and I'm goose-bumpy and fizzy. Maybe this is how it feels to be loved. Or to love someone.

So yes to Beth and her girls. Yes to all-morning fort building. Yes to all of it.

Jake wasn't at breakfast. I think he must be studying in his room. Pete had a plate of leftover bacon, and I waited around in the kitchen to see if Jake would show up.

But now Beth's girls are ready to build the fort, so I hike to Lakeside with them instead of knocking on his door. The girls are a bell curve of excitement. At the front of the pack, Maddie and Catie are interrupting each other to tell me their plans. They've sketched out a two-story tree house, complete with a trapdoor and curtains. They plan to build this before lunch.

Maddie is lugging twine from the maintenance shed up the trail. "We will make a pulley system, like an elevator for food and stuff." She's so excited, she keeps stepping on the backs of my tennis shoes. She's a drill sergeant before battle, a ringmaster before the circus. "The whole thing is going to be as big as Lakeside. Like, I think we should just make a shelter out of the whole campsite."

"And we're building all this out of sticks?" I clarify.

"Sticks and leaves and pine needles," Catie says from behind Maddie. "If we put enough pine needles on the ground, it'll be the softest floor you can imagine. Like God-made carpet."

Beth laughs. "Brilliant!"

"How about you, Jilly? Jenna? Michele?" I call to the girls hiking behind us. "What's going on back there? Do you need to stop and drink some water?"

The Middle-of-the-Bell-Curve Girls are quiet. They're like the privates, subject to the authority of the Drill-Sergeant Alpha Girls. These are the sweet ones, the B+ kids who follow directions and never cause problems. They could spend their morning building a fort or taking a math test or cleaning their rooms, and they would do it with the same reliability and happiness. I was one of these girls, following the Natalies of the world who have the loud voices and good ideas.

"We're doing great! This is fun!" Jenna calls. The B+ kids are always the ones who are hardest to read. They're so concerned about being good, you never know what they're really thinking.

"Harriet? Ava? Are you okay back there?" The girls trailing at the very back are the wild cards, the ones who might go AWOL at any moment.

Some drama went down with Harriet and Hector after he got caught sneaking out. The result is that Hector—who spent the first three weeks worshiping Harriet—now dislikes her very much. And he has proclaimed his love for Wendy in The Light.

"We are perfectly *fine*." Harriet's voice is shrill, like I've asked if she's enjoying getting attacked by spiders. "No, really. We are doing just soooooo wonderful." Then she yells to the forest. "Everything is absolutely, stinking perfect!"

Beth rolls her eyes to me and goes to the back of the group, to the 20 percent of the bell curve with the issues, the ones who could ruin this for everyone else. "Why the bad attitude, Harriet?" I call. "You've wanted to build this fort since Day One."

"No bad attitude here!" Harriet calls, her voice dripping with bad attitude. "Because we *do* need to build a shelter from the other cabins. Especially from the really horrible ones."

We've arrived at the log bridge. While Beth and I position ourselves to help the girls cross the log, Beth whispers, "Help! She will ruin this!"

"I'll try," I whisper back to Beth.

As we get to Lakeside, Harriet has everyone in her cabin—even the Middle-of-the-Bell-Curve Girls—laughing about how we need protection from the other campers, the other *really horrible girls*.

"Why are y'all laughing?" Harriet asks innocently. "Because I'm totally serious. We need shelter! I am going to violently throw up if I have to look at Wendy's face again."

"Harriet, stop." I halt, right before our group hikes up the steep little ravine, right before we get to Lakeside, right before we're at where Jake kissed me two nights ago. "You're being really mean."

"How am I being mean?" Harriet's voice is so sweet, I almost believe she's clueless.

"You know how," Beth says in a low voice.

Meanwhile, the drill sergeant girls are instructing their privates to collect "sticks taller than you!" Like a colony of worker ants, everyone scatters into the forest, finding limbs and lugging logs back to the clearing.

Harriet and Ava make up a song about "Wendy the Wolf" to the tune of "Amazing Grace" and include the lyrics, "Wendy once was lost But now is found Kissing boys on the ground!"

Beth drops her armload of sticks. She looks ready to throw Harriet into the lake. "That is enough! You are done, Harriet. Go and sit on that log. And you'll be cleaning the cabin during Trading Post all week."

Harriet throws the pile of branches she's collected so they land right on Beth's ankles.

"Ouch!" Beth kneels and grabs her feet. When she moves her hands, thin scratches bleed down her shins. Tears are shining in her eyes, and the other girls gather around her. Jilly already has the first-aid kit out. Silently, she opens an alcohol wipe and dabs the scratches.

"That's what's wrong with this stupid place." Harriet's voice is a whimper. "Y'all want us to be soooooo nice. But you refuse to deal with the real problems. Wendy is the one who makes out with boys."

"Come on, Harriet. You and I are taking a hike together." I look at the rest of the group. "Girls, you are doing fantastic. Good work." All of them—the drill sergeants, and the privates, and even wild card Ava—nod back at me.

Because no one wants to be Harriet right now.

CHAPTER 35

"Jesus Loves Me"

We are barely three feet away from the other girls when Harriet starts to talk. It's like the altitude works as a truth serum because the more we hike, the more this becomes a therapy session.

She tells me about how both her parents are doctors and work a lot. She has three older brothers, who are soccer superstars—one is a freshman at Stanford and already leading the team to a winning season. Her parents fly up to San Francisco for every game. Harriet wants to quit soccer because no matter how good she is, she will never be as good as her brothers.

"I've seen you play soccer, Harriet," I say. "You're better than anyone else here. Even the boys."

This makes Harriet cry. She falls down, right in the middle of the trail, and sobs. "You think I'm good?" Her voice is full of venom and self-hatred. "Henry, my middle brother, might play at the *Olympics*. So, no. Really, I'm *nothing*."

I kneel next to her. "You're not nothing. You're *something.* And here at Eden, besides all the soccer stuff, you are a really important part of things. You're a leader in your cabin. You're very enthusiastic. Remember square dancing?"

"Oh my *gosh*." She presses her fingers to her temples, like I'm giving her a migraine. "You have no idea what you're talking about, Poppi. Seriously. I've been in therapy for all of this. It's a *thing*. My parents have abandoned me. My therapist calls this Helicopter Abandonment Syndrome." Her tears run down her long nose and make dark splotches in the dirt. "My mom and dad were always around when I was little. Everyone smothered me with attention. But then my brothers became more interesting. Now, they don't even come to my games. My nanny, Maria, comes or no one comes."

Harriet can be dramatic, but I think she's telling the truth. "I'm sorry about your folks, Harriet. But that's what makes it so important that you're here. At Eden, you get to see who you are away from your family."

"I thought I was important when Hector liked me." She's gut-sobbing now. "I really, really liked him, Poppi."

"You liked him? Or you liked the attention?"

She sniffs. "His attention, I guess." Then she says very seriously, "I want a boy to really like me, to worship me like that. Forever."

"Well, yeah." I smile. "Who doesn't want that, Harriet?"

"Do you want that?"

"I, uh . . ." Her question makes me uncomfortable. I study the roots near the trail to avoid answering. Because, yeah, that's exactly what I want. Right now, in fact. Right now, I want Jake to like me as much as I like him. I can't say that to Harriet, of course.

"Do you want *Jake* to worship you?" She's grinning. Oh man. There are no secrets at camp.

"We're not talking about me. We are talking about you. And the point is that you are not important because *Hector* likes you. You're not important because the girls in your cabin follow you or your parents come to your soccer games. The point is you're important because—"

"Don't say I'm important because Jesus loves me. I really like it when you talk to me like I'm an adult. Please don't use clichés."

"Yes, Harriet. You're important because Jesus loves you." Even as I say this, I wonder if I believe it, if I really know it myself. If I believe Jesus loves me, does that mean He's taking care of me? But I continue with Harriet. "And same to you. Don't be a cliché. Don't start all the mean-girl-hating-Wendy stuff. It's just silly, isn't it?"

"But Poppi, she's a troublemaker. Seriously. Everyone knows what she does with boys when she sneaks out. Kenny is too terrible of a counselor to realize what his boys are doing."

Harriet is smart enough to find my tender spot: Kenny and his boys sneaking out. She's also mad enough to poke that tender spot. But I don't let her distract me. "It's not your job to worry about what happens to Wendy. Or Kenny. Do you get that? Do you understand that if you don't stop the bullying, you will go home?"

She leans back, like my threat is an actual force. Here's *her* tender spot. She really likes being at Eden. "You can't send me home. You need campers really bad. I know Eden might close because there aren't enough campers."

"That's true." Ouch. Now she's jabbing my other tender spot. "But we need campers who want to be here. Will you turn your attitude around?"

Harriet rubs her tennis shoes in the dirt, creating little dust clouds that billow up and catch the sunlight. "Yeah." She coughs on the dust and stands. "I will."

When we get back to Lakeside, the fort is really coming together. The girls have collected armloads of branches, enough to build a little shelter with space for all of us to fit inside. Using the Lincoln Log method, they've intertwined the branches to make walls and used the longer ones for the roof. Now they're tying them all together with twine.

Near the trail, Ava and Maddie are laying out branches one by one. "We're making a door," Maddie announces. Jilly and Catie are spreading pine needles around for the cabin floor.

"Harriet, can you find some tall limbs?" Beth pats her shoulder. "We'll paint our cabin name on a big sheet and hang it up, kind of like a flag. Think you can find some big branches?"

Harriet trudges off and I smile at Beth. She smiles back. Again I have that surging feeling, like strong coffee is pumping through my veins. Harriet will be fine. Jake is waiting back at Eden for me. He danced until two in the morning with me. I feel beautiful and fun and energetic and like I might be falling in love.

CHAPTER 36

"All the Poor and Powerless"

After hours of building—hours of the sun beating down on us at Lakeside—the girls are drooping. I announce we have to stop for lunch.

But they beg to finish spreading the pine needles for the forest floor. They have already spread so many armloads that it really does look like carpet. "Maybe a skunk will have her babies in here!" Catie says. Beth widens her eyes at me because that's exactly what will happen. Then we both laugh because what else can we do at this point?

Harriet has taken over control of constructing the door. When the girls witness their surly leader on board with the fort, everyone shifts to a deeper frenzy.

But by two o'clock, Maddie tells me she's seeing black spots, and my stomach is clenching with hunger. We've eaten the cookies I brought up in my backpack and we've drunk all our water. Beth looks at me. "Maybe you could just run down and get us some lunch?"

"Of course. If I don't pass out on the way there." I'm already heading down the trail. "I'll be back in twenty minutes with lemonade and peanut butter and jelly!"

Down at base camp, I burst through the kitchen door to find Jake inside, talking to Pete. I stand in the doorway, holding it open. We stare at each other. He's holding a bunch of wood dowels we use for doughboys. It's the first time I've seen him since our date.

Pete is next to him—singing along with Rend Collective that's blaring from his phone and mixing Bisquick and milk in a huge aluminum bowl. He dumps in a little powder, then a little milk. More powder. More mixing. I watch them both from the doorway, my eyes adjusting from the bright sunlight.

Pete waves. "Hey, Poppi. Missed you at lunch." He looks back at the bowl. "No leftovers, though. The campers tore through those nuggets."

"No problem. I'm here to grab sandwiches. We're building up at Lakeside." I'm frozen in the doorway, still just staring at Jake, suddenly unsure. I want to kiss his cheek, but Pete probably doesn't know about us yet.

"Hello, Poppi." Jake's voice is oddly formal, like he's talking to a teacher. He turns toward the pantry. "Have you seen the rest of the roasting sticks? I'm helping Kenny get stuff together for their dinner tonight. They're doing doughboys up at Lakeside, and I can only find six of the good dowels."

"The other dowels?" Something is off. He's not looking at me.

Pete groans. "Y'all have got to tell the counselors to put them back when they're finished with them." He follows Jake into the pantry.

"I only need, like, three more." Jake's voice sounds faraway. "You don't have three more?"

"I don't." Pete comes back out of the pantry, shaking his head. "And do you know why? Because everyone wants to make doughboys, but no one wants to clean the sticks when they're finished. They just throw them away."

"Maybe in the office—" I say.

But Pete is still ranting. "I'm like the Little Red Hen in here. Who wants to clean the sticks? Who wants to make the dough?

Everyone's like, 'Let Pete do it!'" He scratches his forehead, leaving a streak of Bisquick by his widow's peak. "But then, who wants to feast on a perfect dough pocket, roasted to perfection? Who wants to stuff their face with that jelly-filled deliciousness? Everyone! That's who!"

Jake grins at Pete. "Dude. Seriously? How are you going to call yourself the Little Red Hen when you are the camp *cook*? Making doughboys is your entire job description."

"Entire job description? All right then, man. You want to get all that corn on the cob ready for dinner?" Pete pushes the bowl away but he's not really mad. This is some kind of bro-joking he and Jake have going on. "Because I really don't feel like shucking that corn all afternoon, man."

"Sorry. I'm headed up to Lakeside to roast some doughboys. You're on your own." Jake comes out of the pantry, hugging a jar of strawberry preserves and the white bucket of peanut butter. He's also got a bag of marshmallows under his arm.

"Lakeside? Wait. Kenny's cabin is at Lakeside for dinner?" I feel disoriented. The kitchen is a cave compared to the brilliant sunshine outside. A fan in the corner is blowing right on us. It's too loud and cold in here. "When did you decide that?"

"They asked me at lunch." He scoops out a huge spoonful of peanut butter and puts it in a baggie. "No one is there tonight, right?"

"You need to use plastic for that, man?" Pete asks. "You can't just take the bucket up there? You have to create more waste that's going to end up in a landfill?"

"Don't get on me about the plastic." Jake opens another baggie and scoops in some jelly. "It's a million times easier for the kids to fill their own doughboys when you just snip off the corner and let them squeeze. This is my doughboy secret. None of the mess."

"I don't care about the mess. I care about that plastic sitting around for the next billion years."

The dark kitchen, the loud music, the noisy fan, the argument over doughboys is causing my adrenaline to ooze out of me and all over this cracked linoleum floor.

"Pete, have you ever seen ten-year-olds trying to fill dough tubes with peanut butter? They spread it all over. Lakeside becomes a huge ant trap. Then we're going to just sit on top of that?" Jake's voice is like Pete's, that smooth, half-asleep guy tone that I kind of hate right now.

"Actually, I need both of those." I nod to the peanut butter and jelly. "I'm up at Lakeside with Beth's cabin and the girls haven't eaten anything all day. We're building this huge fort. In fact, I think they were planning to sleep there tonight." These are actual lies. The girls ate breakfast and cookies. And they don't have any sleeping bags or clothes to camp at Lakeside tonight.

"No problem." Jake's voice is still silky. "I'll tell Kenny we need to do our dinner over at Alleluia." Jake steps back from the counter. He is certainly not inventing reasons to be near me now. Maybe he's even avoiding me?

I dump a loaf of bread on the counter and slap jelly on half of the pieces. Jake disappears outside and the screen door slams. The kitchen feels cooler without his heat in here. I make myself a sandwich, but my throat is too clogged to eat it. I start to spread peanut butter on the other half of the bread.

"Hey, blind man! I found your doughboy sticks!" Pete comes out of the pantry with them. He also hands me an empty box with a pickle label. "Use this to get those sandwiches up to Lakeside. No sense in wasting more baggies when Jake is already stuffing a landfill with them." Pete pokes his head out of the screen door. "Jake! Where did you go? I really need to start that corn."

Just as I'm finishing the pile of sandwiches, Jake comes back into the kitchen. He doesn't even glance at me, just walks over to the dough. "Ah, come on, Pete. You could have made the balls for me. Wolfgang needs me down at the lake."

But Pete pushes past him, his arms filled with green ears of corn. "I've got fifty ears to shuck and boil." He backs through the screen door with Rend Collective playing from his apron pocket. "You can stand there and make twelve stinking doughboys." The door slams and he yells back through the screen, "And don't use any more plastic! Find a box to put them in, man!"

I'm standing so still that if Jake did come close to me, I would topple over. We're both quiet, listening to Pete sing along with "Build Your Kingdom Here." Finally, when the noise of Jake slapping dough in his hands is deafening, I turn to him. "So, how about Saturday?" My voice does not sound casual, as I had hoped. It sounds like it's full of peanut butter.

He disappears into the pantry, taking the long way around the metal table. "Saturday? For what?"

I wait until he comes out, carrying a big jar that once held salsa. "I'm taking you out on Saturday. And it's a surprise too."

He looks at me. His hair does not have any tufts sticking up in the back. No whiskers today either. I would do anything for a pimple on his chin or jelly on the corner of his lip. Anything for the flawed Jake, the one I know and like so much. He's so far from me suddenly. What did I do?

"I'm asking you out on a date." I have no actual idea where we'll go on this date. It's not like I have cool beachside coffee shops I need to show him. "For this Saturday night. What do you think?"

"Ummmm . . ." He doesn't look at me. He just walks right past me, close enough that I can smell his peppery tree smell. "I think I've got a thing on Saturday night." He drops three of the balls into the mouth of the jar, rips off a sheet of wax paper from the roll by my elbow, and lays it over the dough. He looks at me for a long moment and swallows. "I'm really sorry, Poppi."

"A thing? For school?" Suddenly I feel extremely stupid standing here. I want to be back outside, hiking or running or doing anything except trying to get his attention. "Just let me know."

I push through the screen door, letting it smack shut. Outside smells like the pine trees that grow near the benches.

Just then, Pete walks past me to go back into the kitchen. As I sprint toward the trail, I hear him yell, "Aw, Jake. Wax paper? Do you *need* wax paper? You're determined to ruin everything good, aren't you?"

CHAPTER 37

"This Little Light of Mine"

That was days ago, and since then, Jake has avoided me like the flu that's going around Eden. I'm not sure what I did wrong, so I've been hanging around him, waiting for him to talk to me. After every campfire, I stay afterward to collect sweatshirts and flashlights while he puts out the fire. He doesn't say anything to me except "I can grab all that" or "Who's doing worship in the morning?" or "Is Natalie on arts and crafts this week or are you?"

I've also been avoiding the heart-to-heart I promised myself I would have with Bryan. Partly because I don't know exactly what I'll say to him. But I do know we need to have a real conversation. This is the guy who has poured every bit of his life into Eden—and now he doesn't even show up for worship. Something has happened. I want to understand what.

Tonight, I hope to corner Bryan in his office. As I wait for him to finish up a phone call, I scroll through my texts. I haven't checked them in days, which proves that phone addiction is a real thing. Back at Minnesota State, when I was depressed, I checked my phone every few minutes. And during those lonely hours in Mom's hospital room, I constantly felt my phone vibrate, even though it was usually just the phantom buzz of texts that weren't there.

But here at camp, where my phone is always back on my nightstand, the texts I *do* get seem like they're for someone else. While I listen to the drone of Bryan's voice, I scroll through them and wait. One message from Aunt Lily telling me she sent a package with money and old pictures that belonged to my mom. A few more texts from friends back home checking on me. Six messages from my dad, mostly pictures of sunsets or his dog. I don't even have the energy to send back a thumbs-up emoji.

I stretch my stiff neck, leaning each ear to each shoulder. My arms are still sore from working at Lakeside on Monday. Mostly I just want this day to be over, but I can't avoid this conversation with Bryan anymore. He has some kind of answer for me, I know it.

Bryan's call is a personal one. I'm really trying not to eavesdrop, but his loud voice fills the small office. He's talking to his cousin about moving back to his hometown and starting work with his dad.

"I hope to be there by August third," he says. "Yep. I'm staying with my parents for two nights while they do the final inspections on the house. I close on the fifth, assuming the builder is finished by then."

He's building a house that will be finished by August fifth? When our pastor in Eagle built a house, it took over a year. How long has Bryan known he's going to move there?

He goes on to tell his cousin details about the house. It's on an acre of land by some lake. It sounds huge—over three thousand square feet.

"Hey!" Natalie strolls through the door. "What are you doing?"

"Ackgh!" I make a strangled sound. "You scared the daylights out of me!"

"Why are you in here?" she asks.

I point toward Bryan's office. "I'm waiting to talk to him."

"It's Wolfgang." Natalie collapses into the other chair. She holds up a folded piece of notebook paper. Bryan shuts the door to his office with a thud. She glances over her shoulder and rolls her eyes. "What's the deal with him?"

"He's on a call. What's Wolfgang?"

"My secret admirer!" She shakes the paper at me. "Can you believe my luck? It couldn't be someone I might actually *date*. It had to be nerdy, weird Wolfgang." Natalie is biting her bottom lip and looks like she might cry.

"Ah, Nat. You were taking this crush seriously, weren't you?" When she doesn't say anything, I reach over and pat her knee. "Oh, sweetie. Wolfgang is *good*. Seriously, out of all the counselors, I'd pick Wolfgang to be my secret admirer."

"*You* can pick him then." She tosses the paper onto the desk. "He wants me to meet him at Lakeside tomorrow night at sunset for a picnic."

I pick up the letter. Sure enough, he revealed his identity by asking her to do exactly that. "He really likes you. He's just trying to be romantic."

"He's being a cliché. I knew he was cheesy, but a picnic at Lakeside is worse than those 'I Love America' shirts he wears. Ever since I've been coming here, even as a camper, the counselors have talked about Lakeside as a horribly predictable place to take a date. Don't they have any originality in Germany? First the secret admirer routine and now this."

I had actually thought about taking Jake up to Lakeside for our Saturday night date that probably won't happen. The fort seemed cool enough that a picnic there would be romantic. Unless, of course, a family of skunks had really moved in.

I pat her knee. "Please give Wolfie a chance—there might be something between you guys. He's learned so much this summer. Seriously. He's a very smart guy. And funny too."

"There is no way I am going on a date with *Wolfgang*." She crumples the note and tosses it into the trash. "I'm not interested, and I don't believe in giving guys false hopes. Not that there have been many worries about that."

"Just meet him. One of us should have a little romance." My voice sounds whiny. I sit up a bit straighter. I hate whining.

"Still no word from Jake?" Her tone is sympathetic, which is a stretch for Nat when it comes to Jake and me.

"None. But I thought I heard him say his dad is playing a show in Santa Barbara this weekend. Maybe he'll be there?"

"He won't be," she says flatly. "Chloe—one of our friends who used to be a counselor here—is having a barbecue. Jake told me he's going."

"This Saturday night?"

"Sorry, Poppi. This is the part of the movie when Jake breaks your heart. Remember I said it would be horrible?"

"Oh. Well, he did say he had a thing. Maybe this is it." That doesn't explain why he didn't ask me along. Or bother to let me know he was busy.

"I'm going." Natalie stands. "You could come. Pete and Bryan and the girls can handle this place for one night. And Chloe won't mind. There'll be lots of people who used to work at Eden there. Plus, her parents' house is fabulous."

"That would be fun." Maybe I can talk to Jake there. Maybe getting away from camp is what we both need.

"Poppi . . ." Natalie's tone is warning, like she can read my thoughts.

I wipe all hope from my face before I look at her.

She grabs my face and holds it between both of her hands. "Repeat after me. I, Poppi Savot . . ."

"I, Poppi Savot," I say, sounding like the Chubby Bunny.

"Will not waste even one more second getting my hopes up . . ."

"Nat," I say, pulling away my face. "I'm a big girl. Let me do it my way."

"I will not be held responsible for taking you to Chloe's and giving you false Jake hopes. If you're my guest at this party, you better go as a girl who has no time for Jake Bass." She tilts my chin so she can look in my eyes. “You haven’t listened to me about anything else. Listen to me about this.”

“I promise to try.”

“All right.” Natalie grabs my hand and pulls me up. “Let’s figure out what we’re going to wear. You can corner Bryan later.”

CHAPTER 38

"Kumbaya"

Dinner on Thursday is one of those rare nights when every single person is falling apart. It's Week Seven and we have hit We're-All-Tired-of-Camp rock bottom.

The campers are divided between Team Harriet and Team Wendy. Even the boys are taking sides, which is ridiculously bad news. Boys never care about girl drama.

Yesterday I pulled Wendy aside and asked her about sneaking out. When I took her onto the patio outside the dining hall, her eyes were huge. Her dad is a pastor and her mom is a principal, and she's terrified of getting in trouble. Before I had even finished the whole question, she started sobbing so hard that her nose ran all over her purple T-shirt.

Wendy insists that Harriet is a pathological liar who wants to get her sent home. When I followed up with Harriet, she started crying too. Tears seem to be the go-to emotion for the girls this week. In Emmy's cabin, Kate and Ainsley both cried because they didn't want to eat tonight's dinner. This made Skylar laugh, which made the two girls cry even more.

In their defense, the food tonight is a disaster. Pete is grouchy because of some mix-up with Ellie's girls. The story goes that they were trying to make cookies for Jake because he lifeguarded for them last night. The girls had loved night swimming so they decided to make his favorite cookies for him as a thank-you. When Ellie opened the big jar of chocolate chips, they found that a family of beetles had moved in. The girls decided to clean the whole kitchen to help Pete out.

Pete is a bit of a hoarder, and the pantry had gotten out of control with his recycling. Pyramids of boxes toppled over this indoor garden of different-color jars. But the crates were the worst. Banana crates, milk crates, apple crates filled with straw—Pete keeps them all in the pantry where all the meal supplies are also kept, and the little space has become the perfect home for bugs.

Ellie's girls took all the empty crates, boxes, tubs, cans, bottles, and jars down to the big dumpster by the fire road. When Pete found out what they did, he freaked out, and he has been ranting ever since. While he retrieved the recyclables from the trash, the lasagnas in the oven burned. He had to serve corn dogs that had been in the freezer since last summer, and they tasted like wet rags.

It's not just dinner. Tonight's fiasco has been the grand finale to a tedious Week Seven. The kids have mostly forgotten their actual parents, but they're still needy for that kind of unconditional love and affection. This combination makes them stressed out about everything.

The counselors are tired of wearing clothes that smell like campfire, taking two-minute showers, and working twenty-three hours a day. This morning at staff meeting, Aaron launched into a fiery rant about how disrespectful it is when campers keep their caps on during the prayer. Seriously. He almost had tears in his eyes about how offended he gets when he looks around and sees that SOME PEOPLE DON'T EVEN CARE ABOUT GOD. Clearly this had way more to do with the fact that he and Ellie aren't speaking than about what anyone wears when they pray.

I patted him on the shoulder and told him I was tired too. Week Seven fatigue has me feeling like I want to slip into a very dark, very cold room and sleep for a very long time.

My adrenaline from last weekend's date has calcified into bitterness. I'm literally hungry for Jake's attention. I feel like I haven't eaten in three days and he is standing next to me with hot brownies. When he's sitting right next to me at worship or running past me in Capture the Flag, I want to tackle him and yell, "What are you thinking? What changed? *What did I do?*"

But Jake has become a robot to me: I input words and he responds, but with no emotion or flirting. We're sort of like a divorced couple who are trying to co-parent. We're giving each other lots of space, but in such an obvious way, it's ridiculous.

Also, I still haven't had my heart-to-heart with Bryan. He just wouldn't meet with me. I tried to talk to him in the office, emailed him (so weird since we are working at the same camp), and even knocked on the door of his little cabin in the woods. He just didn't answer, even though he was definitely there. I'm not sure why his rejection makes me feel ashamed, but it totally does. What have I done to make both Jake and Bryan ignore me?

And finally, I'm not actively doing anything to save Eden right now. It's like when my mom first got her cancer diagnosis, and she kept saying, "Even when I'm sleeping, those tumors are growing inside me."

Even when I'm staring at Jake, craving him, this camp is dying. Even when Wendy and Harriet are mobilizing troops against each other, August 1 is coming. Even when Nat is ranting about Wolfgang, and Beth's cabin is building signs for the fort at Lakeside, and Pete is threatening to quit, and kids are learning to lead worship and square-dance, Eden is disappearing.

But even in the middle of Impossible Week Seven, I don't feel completely hopeless, not like I did with Mom last summer. Nat was right about me melting. It's the Bible studies, the worship songs—all of that. They're more interesting than before. They're like little bits of sunshine in the dark of Week Seven.

And I really need those right now.

CHAPTER 39

"Do Lord"

"Wow. This place is amazing." I trip on my long, clingy skirt as I walk up the path to Chloe's house. I catch myself on Natalie's arm before I tumble into the luminarias that line the winding sidewalk. I'd rather not be on fire when Jake sees I'm here. Already he might think I'm stalking him.

Or maybe he'll be glad I'm here. He'll smack his forehead and say, "Wow. Week Seven has been so tough, I totally forgot to tell you I'll be at this party tonight. Great you could make it, Poppi. Now, where did we leave off last weekend?"

Natalie rings the brass doorbell. "Looks like there's a ton of people already here. Get ready. You're about to meet Eden's history face-to-face."

A tall girl with a short blonde bob opens the door. She's wearing all black and looks very SoCal—tan, thin, with golden skin and hair.

Then she goes kind of crazy. She screams, "Naaat!!!!" And then this very pretty, very sophisticated-looking girl tackles Natalie in a huge hug that knocks her right into me. Seriously, I have to brace myself so we all don't tumble over.

"There you are!" Natalie kisses Chloe's cheek about six times. "I missed you and missed you and I really hate college for taking you from me. It's horrible and stupid and you should drop out so you can be at Eden right now, fighting during Week Seven."

Chloe throws back her head and laughs. "You are so silly. My real life is too serious without you, Natalie Hatfield. I need you with me all the time. Because, wow! Now that you're standing here, I miss you even more!"

Chloe is a little older than me. She's glossy and pretty, like she might model or have her own Disney show. Suddenly I'm very aware that I've washed this skirt in an outside washing machine that doesn't have hot water, that I smell like bacon and campfire, that I'm wearing a shirt of Natalie's that's two sizes too big, but Natalie insists it looks "bohemian."

But Chloe doesn't seem to care how I look. She hugs me and pulls me inside. "I'm so glad you came, Poppi. You will meet your people here. It's an Eden reunion inside."

"So glad to be here. Because Natalie is right. We do need a break from Week Seven." We step inside the foyer, which is white and elegantly decorated with vases of long-stemmed calla lilies. A winding staircase stands as the focal point in the middle of the marble floor and a massive chandelier lights the whole space. "Wow. Your house is gorgeous."

"My parents' place." Chloe grins. "To be clear, *I* live in a dorm room at University of Nebraska that's as big as your room at Eden."

"Then get your hiney back to camp and live in one of those rooms with us! Because it is not the same without you there." Natalie drapes her arm across Chloe's shoulders and looks at me. "Chloe was my counselor for two summers straight. This girl *reigns* as Eden royalty. Number One Best Counselor to ever write a skit or break up a bunk war."

"Oh, lucky you, Poppi. You get this kind of enthusiasm just a few feet from you every hour of every day." Chloe is still holding my hand and she pulls me through to the living room.

"Wait. I am not finished with my Chloe-adoration," Natalie continues. "Don't worry, Poppi loves it when I get on a tangent."

I smile at Nat. "I do?" We've moved into the massive living room, which is connected to a sprawling kitchen.

"Of course you do." Nat looks at Chloe with little-sisterly admiration. "Chloe is the girl who French-braided my hair every single morning, taught me how to win Flashlight Tag, made me learn to love Bug Juice, inspired me to go on the Longest Hike in the History of Eden, and—finally and most importantly—sent me home for my sassy mouth."

"You got kicked out of Eden?" I ask. "Nat! You've never told me that!"

"Ahhhghhh! Stop, Natalie!" Chloe covers her pretty face. Her ears, which stick out of her blonde bob, are pink. "Could you go at least five minutes without bringing that up? That was seriously a lifetime ago!"

"No, I cannot. Because going home was absolutely what I needed. I learned more from that one act of tough love than anything else in eight summers at camp. I was out of control with the eye rolling and smear campaign against you. You had only warned me every single day for the eight weeks before that."

"Yeah, but if I could do it again, I wouldn't have sent you home." Chloe plops down on a white couch. Natalie and I perch on either side of her.

Through the plate glass windows, I can see the spectacular patio that's crowded with people eating burgers around a big teak table. Behind the outdoor kitchen area is a pool sunken into rocks and waterfalls. Beyond that is a hot tub big enough for at least ten people. No Jake, though. Not eating a burger, not on the patio, not by the pool.

"I'm about to graduate to become a kindergarten teacher," Chloe says to me. Then she turns to Nat. "I've learned that I could've taught you a lot more if I had let you finish the summer. Tough love didn't have to mean sending you home."

Natalie slips into the kitchen and returns with bottles of water for us. "I totally needed to go home. You did your long-distance teaching by writing me letters every day."

"Really? Every day? While you were a counselor?" I twist open my bottle as the two of them reminisce about daily letters Chloe wrote, and how she decorated the envelopes with little cartoons about camp. And how Natalie punished her by not writing back.

While they remember the other girls in the cabin, I crane my neck to see more of the backyard. It's mostly people my age, some a little older. Natalie has told me so many stories about Eden that I feel like I can pick out some of the characters. That must be Jenni, who married her camp sweetheart, Jesus Miranda. By the fire pit are three girls—The Blondes—who Natalie said travel in a pack. Throughout high school, they all came to Eden together. But when they started college at Chico State, they pledged the same sorority and needed to be on campus for summer rush, so they stopped coming to Eden. Also outside is a girl who I think is Lindy, whom Bryan dated for a few summers, until she dumped him to date the cook. Natalie calls this The Scandal of Three Summers Ago.

These are the campers and counselors who could not stop coming back to Eden. Until they did stop. Until their internships started or they needed to go to summer school or soccer camp or to get jobs that paid their employees on time. Gathered outside on Chloe's patio—this was Eden.

I imagine these Eden alums feel about the camp the way I feel about Minnesota—sentimental, like you do about the hamster you had when you were six. How can I get them to care more? to realize Eden is in real danger?

On the other side of the living room, Chloe is in the kitchen, fussing with a big hummus platter as she and Natalie recount every detail about the summer she sent Natalie home.

"I'm not sure how you had time for those letters, though," Natalie is saying. "That was such a busy summer for you."

“Shut up.” Chloe hip-checks her as she brings over the platter with hummus, pita bread, olives, carrots, celery, and radishes. “Just shut your mouth, Natalie Hatfield.”

“What happened that summer?” I ask.

Chloe spreads hummus onto a triangle of pita and looks at me. “I met my boyfriend, Dan, the same summer I sent Natalie home for being a pain in the butt. He was a counselor too.” She takes a bite of hummus and pita, and then, with her mouth full, says, “That’s all we need to say about that summer, *Natalie*.”

“For the sake of Poppi’s education, just one more thing.” Natalie turns to me. “I will give you three guesses who Chloe wasted two years dating because she thought *he* was the one for her.”

“Natalie! Zero people want to hear about this.” Chloe reaches out and actually covers Natalie’s mouth.

Natalie grabs Chloe’s hands and pins them against her back. They’re wrestling like ten-year-olds, and I want to break it up with a “SOMEONE COULD GET HURT HERE.”

“All right, Nat. Who?” I look at Chloe. “Sorry, but she has thing about protecting me from Jake. She’s pathological about it.”

Just then, a guy who looks like a young Elvis comes through the door. He’s balancing two silver platters, one with a couple of hamburgers and the other with crumbs. He has to open the door wide to pass through. “Hey! It’s Natalie!”

With the door open, I can see more of Chloe’s backyard. Immediately I spot Jake. He’s sitting far away from the others, on a black porch swing that’s hanging from a huge tree. The girl next to him on the swing is wearing a white sundress.

And Jake is kissing her.

CHAPTER 40

"Start a Fire"

I lean back into the couch because my body suddenly feels boneless. It's absolutely him. I've memorized that profile from studying it at all those campfires. And he is definitely pressing his lips against hers. His knuckle is resting on her cheek, like he's pressing her face close to his.

I cannot turn away. I can't stop staring straight at the bare tan shoulders of that girl, at her wavy blonde hair and her stupid white strap that's slipping off her shoulder.

"Dan! Dan! The Hamburger Man!" Natalie yells, hugging him. "You made dinner! Y'all are acting like you're an old married couple now, huh? You're outside grilling while your little honey is inside barefoot and making hummus?"

Dan is laughing and introducing himself to me as Chloe's boyfriend, and Chloe makes a joke about how they argue like an old married couple. Chloe and Dan go into the pantry, but I cannot concentrate on any of it because through the still-open door I can see Jake pulling away from White Sundress Girl. I want him to turn and see that I'm here. I want to scream. I want to run all the way back to Eden.

But then Natalie leans over to see what I'm staring at. She sucks in her breath. "Oh, Jake. No, Jake." Her voice sounds like she's pleading. She turns back to me, her hands over her mouth.

It's one of those moments when the nightmare that was playing somewhere in the back of my mind is suddenly real life in my face. Chloe and Dan are busy cutting brownies, arranging them on a plate, and not paying any attention to us. I hope they never turn around. I hope no one ever knows what an idiot I was to fall for Jake Bass.

"Okay." Natalie is taking deep breaths and using her soothing, rational voice. "I'm not going to say 'I told you so.' But I am going to say, 'Now you see. Now you can move on. Remember? This is the disaster movie scene!'"

I close my eyes and try to unsee that kiss. Mom always warned me about unseeing when an animal died. 'Don't look because you can never unsee it!' I can never unsee Jake's profile, her tanned shoulders, that white sundress, his knuckle on her cheek.

"I shouldn't have come," I whisper.

"No, you shouldn't have *hoped*," Natalie responds, rubbing my back.

Dan carries the brownies and pushes his way back through the door. Before he closes it, I have to check to see what they're doing now. Jake is swinging with the girl, and they are both grinning like they're just so pleased. Like they're in some kind of ridiculous commercial for white sundresses and swings and kisses.

Chloe looks at me. "What's wrong, Poppi? You look pale." She comes over to us. "Are you okay?"

Natalie answers, which is fine because my mouth doesn't seem to be working that great. "Who is that girl Jake is macking on outside?"

"I don't know." Chloe looks through the window in the door. "Wait. That one girl in the white dress?" Chloe blinks very fast. "Jamie? Or Johnny? I don't know. She came with a whole posse. I think she said she was a camper back when Jake and Dan and me were all campers. But I seriously don't remember her from then."

"You don't even know her?" This is part of being from a tiny town. Not knowing everyone—especially someone at your own party—feels crazy.

"Nope . . . but now I remember. Over dinner, she was telling us all about this massive crush she had on Jake back in the day. In fact, I think she came here because she was looking for him. Like she has been looking for him for years. Like all she's been doing is looking for him. She seemed kind of obsessed with him."

I giggle, and then I can't stop. This happens to me sometimes and it's the most inconvenient thing in the world. Because obviously I want to throw up or eat three bowls of hummus or pick up the lemonade pitcher and smash it over Jake's head. Really, the only completely *inappropriate* reaction is for me to start laughing like I don't even understand that my co-worker, crush, and guy I believed totally changed my life is making out with another girl *one week* after I told him he had given me the best night of my life.

Natalie puts her arm around me and pats my hair, and I keep giggling because, apparently, I have the emotional intelligence of a two-year-old.

Natalie looks at Chloe. "You get what's going on here, right?"

"I can imagine what's probably happening," Chloe says sadly. "Because we've all seen it before . . . Poppi is the kind of pretty blonde that Jake always falls for."

Natalie is petting my hair like I'm a sick animal. "And then you know what happened next, right?"

"Can I guess, Poppi? You watched as Jake played his stupid guitar and went swimming with no shirt on and told kids about Jesus, and you lived about three feet from him the whole summer. So, even though you tried, you couldn't resist his charms—"

"For the record," Natalie interrupts. "I warned her about this *exactly*. I gave her my Jake speech so many times."

Chloe holds up her hand. "EVEN THOUGH I'm sure that sweet Natalie Hatfield told you *not* to crush on Jake Bass."

Three girls with tousled, long blonde hair, short dresses, and heels pass through the living room. They're all looking down at their phones and hardly notice us as they walk past. Johnny/Jamie comes through the door after them. She's even prettier than I thought. She has wide blue eyes and a button nose, and she's wearing pink lipstick that I imagine is sticky all over Jake's face. She also has that kind of surprised look that girls with really arched eyebrows have, but on her heart-shaped face, it works. "Hey." She smiles at Chloe. "We're all looking for the bathroom?"

Chloe's voice isn't exactly friendly. "End of the hall, turn left."

"Thanks." Then Johnny/Jamie looks at me and sort of waves, probably because I'm staring at her and still grinning from my giggling fit. Should I say something to her? But what? *Hey! You kissed the same boy I did! That everyone did!*

I just keep staring as the girls disappear into the bathroom together. Of course Jake kissed her. She just looks like a girl who has it all together. Her eyebrows alone probably take more upkeep than I've spent on my whole self this summer.

"Now, *of course*, Jake is kissing another girl because he is the guy who needs to make sure everyone loves him." Here, Chloe comes over and puts her arms around my shoulders and hugs me hard. "And you have no choice but to ask yourself, 'At what age did he stop maturing?'"

"Yes! I love that line," Natalie says. "I'm totally using that again. I'm using that for every boy who ever hurts me."

Chloe isn't done. "Poppi, you have to realize that you can't date Jake's *potential*. Recognize that he can be toxic. Even though he does have that thing where he kneels down to talk to kids and you can almost see what a great dad he'll be someday." Chloe squeezes my shoulders again. "But this is what you need to remember—you don't want to have to get him to the great-dad point."

"So many yeses! All the yeses!" Natalie shouts as the bathroom crew comes back out. They travel in a little huddle and stare at Natalie as they pass to go back outside. "Toxic and trouble and all the issues. Are you hearing this, Poppi?"

"Yes. I hear it. And now, I believe it."

CHAPTER 41

"Lord, I Need You"

About an hour later, Chloe's parents come back from dinner. They don't stay outside for long because Chloe is obviously the Martha Stewart of backyard parties.

Eventually, Jamie—apparently that's her name and I'm not really sure where Chloe had gotten Johnny in the first place—and her crew leave. Jamie stops to thank her and apologizes for leaving so early, but her friends hadn't been campers at Eden and they were bored when everyone started telling stories.

Chloe is perfectly cool about the whole thing. But later she admits that she really wanted to say, "Really? Really, you came here for two hours to kiss a guy and now you're leaving?"

I decide that I don't want to see Jake after all, so I hang inside talking to all the people who come through the kitchen to get more drinks. Natalie keeps me company and everyone asks her how Eden is going this summer. She tells them the melodramatic truth that in less than a month, Eden might be bulldozed to become the corporate retreat for a company that makes zillions of dollars storing junk.

Even though everyone is alarmed this might happen so soon, they're only vaguely upset. It's the way you'd react if you found out that your great-uncle who lives far away might die. Sure, it's a little sad, but the sorrow is so removed, it's mostly forgettable.

After the crew finishes the brownies, Chloe pulls out several bags of Oreos and brings them out to the table. Double Stuf Oreos were all the rage when Chloe and Dan were counselors and everyone freaks out about how these remind them of Eden more than anything else.

Eventually I follow the group and the Oreos outside. I notice that Jake is on the far end of the yard, eating cookies with Dan and a couple of other guys. Not looking at Jake is like not looking at a car wreck on the side of the road. Against my will, my eyes keep sneaking quick glimpses. And every time I do, he's laughing or telling a story and not even looking in my direction.

I stand behind the table, listen to everyone's Eden stories, and eat six Oreos. I have to move the package away so I don't stuff down all my sadness and embarrassment and anger with their luscious double stuffing.

Around the table, the Eden stories are like ripples—someone plunges in and that memory inspires a whole bunch more. Remember when Bryan dressed up like Smokey the Bear for that skit about fire safety? Or the year the whole camp stayed up for Lay-and-Pray and there was that massive meteor shower that no one expected? Or when the horrible cook from that summer added the juice from a gallon of pickles to the meat loaf, only he forgot the jar had been sitting in the sun all summer, and everyone got sick?

After everyone polishes off the Oreos, Chloe brings out more chips. The stories start to blend together. And then, as if I have no control over my own body, I stand up and wander over to Jake's side of the pool.

I don't think he knows I saw him kissing Jamie. All night, Natalie has been glaring at him like he really is a poisonous snake, but he hasn't seemed to notice that either. As I get closer, my anger grows in me like a tumor. I can feel it lodged in my chest and suddenly I absolutely, positively have to get all this hate out of me.

When Jake sees me coming toward him, he lifts his chin in that really stupid boy-greeting. "Hey, Poppi. How are you?" His tone is even. He doesn't want to fight, but he doesn't want to hang out with me either.

"I'm really fantastic. Thanks, Jake."

He gives a strange look and then goes back to telling Dan about his upcoming exam. I listen for a moment, scanning my brain for the perfect words for Jake.

Dan smiles at me from where he's sitting with his legs in the pool. "Had enough of memory lane over there, Poppi?"

"Not at all." I smile. "They're great stories. I'm just here to talk to Jake."

Over at the table, Natalie stands on a chair. "Poppi! What are you doing?"

"I'm fine!" I call back. Because, suddenly, I know exactly what to ask Jake. Why did he kiss me in the first place? Why did he make so much effort, with the night out and the dancing and the music, if he wasn't really interested?

Jake looks at me, his eyebrows lifted. It's our co-worker shorthand for "What do you need?" I glare at him, which he probably doesn't know yet is our shorthand for "You are my least favorite person in this world."

The tumor that started as anger in the pit of my stomach has grown to be something bigger. Maybe Jake gets away with these games with other girls, but I am running a camp with him. Not only that, I'm trying to *save* a camp. Taking me out for kissing and dancing got in the way of that. He couldn't respect that I wasn't interested—he was selfish and egotistical, and he needs to know that's not okay.

"I need to talk to you," I say.

Jake looks at me like he really wants to jump in the pool.

Or maybe, like he wants to push me in.

CHAPTER 42

"Every Move I Make"

Chloe comes up behind me. "Hey! Dan!" She reaches for his hand. "I need your help. Emmy and Beth just called and they're on their way."

"Who?" Dan stands and does a dance to shake the water off his legs.

Chloe wipes a black smudge from Dan's cheek and keeps talking. "Emmy and Beth. Remember sweet Beth? Her parents are Mike and Eva—the ones who always come up to Eden to volunteer? Mike played the guitar a few summers ago? Beth is his daughter."

"Oh, yeah. I know Beth. She's old enough to be a counselor? Man!" Dan shakes his head. He's one of those guys who has a permanent smile on his face. Even though he has Elvis's same sleepy eyes and cleft chin, he's the jolly version of Elvis. "I still see her as a little kid. Is she even old enough to drive?"

"Well, kind of," Chloe laughs. "She actually just called to say she got really lost. But they're back on track and will be here in about ten minutes."

Jake stands and brushes the water off his calves too. "I'll grab some hot dogs for them."

"No, that's fine, Jake." Chloe catches his sleeve. She smiles at me. "We can do it." She turns back to Dan. "Can you put a couple more burgers on the grill?"

"Will do." Dan glances at his phone, then at me. "It's getting late. What do you think, boss? You're okay with your counselors out this late?"

"More than okay," I say. "Pete and Bryan are with the boys and Ellie is with the girls. And Beth and Emmy need a break. It's been The Week Seven World War III for their cabins."

Dan laughs. "Seriously. I miss The Week Seven Wars. The real world is stupid compared to camp. I wish I could go back for the rest of the summer."

"We could just ditch our internships," Chloe says as they walk away. But of course, she's kidding.

"What's going on, Poppi?" Instead of looking at me, Jake studies the fire pit.

"What's going on with *you*, Jake?"

"Not much." His phone buzzes. He pulls it out of his pocket, smiles, and then starts thumb-typing.

"Who's that? Your new girlfriend? Is that *Jamie*?"

Jake's head snaps up. He looks more surprised than the day I smacked the wasp. "Wait. What did you say?"

"Is Jamie coming back for more?"

"It's my mom." He holds out the phone. The screen does say "MOM," but obviously, that's not my point.

"Well, here's what you can tell your mom. Tell her that you need serious help. You have this weird, perverted impulse for every girl to love you. Tell her you cannot control yourself, and you kiss all of us, and then you immediately lose interest."

He furrows his brow and stares at me for a couple of moments. Then he puts away his phone and says, "I am very sorry, Poppi." He sounds like he almost means it. He runs his hand through his hair and looks past me. "I wasn't trying to hurt you by kissing Jamie."

His eyes flicker to mine, then back to the fire pit. "I've known her for a very long time."

"How does that even matter?"

"That totally matters. That kiss was a thing from a long time ago. So it wasn't like a real kiss. It was more like . . . more like . . . finishing something . . ." He's fidgety. He keeps shrugging his shoulders, like his shirt is too small. Squirming like this, he looks pathetic.

Knowing I have the power to make him look this pathetic makes me dislike him even more. "Look, I don't even care, really. Seriously. Kiss everyone. Kiss every girl you meet. Take us all on super-romantic dates and then make all of us feel really special. And then, definitely, keep moving on to the next one. Because you have a *lot* of girls to get through—"

"Stop." He's not squirming now but is glaring at me. "You want to talk for real? Okay, forget Jamie. Seriously. It was just a kiss. But Poppi, you have to stop this. You need to calm down because you're acting ridiculous—"

"You want me to calm down?" I laugh really loudly and the crowd's chatter behind me stops. "Ha! I'm not the one who acts like I'm in heat." I say this way louder than I mean to.

Chloe's friends at the table are suddenly silent, except for a few giggles. Even in the shadowy light, I can see Jake's cheeks and forehead are red.

"Please, Poppi. Please don't embarrass us. You'll regret this later."

"I'm not the one who is embarrassing myself. You are the one who is . . . *toxic*," I say, thinking of Chloe's word.

"Stop yelling and realize it's not that big of a deal. It was just a *kiss.*"

"With me or with Jamie?"

"Why does that matter? And why do you need to talk about this right here? Can't this wait until we're back at camp?"

"It totally matters. Because, unlike *you*, I don't believe that the word *just* belongs with *a kiss*. A kiss always means something. At least it should."

"You are not being rational. I can't talk to you when you're like this." Jake steps toward me. He's talking out of the side of his mouth, quietly, like we're at campfire and don't want the kids to hear. But that doesn't stop me.

"You can talk about it now or you can talk about it later. But you *will* talk about it, because you live with me and you work with me, and there is too much weirdness between us. And that weirdness is all your fault."

"Or maybe you could just ignore your *emotions* for once? Maybe you could control your anger so we can work together for three more weeks?" I don't think I've ever seen him mad before—really mad.

"Are you really, actually, serious right now? Ignore my emotions so we can work together? We were working together fine before. *You* are the one who changed everything. You are the one who insisted on *waking up* my emotions. You strategized an entire evening—like an intentional eight hours of both of our lives—with that exact goal."

"Aghh! Come *on*, Poppi. I said I was sorry." He looks to the sky. "Believe me. I am so sorry I kissed you. Of all the girls in the world, that was really stupid. Now, I can either stand here and beg you to forgive me. Or you can just see that it wasn't a big deal."

The tears are just about to explode down my face, and I know that when they do, there will be no stopping them. It will be a repeat of that night on the patio, but it will be so much worse now because I'll be crying about Jake—*to* Jake.

"I forgive you," I manage to say. "But I really would suggest you look into some help for your issues with women."

He squints at me, like I'm so painfully ridiculous, he cannot even open his eyes. "Are you really being serious right now?"

"I'm sure a therapist could help you look closely at why you need girls to adore you." Then, because I dislike him so much—and my heart can be small and black and cruel—I keep going. "I'm not saying it's because your dad is an actual celebrity that you keep trying to find that adoration for yourself, but—"

"I need help with *my* issues? Really, Poppi? Because I have never met anyone looking for a savior more than you." He leans close. "I'm sorry, but I can't be that for you. I can't keep giving you 'the best night of your life.'" He makes air quotes around the last part.

The jerk. My heart is pounding and I'm dizzy and my eyes can't focus right. "Do. Not. Talk. To. Me." My voice is raspy with feral anger. I'm kind of even scaring myself here.

"Fine. I won't." Jake stomps around the pool. "We just won't talk. That's a fantastic strategy for working together," he calls over his shoulder.

Then he storms past the group and slams the door.

CHAPTER 43

"Jesus Paid It All"

Okay, give me the details. What did he do now?"

I wipe my eyes, take a deep breath, and turn from the pool to see Chloe standing right behind me. Her forehead is wrinkled. This must be the way she looks at the kindergartners she's interning with—a mixture of sympathy and curiosity.

I take a deep, shuddering breath. "Jake? Oh, nothing. We were just arguing about some camp stuff."

"Yeah, right. I worked with Jake for years. Let me guess. You called him out for kissing that girl, and he hates to be criticized?"

"I guess. Actually, I'm not really sure what happened." My voice sounds jagged. "I haven't dated a lot, but I felt like our night together was really amazing." I suck in all the snot that's trying to run down my face. "I guess we had different impressions of what was supposed to happen next."

"You should put that on a T-shirt. 'I dated Jake Bass and liked it.' You could sell lots of those." She nods to the big wooden table, where Brooke, a girl with a pierced nose, and Bella, a tall blonde, and a few others are watching us. "You could probably sell about five of them over there alone."

“I just feel so stupid. Natalie warned me. And then Jake accused me of falling too hard and wanting him to be my savior.” I drag my toe across the reddish-brown concrete. It glistens under the twinkling lights that are strung across the pool.

“I’ve never heard him say that one before.” She sits next to me on a rock. I watch her shadow’s reflection in the dark water. “Usually, Jake just gets bored with a girl. At least that happened with me. He lost all interest. I would be talking, and he would clearly be thinking about who had won the Rangers game or whatever. Then I would freak out and that would drive Jake crazy. But really, he was just done with me. No interest at all.”

“I didn’t even get to that point with him. I just make him very mad.”

“Can I explain something about Jake to you?” She sits down next to me. “I learned a lot from dating him. I have a different perspective than Natalie. A deeper perspective.”

“Yeah? Any hints on how to survive the rest of the summer with him?”

“No. Because he can be really impossible. But it’s worse news. Because Jake has this other side.”

I look at her pretty face, glowing under the lights in the palm trees. She has no pores, just smooth, radiant skin. “And you got to see that part?”

She studies the pool, her bottom lip sticking out. “The other part is like Dan—sweet, hopeful, and protective. When Jake loves something, he’s loyal to a fault. Just look at how he is with Eden. He’s so devoted that he’s impossible to work with.”

I nod. Because, obviously. “Totally. He overthinks everything about Eden.”

“Jake loves more fiercely than anyone I’ve ever met. Seriously. If you could see him with his mom and his sister, you would understand what I mean. He has this steely commitment. The girl who finally gets through all his other issues is going to enjoy that.”

"Good luck to her," I mutter. "I wouldn't have the patience. We are the two most incompatible people ever. We drive each other crazy. We're *combustible* when we're together."

"Are you really sure about that?" Chloe looks at me for what feels like a long time. The only sound is the bubbling spa. It feels too intimate to talk like this with someone I just met. I want to be back at camp, cowering under the covers. "That's too bad," she says, finally.

I don't respond. I don't want her to say that I should be that girl—the girl willing to put up with Jake's issues. Because clearly I have enough of my own.

Chloe stands. "I really am impressed you have the guts to argue with Jake. I never could." She turns to me before she goes back to the table and to her party. "All of us were watching you over here. We've decided that if you can make Jake that mad, you're also the only one he'll fall for."

CHAPTER 44

"Build Your Kingdom Here"

"What were you *thinking*?" Natalie asks. She's gripping the steering wheel so hard, we'll surely get in a wreck. She'll plow into a median and smash her car, and we'll both end up in the ER tonight instead of getting back to Eden.

"You've got to loosen up, Nat. Seriously. You can't drive this tense all the way back to camp." She shakes out one hand as she merges onto the highway. "Trust me," I add, "a barbecue is the next right step. Eden needs a huge, end-of-the-summer fundraiser. It's brilliant!"

"But did you have to promise so much? Poppi, those people are emotional and nostalgic—and now they believe you can really save the place they love."

"Right. That's good news. They need to believe that."

"But hello! You can't! You're not Superwoman. You don't have the power to make thousands of dollars appear out of thin air. You do *not* have the authority to make the Association say no to STUF."

"When did I say I would make thousands of dollars appear? I said I would organize a barbecue. That's different. They're the ones who will make thousands of dollars appear—when they come and rally around Eden's success on July thirtieth."

"It will never work, Poppi. Five years of decline. Summer after summer of fewer kids coming back to Eden. Three years of not paying the staff on time. One barbecue can't turn that tide."

After Jake left, the party changed completely—for me, at least. Jake leaving felt like a storm cloud moving past and revealing brilliant sunshine. I started to have fun. I sat at the table and laughed at all the stories. At one point, I looked at the faces gathered around that table and realized that Chloe's friends have parents and money and passion and a long connection with Eden. One day they will all have kids of their own, and they will want to send them to camp. *These* are the people who should be giving the money to save Eden.

So, I told everyone, "We'll have a big barbecue with auctions and a band, and everyone can come back and celebrate Eden. We can do this together! We can save it from STUF!" They loved it. All of it.

Natalie points to the clock on the dash. It's after two. "We can forget about sleeping tonight. You told them we'd email them information by Monday." Her shoulders are around her ears, like she's holding a big breath. "Fund-raisers take time and money. And we're getting a *band*? Where are we going to find a band? Where are we going to find the seed money for this big party we're suddenly having?"

"You heard Beth. She said the Association churches would do a special offering for our seed money."

Natalie is quiet for a few miles. But then she says, "Bryan will never agree to this, you know." She looks at me. "You said he wouldn't even talk to you about Eden. No way will he get behind a fund-raiser."

"Then I'll just go over his authority." I lean my head against my seat belt strap because suddenly I'm very tired. But I continue, "Pastor Sean will be the first to jump in to help. Mike and Eva will love the idea. Before the weekend is over, Beth will have talked them into it. I know all of them will help with everything."

"I don't want to let all those people at Chloe's down," she says quietly. "I've known them my whole life. I love them."

"We won't, Natalie. They want to save Eden, but they're too busy to realize what's going on here. A crowdfunding message on your phone isn't the same as standing at the place where you made your first real friend. A picture on Instagram isn't the same as singing camp songs with people you've known for a decade."

"Jake's going to ask what our actual goals are." She holds up a white-tipped nail. "And I know you two are fighting, but it's a good question."

"Okay. What about if we could raise thirty thousand dollars and get a hundred kids to register for next summer? That will be enough to prove that Eden is viable."

She yawns loudly. "The Association will say no to five million dollars for that?"

"They'll absolutely say no," I explain, "because this will prove that Eden could have a real future. It could fill a niche that Southern California is missing, as a Christian retreat center. Next winter, I'll travel to colleges to recruit good staff and ask churches to do Sponsor-a-Camper. Seriously. I'm really, really excited about Rehab Eden."

"'Rehab'? You're so L.A." She pats my hand. "Eden will be your life."

"It will be," I say.

As I say it, a chill passes over my shoulders.

It's the exact same feeling of *knowing* that I had on Day One at Eden, when I already recognized what the canoe shack looked like, even before I saw it. It's that feeling that, no matter what, I should stay here.

And I really hope that this feeling is true. I really hope it's from God.

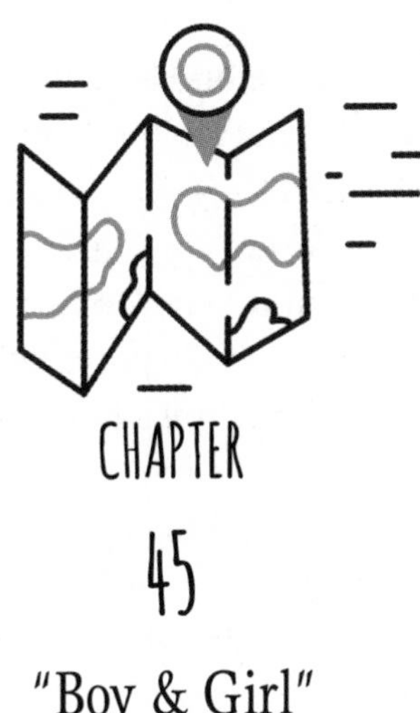

CHAPTER 45

"Boy & Girl"

"Thank you," says Wren, a ten-year-old red-haired camper, as she bows deeply. We're all gathered at campfire worship at Lakeside, and Emmy's cabin just finished a skit about turning the other cheek. The play's climax included a fake slap that made the campers gasp.

Wren keeps bowing and we keep clapping. She's standing on a stage that Beth's cabin built. After they finished the epic fort, the girls just kept adding on. Now, they've constructed a cool stage that even has a tin roof. The girls are so incredibly proud of their work that they hike up here nearly every day to admire it.

Wren bows again, so deeply this time that her thick braid flips over her shoulder and touches the ground. "Before we go," Wren says to the group, "I would love to share a poem I wrote." She clears her throat and closes her eyes.

Forgive! Forgive!
This doesn't make you weak!
God tells us over and over
To turn the other cheek!
When they do you wrong,
Forgive them and you will be strong!

The campers and counselors clap louder. Charlie and Ryan are cracking up on my right, and I shoot them a warning look. On my other side, Natalie is kicking my shin. If I turn even one centimeter toward her, we will make eye contact, she will make a crazy face, and I will start laughing too. Wren's poetry always does this to us.

Last week, when Wren read her poem about trusting God (which included the lines "God might lead me into a lion's den But He will say, "It's okay! I got this, Wren!"), I glanced at Jake, and when he winked at me, I had to bite my lip to not laugh.

I will not be glancing at Jake tonight. After Saturday night there is no warmth between us. Our fight has sucked all the oxygen out of this place—out of this *forest*.

"Let's end by singing 'Kumbaya' for our closing song." I watch Jake as he picks up his guitar and starts to play. After we sing a couple of verses, he says, "Counselors, when you're ready, you can lead your kids back to your cabins."

We sing all the verses. Eventually, the counselors start to stand and collect their kids. Natalie and I hold up flashlights so everyone can find their way over the tree roots. The kids, who are mumbling along with the words and yawning, shuffle down the trail and back to camp.

As I listen to the words of the song, I roll my shoulders and think about the words. *Come by here, Lord.* Yes, that. *Come here, Lord. We need You.*

I sit up straighter and look around, feeling a little silly for taking the words to an old song so literally. We're not like—really—asking God to come here, are we? And what if we are? What does that even mean? Or if He's already here? What difference does that make if He is or not?

There were fewer kids at campfire tonight than last night. A stomach virus has been going around for the past two days and kids are getting sick at the rate of three or four a day. Eva has been on the phone, notifying parents and helping distribute ibuprofen.

If there was any doubt we're all sharing each other's germs, Charlie asked me last week if he could have a new toothbrush. He had been borrowing from different guys in his cabin for the past eight weeks. *Eight weeks!*

Ascension, one of the congregations in the Association, has a parish nurse who is on call, but without an official nurse on staff here, Pete, Nat, Jake, and I have been taking turns sleeping in the makeshift infirmary and tending to the puking campers. We've divided Lord of Life (an empty boys' cabin from Eden's heyday) into male and female halves of sick kids.

The only good news about this tummy bug is that it passes quickly. The really, really bad news for Eden's outdated septic tank is that this flu is violent. After three days of this, the bathrooms are seriously rank.

Natalie yawns as we sit back down near the dwindling fire. "What time am I supposed to relieve Pete with the sickies?"

I look at my clipboard. "At ten. Can you help me figure out a couple of logistics for the barbecue before then?"

"Yep." She rubs her eyes. They're shadowed with dark circles from fatigue and smeared mascara.

"Thanks. I discovered some old pictures in the office. I'm going to put them on Eden's social media sites to get alumni talking. I need you to help me with the dates."

"Ooooh. I love that." Natalie stretches out on the log while Jake throws sand on the fire. "Nothing goes viral like old pictures of awkward hairstyles and serious orthodontia."

"It was Eva's idea. She thought of it when we were working in the office together yesterday." In the old storage room, we discovered boxes of files, faded pictures, an ancient popcorn machine, and about two hundred of the doughboy sticks we can never find when we need them.

Jake sits down and Natalie rests her head in his lap. "Wake me up when you're ready to talk about those logistics, Poppi," she says. "I'm sneaking in a nap. Tonight will be a long one." She cracks open one eye. "How many kids are in the infirmary now?"

I look at the page with campers' names scrawled on it. "Fifteen? Sixteen?"

"Sixteen." Jake pats Natalie's head. These two really are like brother and sister. The day after Chloe's party, Natalie ranted at him about kissing Johnny (as Nat still calls her). Then—poof!—the whole thing was over between them. There's only awkwardness between him and me.

He glances at me as we both stare at the red, flickering coals. Even though I was so mad at him this weekend, I'm pretty much over it. Or more accurately, I don't have the energy for the kids and the barbecue and the hiking and planning—and to stay angry at Jake. Time always feels weird at camp. Chloe's party seems like it happened months ago.

Jake clears his throat. "You were right about something."

"What's that?" My voice sounds way less interested than I actually am.

"Wolfgang and Kenny. Giving them a little more freedom has been okay. More than okay. They're good counselors."

I snuggle into my sweatshirt and smile at myself in the dark. An actual Jake compliment. "I hope they do okay on the canoe trip."

"I don't know how they'll do. I don't know how anyone will do." In his lap, Nat begins to snore softly. He brushes her hair back from her forehead. "Have you considered canceling the trip?"

I look over at him. The fire has died, so I can only see the shadows of his profile. "Have I considered canceling the trip that every single kid has talked about all summer? the one that's a huge Eden tradition and no one wants to miss?"

"Is that a no?" There's a smile in his voice.

"Correct. That's a no." I keep my voice even. No smile in mine. Every summer the whole camp spends Week Eight on a canoeing trip. Since Day One, the kids have talked about who their tent partners will be, who they'll canoe with, and who they'll push into the lake. "I don't know how many times Aaron's boys have told me that the only reason they come to Eden is for the canoe trip."

"Yeah, but we didn't plan on the flu hitting now. So many kids will have to miss. Maybe if we shortened it to just one night, the sick kids wouldn't be so bummed."

"Natalie has it mapped out. It will take a full three days to do all the stops she's planning."

"But we'll have more than a dozen infirmary kids still here." Jake is studying me. His gaze feels like a camera, focused right on my face. "Who'll take care of them?"

"Me. I'm staying here. That's always been the plan. I'll do infirmary and keep tracking on the barbecue stuff. You, Nat, and Pete will do the trip."

"You can't do all that. The infirmary kids need at least two people—one to hand out Pepto and one to clean the bathrooms."

"I can ask Eva to stay." In my peripheral vision, I see a shadow moving behind Jake: a raccoon, who is surely hoping we'll pull out s'mores and leave some chocolate behind. "But even so, this is a big week for barbecue stuff. I've got hundreds of old pictures to post. I really need to find a band." I nudge Nat awake. "Hey. Will you skip the canoe trip to stay here with me and the sickies?"

"Nope." She shakes her head. "Absolutely not. I am going canoeing."

"What?" I'm not used to Natalie being so decisive. It takes her half an hour to get dressed in the morning. "Why?"

"I always go on the canoe trip. I am not missing it."

Jake taps her forehead. "What's up, Nat?"

"Nothing's up." She opens her eyes. They're wide and innocent. "You should be glad that I'm volunteering to go. It'll be the worst canoe trip in the history of Eden—half the kids will get the flu out there."

"I'll stay here and run the infirmary with you," Jake says to me. "Beth, Ellie, and Aaron have been on the trip so many times, they'll be fine out there. Plus they'll have Pete on the trip. And I'll send

Bryan in the van to check on them. If any canoe kids get the flu, Bryan can bring them back."

I nod. "He can go out on Tuesday. If anyone's going to get sick, it'll be by then."

"We could also park the camp truck out by the White Trail with supplies. It'll be there if Wolfgang needs to bring any kids back the next day."

I look at him. "Yeah. All of that will work. Good plan."

We lock eyes for a little longer than a second and I can just barely make out his face. I look back at the cold fire pit. He turns to stare at it too. Maybe he's thinking about our fire the night of our Truth or Dare kiss. Or maybe he's remembering the blazing bonfire at Cove and our night of dancing.

Or maybe he's remembering the fire pit at Chloe's, when I told him he was toxic. I cringe. He doesn't feel toxic right now.

"Good night," Jake says. He picks up Natalie's head, stands, and then gently places it on the log. He glances back at me one more time, stuffs his hands into his pockets, and disappears into the dark.

CHAPTER 46

"Rock-A My Soul"

Camp just isn't the same without kids here, is it?" Eva says as we walk back to the parking lot. She's been here all day helping me schedule social media blasts and press releases.

Eva is incredibly organized and she marched right in and sifted all the old pictures into piles for each decade. Then she took snapshots of them with her phone and posted them on all Eden's social media places. By the time she was finished, the "Save Camp Eden!" Facebook page already had over a hundred new likes.

"It's quieter, that's for sure. And definitely not as fun. I'm not sure if the kids who are left here feel worse about the tummy bug or about missing the trip." I check my watch. In fifteen minutes, I'm supposed to relieve Jake with the flu victims.

"Are you sure you don't want me to stay the rest of the day?" Eva touches my shoulder. "You look tired, Poppi. It would be no problem."

"I'm fine. You take Marie to her ballet lesson." The Brownes only live a few miles from Eden, and their younger daughter has ballet on Monday afternoons.

"Please call my cell if anything changes." She squeezes my shoulder. "Any word from the counselors? Have the kids on the canoe trip come down with the bug?"

"No, but they just left this morning. We'll know more tomorrow, when Wolfgang comes back for supplies. Bryan drove out there with dinner for them, but he didn't have much of a report."

She rolls her pretty green eyes. "Does he ever have a report?"

I smile. "Unfortunately, no. Communication doesn't seem to be his strength."

"Among other things that are not his strength." She opens her car door and slides behind the wheel. "Can I pray about the kids—about tonight?"

Her question surprises me. I thought she had forgotten about praying together. I want to say yes because I really am worried about the kids. And I think Eva would be a good person to talk to about everything happening between God and me. Except no. Holding hands with Eva, talking to God out loud with her—it seems too intimate.

I shake my head. "I will be absolutely fine here with the kids. I promise." Really, I'm much more worried about the ones on the trip. And about Natalie. She was acting very distracted this morning when they left. She kept watching Wolfgang. As the group paddled away, she was so focused on him, she almost capsized her canoe, which also held all the sleeping bags.

Eva leans over and hugs me one last time. "I'll monitor that Facebook page. You call me if you need any help at all with anything."

"I promise I will," I say. "But you've done so much already." I hug her back, feeling really grateful for Eva and Mike. "You guys are the very, very best."

Her SUV roars to life and she waves as she heads home. This week the four other Association members have called me about the barbecue. While they do support the fund-raiser, they're full of questions: How did we decide on one hundred campers? Why thirty thousand dollars?

"Those are sustainable amounts," I kept telling them.

I learned about the word *sustainable* when Mom was sick. *Sustainable* is a really big word for cancer doctors—actually for anyone trying to figure out how they can help the dying live longer. There's *preventive* care, *sustainable* care, and *end-of-life* care.

Because insurance companies don't seem to realize they're dealing with actual, dying people, they make you classify every kind of treatment. Each time I called RedLife Insurance, the agent would ask me, "Are we classifying this as sustainable care or end-of-life care?" Is this night nurse there to help your mom live or die? Do you need a bedpan to help your mom live or die? It was so awful—but the categories have stuck.

Now I classify Eden with these same labels. We're not quite to hospice, where we give in to the bulldozers. And to reach preventive care for Eden, I think we would need something like fifty thousand dollars. But to sustain this place, we could get by with thirty.

I climb The Hill to the extra boys' cabin, Lord of Life, which is gross Germ Central right now. Butterflies are flapping around in my stomach like I ate cocoons for dinner. Even after all that Jake and I have been through in the last week, electricity still passes between us. He can feel it too. I can tell by the way he watches me.

This morning I dropped off Sprite and crackers for the kids' lunch and dinner, but I haven't heard from Jake or his charges since then. And as I step into the clearing, I hear strange noises—shouts, laughter, and squeals.

This morning in the infirmary we had fourteen kids too sick to raise their heads. Now it sounds like a Chuck E. Cheese's party.

Jake is standing on the concrete step outside the cabin. He looks up when he sees me. "There you are." Then he swallows hard and says, "Please help me."

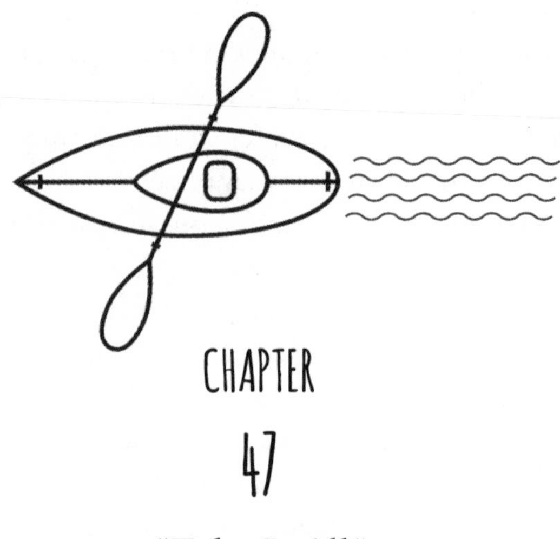

CHAPTER 47

"Take It All"

I sprint to the cabin. "Here I am," I say, out of breath. "What's going on?"

His eyes look tired. Actually, he looks completely exasperated—nothing like his usual confident self. He is Imperfect Jake at this moment. Not only are the tufts of hair sticking up on the back of his head, but he didn't shave today. Or maybe yesterday either. His navy Eden T-shirt—the one that usually makes his eyes look like the exact color of a Minnesota lake—is wrinkled and the neck is stretched. Also, white stains dot it. Bleach. Clearly he's been doing some heavy-duty cleaning in the bathrooms. Actually, he looks kind of homeless.

"What is all that noise?"

"Apparently the Virus of Death morphed into a twelve-hour bug." His tone is one long sigh. "It's nothing like what those kids had a few days ago." Through the door I see the campers sitting on their beds playing UNO. Maddie and Ava are yelling at each other. Ryan and Camron are wrestling on their bunk beds. Only they're not just wrestling. They look like they're really trying to beat each other up.

Charlie sits cross-legged on the steps next to us. A trail of mosquito bites cover his legs, and he's picking one of the scabs. "Will *you* let us go swimming, Poppi? Jake won't let us do anything. We've been inside all day."

"You're outside now," I point out.

"Only because I'm being punished," he mutters. He holds up bloody fingers from the picked scab. "See how bored I am? I'm actually making myself bleed."

I hand Charlie tissues from my backpack. Then I look at disheveled, tired Jake. "The kids are better? All of them are cured?"

"Some are. Some are on their way. But they're all revolting about needing to stay inside until they're back to a hundred percent."

"We can't even play catch," Charlie whines. "What are we supposed to do all day? Pick our scabs?"

"It was that attitude that got you this punishment in the first place, Charlie." Jake's voice is low. It's his I-am-truly-d-o-n-e-DONE voice. "You had better change your behavior right now. Am I making myself very clear, Charlie?"

Charlie smears dots of blood on the tissue, making little designs.

Harriet bursts outside with Wendy right next to her. World War III has passed, and the two of them have become best friends. They're even wearing the tie-dyed shirts they made last week in arts and crafts. Harriet's is decorated with perfect pink circles. Wendy's is a brown mess of botched designs.

"Jake," Harriet announces, "me and Wendy are going to the bathroom. And I'm telling you right now that we will be in there for a while."

"You know the rule, girls." He puts his hands on Wendy's shoulders and steers her back into the cabin. "One at a time in the bathroom."

"We *have* to go together." Her face is glowing with excitement. The fever she had yesterday has completely disappeared. "Wendy thinks she just started her period."

Wendy nods like Harriet has announced they're going to Disneyland together. Jake drops his hands from Wendy's shoulders. He looks at me. His face is ashen.

"Oh, this is so gross!" Charlie scrambles up and tears back inside. "I'm going back in."

Geesh. You'd think we were in biblical times and the poor girl was unclean. I touch Wendy's shoulder. "Thank you for letting me know, Harriet. I'll take care of her now."

"Poppi, I don't think you understand." Harriet looks me in the eye and speaks very slowly, like she does when she's trying to talk an adult into something. "This is Wendy's very first time. She doesn't know *anything*. Like, her mom is one of those who has avoided the whole topic."

"Ah." I nod. "Trust me. I've done this talk before. She's in good hands."

Jake tries to scoot back into the cabin, but Harriet grabs his arm. "Jake. Please? I really think I should go with them. My mom's a doctor and she's taught me everything. A girl's first experience with menstruation is extremely important. She needs to understand how her body is changing."

Jake closes his eyes. I get the feeling he's imagining himself in some all-male society where the only bloodshed comes from games of football. He peeks at me. "You'll take care of this? Right?"

"Of course." I smile at the girls. "Wendy and Harriet. Let's go back to my cabin and—"

"Jake!" Harriet barks. "Right now you are teaching Wendy that menstruating is something to be embarrassed about. A women's monthly cycle is a beautiful process that God invented so females—"

"Okay, okay." Jake waves his hands. "I get it. It's nothing to be embarrassed about. It's fine. It's great. I'm very—um—happy for you, Wendy."

"But you're not going to call my mom, are you?" she asks. "Because I want to do that. I mean, I know we're not supposed to use the office phone, and if we have an important message, you're supposed to call." Wendy stands up straighter and she is grinning so much, I can't help but smile too. "But maybe for this, I could tell her? Instead of you? Please?"

"Yes. Fine." Jake's face is red and his eyes are watering. "You can call her. Whenever you want."

Harriet steps toward Jake again. She's kind of crowding his personal space, but that's totally Harriet. "Wendy and I are going to my cabin for just a bit," Harriet says to him, but really it's to both of us. "I have a really good article that my mom sent with me that explains the difference between pads, panty liners, and tampons. I need to show her all the options she has."

Jake swallows hard. He manages a weak "Go."

"Wendy?" I ask gently. "Are you comfortable with going along with Harriet to see the article? I'll be over there in just a bit." Jake is a mess. He needs help.

Wendy is hopping from one foot to another, so very excited about this moment. Attention from Harriet—not only a year older, but the girls' leader and an expert on periods—is about the best present she could hope for.

"Okay," Harriet says, as they walk away. "First, there are these really big pads. I prefer to use minipads myself . . ."

I turn to Jake. "Sorry you had to go through that—"

Something's very wrong. His eyes are red and watery, and he's cringing. His face looks green.

"Jake? Are you okay?"

Instead of answering, he coughs violently, leans over, and throws up all over my Chacos.

CHAPTER 48

"Tear Down the Walls"

I'm warning you, Charlie." I push apart the heavy tarps draped in the infirmary. When the flu first started, Jake strung these musty tent tarps to divide the male and female sleeping areas. They make it smell like an attic in here. "If you don't lie down and close your eyes, you will not go swimming tomorrow."

"Why are you so mad? I'm just going outside to get some water." In Charlie's eyes there's a spark of mischief—the spark that has fueled four hours of pranks and arguing tonight. I'm about to string *him* from the ceiling.

"It's after midnight and you have to get some sleep. Do you understand?"

He collapses against his pillow. "But I'm thirsty."

The boys giggle, like they're a laugh track. At this point, anything—anything except spending another day cooped up—will set them off. They all have a bad case of cabin fever, and I'm their warden.

Jake is the only one who's actually sick at this point—and he's really bad. After he wrecked my shoes, he disappeared into the bathroom for almost an hour. I was so worried about him that I sent two groups of boys to make sure he was okay. Their reports were not pretty. Apparently Jake lost a lot more than his dinner—it sounds like he emptied his entire large intestine. And my reports were from ten-year-old boys, so the details were very graphic.

The poor guy. When he came back to the cabin, he collapsed onto the cot, shivering. He wrapped himself from head to toe in a flannel blanket. I know he has a fever, and every time I have a spare second, I've tried to make him swallow either Gatorade or some Tylenol. No luck. He just pushes them away and falls back asleep.

The kids aren't helping the situation. About an hour ago—when the campers couldn't get to sleep no matter how much I threatened—I had to resort to bribery. I promised we'd spend tomorrow at the lake. How I'm going to pull off lifeguarding for fourteen kids so ecstatic to be outside they'll forget basic safety is tomorrow's problem.

Someone coughs—a loud fake cough. Everyone giggles. I poke my head through to look at Charlie. He grins at me and coughs so violently it sounds like he's choking.

"Charlie!" I hiss. "Go. To. Sleep. Now."

He grabs his throat. "If you don't let me get more water, I'll cough all night and keep everyone awake."

"Fine. And since you so obviously have a cold now, there's no way you can go in the lake tomorrow. You'll sit on the shore while the rest of us swim."

He tears off his sleeping bag. "You can't do that."

"I can, and I did." I shine my flashlight at the boys. "Wolfgang is bringing the camp van back tomorrow. Those of you who go to sleep now might be able to join the others on the last part of the canoe trip." A hush falls over the cabin. It's finally as quiet as a real hospital room. "Those who want to cough and giggle can stay here and do that with me for the next *two days*."

Finally—in unified disgust of my unfair rules—the kids sigh and fall sleep.

CHAPTER 49

"Sinking Deep"

Suddenly I wake up and realize I never gave Jake any medicine. I stumble through the drapes to his cot. It's empty. I pat around the covers. Maybe he's scrunched down there, shivering. But his whole bed is cold. My watch says it's after two.

The door to the cabin is standing open. All the kids are asleep, even Charlie. He doesn't look so naughty snuggled in his sleeping bag and breathing softly. He's probably dreaming of ways to terrorize me tomorrow.

I tiptoe through the door and out into the cold night. I zip my yellow fleece as high as it will go. It covers my mouth and I breathe hot air into it to keep myself warm. A fat raccoon is standing on its hind legs, watching me.

"Hey," I whisper. "Where did Jake go?"

He blinks his beady eyes and scampers toward the girls' cabins to scavenge for candy.

There's a rustling around the corner. I step off the concrete stoop and pine needles poke my feet as I creep around the corner of the log cabin. Swaddled tightly in his flannel blanket and vibrating with chills is Jake. I drop onto the dirt next to him. "What are you doing out here?"

He cracks open his eyes. They're bloodshot. "Poppi," is all he croaks before he drops his head back onto the dirt. It clunks. He doesn't even wince.

I touch his cheek. It's burning with heat from deep under his skin. "Oh, Jake." I feel in my shorts pocket for the pills I slipped in hours ago. "You have got to take some medicine. If you don't get your fever down, we'll have to go to Urgent Care." And I don't have anyone to stay with the kids. I'd have to run out to Bryan's cabin in the woods and get him to drive Jake. All that is so complicated that I know already it won't work. *Please, God. Get his fever down. Help me, Lord.*

Jake blinks. "I came out here for water."

I run to the cooler, grab a Dixie cup, and pull the spigot until some sloshes inside. I rush back to Jake and hold it to his lips. "Drink this."

He squeezes his eyes closed. "Can't."

I remember a trick I used with Mom when she was too weak to swallow her chemotherapy pills. I would prop her head up with pillows, open her mouth, and pour the water down her throat. I got pretty good at figuring out the exact angle so she wouldn't choke.

I don't have any pillows—and even if I had a stack of camp-issued ones, they wouldn't be fluffy enough to elevate Jake's heavy head. I scurry behind him, lift his head, and place it in my lap.

His temperature feels like 103—maybe 104. "Just open your mouth. That's all you have to do."

He doesn't. I tilt the cup to his mouth and let some of the cool water run over his lips. That does the trick. He opens his mouth and gulps.

"Careful," I say. "If you drink too much"—he sits up, gags, and heaves the water back onto the dirt—"that will happen."

He drops his head back into my lap and looks up at me. "Sorry."

I smile. "You didn't do it on purpose."

He stares at me, upside down and backward. "I'm cold."

"You're so sick." I hold my hand to his cheek. "And dehydrated. Your body's working hard to fight the infection and you're not getting any liquids." I push the pills between his lips. "We've got to get this fever down so your body can do the other work." This time he swallows the water and medicine in slow sips.

"Go back to sleep," I whisper. With the backs of my fingertips, I smooth his hair away from his forehead.

Still lying on the ground, he closes his eyes. "I like that."

My own face heats as my mind understands what my body feels. This whole situation is intimate—more intimate than even Lakeside or dancing at Cove. Now I see those things were orchestrated intimacy.

This is Jake, unarmed. He doesn't have the energy to stand, and he certainly can't play his usual role of romancer. He needs me. For the first time since I met him in the parking lot almost two months ago, he's helpless.

I run my fingers over his face and through his hair. Even after his breathing becomes raspy with sleep, I don't stop.

Watching him reminds me of when Mom was really sick. Those months are a montage of ugly scenes: when she couldn't make it to the bathroom, and then I spilled an entire bedpan of chemo pee all over her bed; home health care bringing the hospital bed into the living room; spooning avocados and buttered oatmeal into her mouth; morphine; and so many visitors. Psalms, hymns, days that felt like nights that faded into nights with all the lights on at 3 a.m.

During those nights, Aunt Lily and I sat together on the couch and talked about everything. She told me the same lessons she teaches the anxious kids at her school: "Focus on the next right thing"; "Trust God because He knows the long view"; "Always hope for something better."

Right now, breathing the clean air scented with pine from all these trees, is the long view. Jake, Natalie, Eva, the counselors I love so much, the kids I adore, this peaceful place, this moment.

These were all waiting for me. I see this with the same certainty that I can see my fingers on Jake's forehead. All of this was God's long view.

For the first time in months, the straitjacket around my soul eases and I can breathe a bit. This place, this time, *this* was the something better.

I can feel this truth like I can feel the cold air all around me. God knew all this was coming. I just couldn't see it. Tears are in my throat, then in my eyes. The very worst happened with Mom—but it's okay. I close my eyes. *This is okay, God. I didn't see this was all coming. Everything feels okay.*

That prayer, just thinking those thoughts, starts the tears down my cheeks. Tears of sadness and thankfulness and happiness and relief. *Thank You, God. Thanks because right now, I do feel loved. Right now, it feels like You are taking care of me.*

"Are you crying?"

I look down at Jake and see his face is shining with tears. My tears. "Sorry." I wipe his cheeks. "I was—" I laugh and sniff. "Nothing."

"You were crying." He touches my knee.

"Hey!" I feel his forehead. "You don't feel as hot. Maybe the Tylenol is starting to work. Drink some more water. Hydration is the only thing that's going to get you over the worst of this."

He takes small sips and hands the cup back to me. "C'mon. Tell me why you were crying."

The night is quiet except a rustling. Probably that raccoon feasting on Nerds over at the girls' cabins. Oh well. I don't want to move from this exact spot.

Usually when I'm with Jake, a sort of drama hangs between us. Maybe fear? But I don't feel afraid right now. I'm completely relaxed. "I was thinking about what it was like when my mom was sick."

He swallows hard, the way you do when your throat hurts. "Yeah?"

"I was looking at you, and thinking about—" I study the black sky, and Chloe's words are in my head. *Toxic. Has issues.* I stop talking and look at Jake there. And suddenly, two thoughts appear in my mind. First: Jake cannot be my savior because he is not perfect. The second is connected to the first: I need to forgive him for not being perfect.

I don't say this to him. I don't say anything. Instead I picture myself taking him off a high pedestal and looking him right in the eye. Like this, eye to eye, we are two humans who need each other's forgiveness. I need his forgiveness for all the mean things I said to him. He needs my forgiveness for being a jerk.

And right then, Jake does sit up and moves to sit next to me. He looks me right in the eye. "Yeah?" he prompts.

"I realized I've been asking God this question since my mom died. Deep in my soul, I've been saying to Him, 'Will You really take care of me?' Only, I haven't been saying it that clearly. Instead, it's been this question—a question of my faith."

"Of course you have been."

"The answer has felt like no. No, He won't take care of me. He just felt so far away."

"Yeah." Jake is quiet for a really long time. Then he says again, "Yeah."

I love the way he says that second "yeah." He gets me right now. And it feels so nice to be gotten.

"Then, tonight, everything just kind of broke loose inside me. Tonight, I realized I couldn't do anything to really help you. But then, I started to pray. And guess what? I don't know anymore if we can call every little thing bad or good. I'm starting to believe that God is revealing everything a little bit all the time."

Jake slides his hand over my yellow fleece. His palm moves across my back and around my waist. We sit like this, in a side hug, and listen to the rustling and stare at the glowing white moon. "So, you didn't tell me the answer. What are you thinking right now? Will God take care of you?"

I turn to him and we are so close, our noses are almost touching. My arms and legs and hands are all buzzing to be sitting like this with him. "Tonight I see the long view. Tonight feels very much like He is."

"And maybe for tonight, knowing that is enough." He pulls me closer to him.

"You're going to give me the flu." But I drop my head on his shoulder anyway. It lolls there, boneless and peaceful.

He squeezes me closer to him. "If you don't have the flu by now, you're the only one immune to it."

I listen to his heart. I have no control over its beating. I'm not in charge of how long Jake will keep his arms cocooned around me. But God is.

I stare at the big marble of a moon and listen to the woods, and breathe in and out this beautiful night. *For tonight, this is enough, Lord.*

CHAPTER 50

"Be Like a Tree"

"There are more germs in that lake than there are in a toilet bowl," Maddie—Harriet's old best friend before she aligned forces with Wendy—says to me.

"But you've swum in it every day this summer." As I talk, I scan the lake for ten bobbing heads, making sure all the campers are safe. "Why are you worried about germs now?"

"Maybe because I don't want to get sick again?" Her words bite with sarcasm. All morning, she's been pouting, sitting on her towel, and looking for a fight.

"But you didn't get sick from the lake, Maddie."

"Maybe I did. You don't really know, do you?"

I don't say anything because it isn't me that Maddie wants to argue with. She's mad for lots of reasons: because she doesn't like she's lost Harriet, because she's not on the epic canoe trip, because she's sick of being sick. Whatever Maddie's issue is, she's decided that the biggest deal in the history of the world is that Lake Eden is full of bacteria and we shouldn't be swimming in it.

Lanie and Lydia are sharing Maddie's towel and watching me with interest. Is Maddie crossing a line? Will I let her?

"Think about it," she continues. "Nate saw a dead fish floating in the water yesterday. What killed it? Bacteria, right?"

I blow my whistle. "Ryan! Get out of the deep end or get out of the lake." I look back at her. "Maddie. I don't know what killed it. But the lake is full of its own ecosystem that balances all of it out."

"That lake is full of urine and feces—that's what that lake is full of!"

Lydia and Lanie love this. They start laughing and can't stop.

"Ewww!" Lanie says. "It totally is. I mean, fish poop in it, right?"

"And people pee in it," Maddie adds. "At least I know that Wyatt does."

"Enough!" I scold her. Everyone picks on Wyatt, a skinny kid with scabby elbows and a nose that's always running. But there's something especially mean about Maddie's dig. Maybe because right at this moment, Wyatt is floating by himself in an inner tube, watching while the others play Marco Polo.

Jake stirs next to me and pulls a towel over his face. A moment later, he starts snoring again. It was a long night for both of us. His fever did come back, and I was up until sunrise dosing him with Tylenol until it broke again.

After our talk last night, I expected him to act like nothing happened or to avoid me. That second option would be pretty hard, even for Jake, since I'm the only other staff member here. Unless you count Bryan. Of course, I don't.

But actually, neither has happened. All morning Jake has been sweet. I am so glad the awkwardness has evaporated between us. We're a team again.

"Jake! Hey, Jake!" Charlie yells. He's standing at the top of a hill by a clump of trees. It's near a cliff that juts about ten feet above the lake.

"Jake's sleeping," I call. "What do you need?"

"I'm awake." Jake sits up. The towel falls from his face, and he rubs his eyes with his palms. "What's up, Charlie?"

"The tire swing." Charlie points to the top of a tree where an old tractor tire is tied to a rope. "Can we get it down?"

Jake yawns. "I thought Poppi made it clear you weren't getting in the water today."

"Okay, yeah. Whatever. I am not getting in the water. But we haven't pulled the swing down yet this summer. I can help push the other kids." Charlie grits his teeth. "And I won't get in the lake the whole time. I *promise*."

"What do you think?" Jake looks at me. "Want to referee the swing?"

"Sure. Yeah. I don't mind." I glance toward him. Then, before I can stop my mouth, I blurt out, "Can we talk about Chloe's house?"

"What?" Jake sits up quickly. Now he looks fully awake.

I look to see if Maddie and the girls are listening, but they've run over to the tire swing, Lydia and Lanie trailing behind Maddie. "Chloe's house? We need to discuss it."

"Of course. Yeah. Now is good." He swallows hard. "I'm the one who needs to apologize. I caused all the problems. I know that."

"Apology accepted. But I'm confused about why. Did I do something stupid at Cove to make you mad? You were completely different after that night."

"No." He shakes his head. "Please don't think you did anything wrong. Kissing Jamie was the single stupidest thing I've ever done. An epic lapse in good sense. I'm so, so sorry. I know Nat has told you I'm some kind of a player, but I've never done anything *that* stupid before."

He's biting his bottom lip. He looks genuinely afraid. I can feel his fear. Because of that, I believe him that the kiss was a mistake. I believe he's truly sorry.

"I forgive you." Immediately—as soon as I say it—it's true. An itch has been inside me since I saw Jake kissing Jamie. But his apology was a salve for it. "I want to move past that kiss."

"Thank you." He reaches for my hand. "Because the kiss with Jamie meant nothing. It was a dare leftover from when we were kids. I had forgotten all about it. But then she busts into Chloe's backyard with this story about settling an old score."

"I told you that Truth or Dare was a dangerous game." I'm not smiling. "Eden is the last camp in the world where people still play it."

"But it wasn't really about the Truth or Dare. Or Jamie, even. She showed up at the right time, but kissing her had a lot more to do with you than it had to do with her. After our date, I needed to get you out of my head."

"Yeah. I got that message. Why?" I hear his words from our fight echo in my head. "Because you thought I was looking for a savior?"

"Oh, man." He rubs his eyes with his palms again. "This is really hard."

"Let me guess," I say, thinking of Natalie's movie scenes. "It was that you lost interest in me?"

"No. Not with you." He fills his lungs with air and then whooshes it out. "I'm not saying that hasn't happened before. But everything has been different with you, Poppi. Way different."

A flutter—like a pinwheel—is spinning in my chest. I really like what he's saying, where this is going.

"After Cove, I could feel how much I liked you. And how much you liked me. When I thought about it, I realized that we couldn't be together. For three reasons."

"Okay. Lay them out. And hurry." Over by the cliff, Charlie is lining the kids up for the rope swing, and I need to get over there. I have—maybe—one minute before the kids start jumping in unsupervised.

"One, when you said that had been the best night of your life, it hit me how serious this was getting, really fast. I could feel you really liked me. Two, I loved you liking me so much. So, yeah, if you were looking for a savior, I was looking to be one. And I've done that enough to know it doesn't work."

"Poppi! Can I go first?" Ryan yells. Suddenly the tire swing is better than all the iPads in the world. All the campers are climbing out of the lake, dripping wet and trying to climb on.

Jake and I stand. "Be careful," he calls to the kids. He looks at me. "They need help."

"Wait. What's the third reason?"

He tilts his head at me. This isn't something I want to hear. The pinwheel freezes. "I couldn't just have a summer thing with you. It would be more than that. But I can't imagine a future that includes both of us." He shrugs. "What would we do? Long-distance dating for years, until I finish college? That would be stupid."

"Maybe not," I say automatically. Then I remember what I realized last night with that prayer. "But if we're supposed to be together, it would work out. Somehow."

"Can I just test it first?" Charlie calls. "Come on. I won't even swim or enjoy it or anything. I will just drop into the water, and then I will get straight out. I won't even smile, Poppi."

"He's grounded from swimming!" Ryan yells, hopping on the swing. "I'll go first."

"No!" I call, marching over to the crowd. "We don't know if it's safe."

"Hey." Jake puts his hand on my shoulder. "Come back here. We're not done."

I nod to the swing. "According to the kids, we are."

"It's safe!" Charlie is trying to pull Ryan off the tire. "And I'm the one who found it!"

Over at the swing, the boys form a tight circle around the rope. Behind them are the girls. Jenna cranes her neck. "You swing on it into the lake? I want to see how it works."

"Oh, it's so awesome!" Charlie says. "For a second, you feel like you're flying."

"Guys!" Jake calls. "Hold on. There's a trick to this. You've got to know when to let go." He turns to me. "You want to go first?"

"You can." The swing isn't my thing. Too dangerous.

"You're thinking about the fish poop, aren't you?" Maddie asks, smirking.

"Ha ha." But I actually am worried about looking silly in front of Jake. Sailing over the water would be a moment of no control. I'm not sure I want to do that in front of him. I'm not even sure I want to experience that.

He grins. "All right, guys. Watch and learn." Jake peels off his shirt. The boys move away as he catches the rope and pulls his legs onto the tire.

Jake runs backward with the swing and leans back onto the tire. When he's up the incline, he lets go and whoops as he sails over the lake. When he's several feet from the cliff, he drops through the tire into the water with a splash.

We all clap because it really does look that fun. He emerges from the water and shakes out his hair. "I forgot how great that is." His eyes find mine on the shore. "You need to try it, Poppi."

Ryan runs back up with the rope. I grab it from him and look down the cliff. "Was it scary?"

Ryan hops on the swing and rides into the water. He screams the whole way. When he splashes, everyone cheers again.

"Not scary at all," Jake says climbing back up to us. Then he grabs his towel and rubs his hair with it. "Come on. Try it." He rolls up the towel and snaps near my thigh. "You have to."

"I liked it better when you were sick," I say, as he snaps the towel at my bottom.

He winks at me. "Oh, me too."

I have to laugh. "Okay!" I call to the boys. "I'm next." I peel off my T-shirt and shorts, adjust my bathing suit, and climb onto the swing.

Then I hold onto the rope, throw my head back, and enjoy the crazy, exhilarating ride.

CHAPTER 51

"My God Is So Big"

"*Achtung*, baby! *Achtung*, Camp Eden!"

I open the kitchen screen door to see the orange camp truck coming around the corner, crunching gravel in the parking lot by the dumpsters. Wolfgang is hanging out of the open window, yelling, "Helloooooooo! *Achtung*, Camp Eden!"

Bryan is also in the kitchen, making himself a ham sandwich. Usually he just eats in his own house, but today he's been around more than usual. He's been chatty too. He asked Jake questions about UCLA and what he's studying.

They sat together at lunch and Jake told him everything. The two talked like they're old friends—which I guess they are. But it bugged me. The more I watch Bryan, the more I blame him for Eden failing. He has zero interest in the kids. As Bryan was walking past last week, Jackson tripped and wiped out on The Hill. Bryan didn't even stop to help him up. Every time I've asked him to lend a hand with KP or with evening worship, he says he's got something else going on. What on earth could he have going on? Bryan finishes up with the mustard, walks past me, and heads up The Hill, away from the incoming van.

"Hi, Wolfgang!" I call, waving from the kitchen's porch. "Welcome back!"

He is singing a polka tune with German lyrics. He drops the big white cooler he's carrying and it clanks to the dirt. "Poppi! The campers? How are they? Still sick?"

"They're better. And every single one of them wants to go back with you." I hold the door open as Wolfie drags the cooler into the kitchen. "What about yours? None of them had to come back?"

"If they are sick, it is not bad. And they're not letting us know it. They don't want to have to go to bed. The canoeing is too fun!"

I laugh. "I'm so glad it's so fun. And it looks like, in the end, all the kids will get to go on the trip. Jake said he would drive the van out there later today and stay to help you."

"This canoe trip is the very best part of the summer." He hugs my shoulders as he walks past. "We are all loving it. Everyone is getting along and laughing. The lakes are all so very beautiful."

"You made it all the way to White Trail this morning?"

"We made it. All of the kids are becoming professional paddlers." Wolfgang comes around the corner with the ice bucket and dumps it into the cooler. While I fill the first cooler with hot dogs, balls of dough for campfire pigs in a blanket, and hamburger patties, he retrieves another cooler from the truck.

I dump Kool-Aid into the big cooler and stir until it's an orange funnel, then I stick the spoon in the Kool-Aid tornado to taste. "How's Natalie? Not sick?"

Wolfgang is grinning. "This is the most important part of the trip for me." He nods sharply once. "Because now Natalie has become my girlfriend."

I cough on the drink. "Wait. *What?*" Wolfgang pounds me on the back. "Did you just say that Natalie is your girlfriend? When did that happen?"

"Poppi, I must tell you that from the very second I saw Natalie Hatfield, I knew that she is the girl I will love." Wolfie's eyes are wide, even a little crazed. "She is beautiful and funny. I know that

God has brought me to Eden to find her. I have loved her in the far-off way all summer. But now we are loving close-up."

"What are you saying? That Natalie is loving you close-up too?"

"Not at first." Wolfie holds up an index finger. "At first she was seeing me as this very weird German guy. But then, we spent so much time together. I told her every day how much I liked everything about her. Then she heard my truth. On this trip, she finally said that, yes, she would be my girlfriend. Forever. She will be my girlfriend and then she will be my wife one day."

"Wow. This is so crazy. You have to slow down." Natalie was weird about wanting to go on the canoe trip. Did she know this was building with Wolfie? Is that why she went? "How did all this happen?"

"I have the canoeing to thank. So much time together I have been telling her I love her. She said I have worn her down."

"But won't you go back to Germany after this summer? What will happen then?" I think of Jake's Reason Three. This is the problem with every camp relationship. At the end of the summer, everyone goes back to real life. Wolfie is going to another *country*.

"Poppi." Wolfie grabs my hands. "When you know it is love, you *trust* it is love. I will do anything to be near Natalie. I will trust the feeling I have right now, deep in my heart. I will stay in the United States! This!" He pounds his chest. "This feels like the right thing to do next!"

CHAPTER 52

"10,000 Reasons"

What, exactly, are we hoping to find in here?" Jake asks.

This afternoon he and I are scavenging in the office, looking for treasures we can auction off at the barbecue. In a few minutes, Jake will take the camp truck out to White Trail to help with the canoers on their last night. "Anything Eden people will like enough to buy," I answer.

Jake picks up a handful of confetti. There are buckets of it in Eden's office. Sparkly gold circles. Tiny red diamonds. Glittering green shamrocks. He inspects the glittery stuff in his hands. "Oh, wow! Hey! I remember all this. It's from a musical we did one year for Parents' Lunch."

"You were all leprechauns?" I toss a handful of the shamrocks at him.

"Ha ha." He shakes the stuff out of his hair. "I think it was about Noah. Or rainbows. I don't know. My job was to sneak into the audience and dump buckets of confetti over the parents. It was awesome."

"Why is it still in here? Did someone take the time to pick up every piece?"

"We must have had lots of extra? No clue. I was like ten years old."

"Do you think anyone would pay for it? I could put it in cute containers and try to sell it."

"No one would pay for confetti." He holds up a trail map. "Maybe this, though." It's huge, almost as tall as Jake, but the top right corner is ripped. "If I tape it up? Someone would bid on that, huh?"

"I bet they would. There's some frames over in that corner. See if one fits. I don't know what else we'll do with them."

As he sorts through the frames, I paw my way through a huge bin of Eden sweatshirts. "These are good, right?" I ask, holding up a bright purple one with a hood that reads "Camp Eden—2014" across the chest.

"Oh, yeah. People loved those back in the day. 2014 was a good year. Natalie alone will buy six."

"Did you talk to Wolfie when he was back here?" I ask. "About him and Natalie?"

"There's a him and Natalie?"

"Apparently they're a couple. Like a serious couple. He's saying he's not going back to Germany at the end of the summer."

"Really?" Jake sets down a frame. It's spray-painted gold and I can't imagine what it's doing in the camp office. "Wow. There goes Reason Number Three, huh?"

We look at each other for a moment. "Yeah. I guess so." And suddenly, here it is between us—the hanging end of this morning's conversation.

"Leave it to Wolfgang to not care about whether a future makes sense. Actually, leave it to Natalie too. They'll make a good couple."

"Yeah," I say again. "Maybe they're just not scared."

"We're scared?" Jake says this in a casual voice, like we're talking about whether to put the Smokey the Bear costume in the auction. "Our three reasons mean we're scared?"

"Maybe we're scared. But to be clear, they were your reasons."

He pokes his tongue in his cheek and looks at me. "I guess they were my reasons."

"But I agree with Reason Three. I can't imagine a future that includes both of us. Reasons One and Two? I'm not sure about."

He lifts the glass from the frame and smoothes the map. "So, here's the deal about Reasons One and Two. I've learned that I have to stay away from a girl who needs too much. I love to be the one to make her happy. I believe I'm solving her problems, but it's always a crash-and-burn situation."

"Am I a girl who needs too much?"

"You know what? That first day I met you, I guessed you were. I didn't want to get involved in your Team Eden plan. Right away I could see how much I would like being the one to help you with that, the one to give you all the answers and strategies. That's, like, electrifying for me. To be the guy with answers? I need it."

"And now?"

"And now I'm tired of talking. We are who we are. Talking about who we are isn't going to change that."

"But I like talking about it. I like to understand you."

"And I like to date you and kiss you and dance with you. We've talked a lot today. Now let's do the other things."

"You want to date and kiss and dance right now?" My voice is so thick with flirting, I'm purring.

"Well, yeah." He grins and his smile is boyish and very cute. "But I was supposed to meet everyone over at White Trail five minutes ago." He twists his wrist and shows me his watch.

"Oh, yeah. We'll finish this later?"

"Later we'll have fun. My dad has a benefit at the Beverly Hilton this weekend. Will you go with me?"

I have to grin because being with Jake is my favorite place to be. And this is another actual date. But I have to ask, "What about Reasons One, Two, and Three?"

"We've just discussed One and Two. So, we're good on that. And didn't we decide that Natalie and Wolfie taught us not to worry about Reason Three?"

"Not really. We didn't decide that at all."

He leans over and kisses my nose. "Be there by seven on Saturday night. I'll already be in L.A., but I'll give you the address. Get ready to have fun."

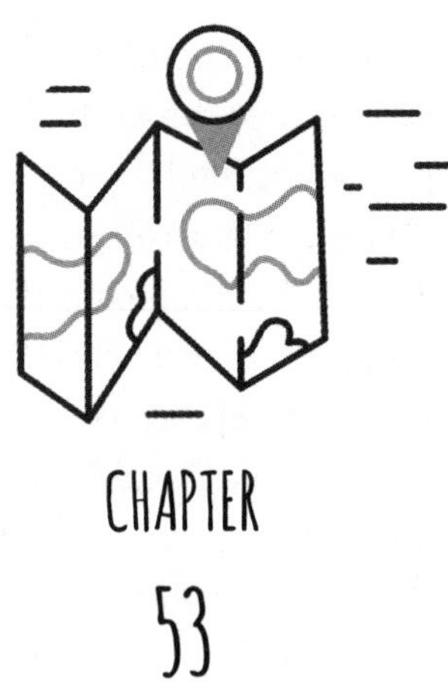

CHAPTER 53

"Lead Me to the Cross"

After Jake leaves for White Trail with the rest of the supplies, Eva comes out to camp and we sort and photograph the auction stuff we found. We post everything on the "Save Eden" page much more quickly than I could have by myself. We're a good team.

When it's getting close to dinner, she stretches out and looks at me. "I brought my suit. Want to go for a swim? I really miss being in the lake."

I smile. "Go ahead. I swim in the lake a couple of times a day. I should probably email some more places to try and find a dunking tank. But you should go and enjoy it."

Eva grabs a black bag with a towel poking from the top. "I will. I always feel awkward swimming when the kids are here." She walks toward the door, but then she turns. "Take a little time to yourself too, Poppi. You should go for a hike. Or just lie down in the sun and enjoy God's best work. Just for a couple of hours, experience the peace of camp—without having to answer questions."

"That's a really good idea." I picture myself on the trails, not cheering on campers or supervising counselors, but thinking. And praying. I'm twitchy from everything going one with Jake, like an

ADHD kid in a cabin full of puppies. I need to stretch out my legs and my soul. "I do want to go for a hike."

I head to the kitchen and fill my backpack with two apples, three water bottles, a baggie of pecans, and two baggies of granola. I'm glad Pete isn't here to berate me for the excessive plastic use.

While I'm packing up, Bryan wanders into the kitchen. I ask what he's planning to do today, and he says he's meeting someone. Then he heads outside, sits on a picnic table, and types on his phone.

As I'm leaving, I see Hilary Steinmal, the woman from STUF, arrive in a silver BMW convertible. Pulling into the parking lot behind her is a pickup truck that reads "C&H Services—Anaheim." I'm just about to head down to ask who they are. Instead, I pull out my phone and Google C&H. Their website says they're a demolition company. Probably the exact company that's supposed to destroy the patio I'm standing on right now. I want to run down to the lake and get Eva. But what can she do? Block them from the property?

Bryan leads Hilary and two guys in black polos and jeans up The Hill. When he sees me, he does not smile.

One of the guys nods to me. "Hello there. I'm Carl. How are you doing on this fine afternoon?"

By the panicked look on Bryan's face, I'm guessing Carl didn't get the memo I'm Enemy Number One. "Hi, Carl." My heart is pounding. "What are you doing here?"

Hilary steps forward, grinning. "Hi, sweetie. We're just here to dream and plan." Her smile is exactly like the one Cruella de Vil must have had when she first saw the Dalmatians. "I just love the imagining part of any project," she gushes. "But please, don't mind us. We won't get in anyone's way." She shoots Bryan a look. "Right? The campers aren't even here today, am I correct about that?"

"Everyone is gone," he confirms. Even slimy Bryan looks uncomfortable. Good. I hope this is so awkward for him that he realizes what he's doing is wrong on like five million levels.

"But the sale isn't final," I say. "You can't be here." Eden feels like a very small child I must protect from violence. "You don't even know we're going to sell the land to you."

"Just dreaming." Hilary's grin is tight. "Our whole team is excited to move our corporate offices, and Eden is just a fantastic place to envision the perfect layout, isn't it?"

Bryan takes Hilary's elbow and moves past me. Carl and the other guy don't look at me as they file up The Hill.

I bite my lip until I taste blood. What I really want to do is trip all of them and tell them they are not allowed to pull out their measuring tapes or snap pictures or even take one more step on this property.

Instead I run for the trails. More than ever, I need to get out of my own head.

For this hike, I chose the triple black diamond of Eden trails: Flowerhead. It's pretty much vertical the whole way to the top, and today I want to do it faster than ever before.

I tear up the side of the hill, trail-sprinting over dead trees and little streams and through thick branches. Natalie calls trail running "using all the muscles you didn't know you had." Exactly. Even though my legs are strong from a summer of hiking, Flowerhead is so steep, I'm panting.

But I need to run this hard to get away from Bryan, away from the nightmares where Hilary gets Eden and Jake leaves at the end of the summer. I need to outrun the lead ball of anxiety inside my belly. My legs need to feel, reach, stretch, and hurt.

Because the thing that broke free when I prayed last night terrifies me. It feels like I've walked through a doorway and on the other side of it, everything changes. This is like standing in a new room. Now that I've seen it, I cannot go back to the old one.

If I believe what I told Jake—if I believe that yes, God has been taking care of me—then can I trust that He will *keep* taking care of me?

And what does that mean? How do I even *do* that? Am I supposed to wait for feelings and nudges and trust they're from God? How do I know which are the right decisions and which are the wrong ones?

Because I'm pretty sure that my decisions would always be wrong. I truly am a mess-up. I know that about myself. I couldn't keep Mom alive. I can't keep Dad from drinking. I failed at school. I don't want a normal job.

"HELP ME KNOW, LORD!" I look to the sky and yell, "DO YOU HEAR ME, GOD? THIS IS ME CRYING OUT THAT I DON'T KNOW WHAT YOU WANT ME TO DO. I NEED HELP!"

Nothing.

But yelling at the sky—actually—feels very good. Something inside me is pulling and shifting. I fall down to my knees, right here next to a sticky old log, and I look up to the sun and call, "THIS IS ME SAYING THAT I REALLY WANT THE LONG VIEW TO BE JAKE AND EDEN. PLEASE GIVE ME THAT." The trail pebbles dig into my knees like little wasp stings. But I want to feel this pain. I want something that is real. I want an answer.

The forest is absolutely silent. Not a falling branch, or chirping bird, or scampering spider.

"WHAT DO YOU WANT ME TO DO? PLEASE TELL ME, LORD. I DO TRUST YOU AND I DO KNOW YOU WILL TAKE CARE OF ME. NOW, TELL ME. IS IT JAKE? WHAT'S NEXT?"

I can hear my own breathing—and nothing else.

I begin to hike back down the hill, chugging water and eating every bit of food from my pack. Yellow spots float in front of my eyes, and I can almost see the separate rods and cones that make up the trail. My throat hurts from screaming. Or from the flu. I'm miles from camp and suddenly I am crying.

As I step between roots and loose gravel and tangled branches, I get my answer, the only little one I ever hear. *I will take care of you.*

CHAPTER 54

"Priceless"

For the third time, Natalie finds the perfect outfit for me in her trash-bag luggage collection. At least I hope it's perfect. Up until now, my "fashion sense" has been to look like I'm not trying that hard. This way, if I get something horribly wrong, people won't notice. Natalie's white sparkly dress is the opposite of not trying hard. It's like a neon, glowing billboard that screams, "I'm the girl who is trying the very hardest."

Jake had an exam for one of his classes, so he's been at UCLA all day and is meeting me at the event. All afternoon, Natalie has delivered a steady stream of information about what I should expect tonight: "Beverly Hilton. A benefit for the farmers who lost crops in the drought. Not very Hollywood of a venue—I'm guessing no celebrities. Well, maybe some F-listers. But no one to bring in the media. Not for farmers."

"Hey!"

"You should be glad. You're nervous enough already. Everyone kicks it up a notch when the media is there. You'll have to valet. Go straight to reception. Look for signs in the lobby. I'm sure it's in the International Ballroom. Grab a gift bag."

"Gift bag?"

"Calm down. It'll be something down-home to fit the feel. Think *Rhinestone Cowboy*—BeDazzled belt buckle or something. Smile a lot, and DON'T SLOUCH!"

Two hours later, after primping and prepping and driving through the traffic of L.A, I find the Beverly Hilton and hand my key over to the valet attendant. As I'm walking into the International Ballroom, I glance in a mirror, only to see that my shoulders are rounded like I have osteoporosis. Oh, geez. I'm not really the Instagram Poster Girl for Fun Date in Beverly Hills. More like So Wrecked with Nerves, I Can't Even Stand. I take a deep breath and stand up straight. The Beverly Hilton is Jake's actual real world. I have to try to fit in.

The ballroom, the guests, the *feel* is elegant and sparkly. There's an orchestra playing a swingy country song and hundreds of guests are mingling under a gigantic image of George Jackson Bass smoking a cigar. The men are in tuxedos and almost all the women are in black. I sure hope Natalie's right about this white dress.

Then I find Jake in the crowd, and we lock eyes. He's smiling at me. And with that smile, I am so glad I came. It's the grin he gets when he's teasing me—his eyes crinkle and his smile is so wide, all his teeth show. Suddenly, there is absolutely no place I would rather be than here. Maybe I don't fit in with Beverly Hills. But I really want to fit with Jake.

Several eyes follow Jake as he walks to me. People might be staring because they know he's George Jackson Bass's son, but it's not that kind of watching. These are female eyes that are not considering him as someone's son. A girl my age in a red dress actually licks her lips as he passes her.

It's because Jake *is* the Instagram Poster Boy for Hot Guy in a Tux. His hair is gelled and his jaw is smooth. His straight shoulders—the same shoulders that carry campers in Red Rover and paddle kids around the lake—are horizontal under his black jacket.

He takes my hand and pulls me to him. "You are stunning," he whispers in my ear.

"Me? I'm not the one everyone is checking out here."

"Oh yes, you are." He kisses my cheek. "I was afraid you wouldn't have anything to wear. But you most certainly do."

"It's Natalie's." I'm smiling all over the place, because that is just what you do when you're breathing the same air as Jake Bass in a tux.

"That dress is having the best night of its life." He's grinning too. "This is a different version of you. A more sophisticated one. It's like grown-up Poppi."

"Jake Bass, that is the most perfect thing to say."

"Not toxic?"

I shove his shoulder. "Shut up."

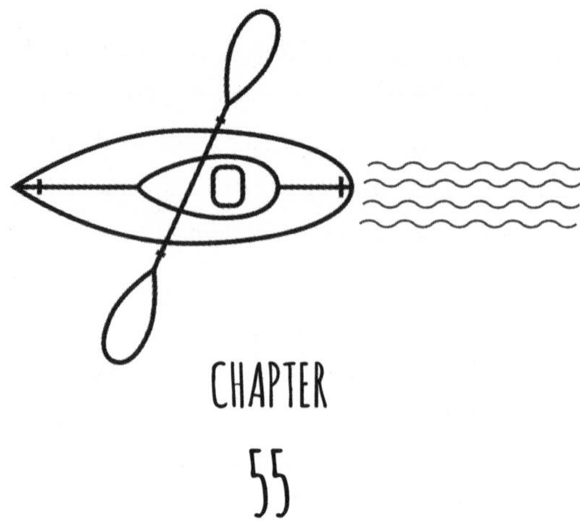

CHAPTER 55

"Brothers & Sisters in Christ"

Jake's sister, Savannah, flew in from Dallas for tonight. She looks just like Jake, only she is even more of everything that he is. Her blue eyes are shadowed in smoky makeup and look indigo in the soft light. Her cheekbones are contoured and appear even more pronounced than his. Her long, shiny hair is perfectly tousled, making her more sophisticated than even tuxedoed Jake.

"It is so nice to meet you, Poppi," Savannah says, with a deep southern accent. "You and me could sit down here and talk for sixty hours about everything at Eden, couldn't we?"

I laugh. "We sure could. I love it there."

"Me too, of course." She leans closer to me. "I am just so happy you're there this summer. That place needs some serious help, doesn't it?"

"Yes, it does," I agree. I like her. She's like her mom. Both Honey and Savannah are so at ease with themselves that I can't help but relax too. Even here. Even when I've landed in the middle of people who have five hundred extra dollars that they don't mind paying to breathe the same air as GJB.

Savannah has brought her boyfriend, Addison. He has very white, clear skin and eyelashes so long, he's almost pretty. He's also polite, and so southern that I keep expecting him to call me "ma'am." Savannah explained that she met him at her summer ballet program, where he helps with the sets. Jake chats with Addison about his favorite restaurants in Dallas. Watching them talk, I see that Jake also inherited the Bass knack for putting people at ease. Their whole family is especially talented at making everything look effortless.

With Addison in tow, Savannah strides straight to the chairman of the Farmers Union, and I hear her introduce herself as GJB's daughter and tell him how sad she is to hear about the damage the drought is doing to farms. I watch from a few feet away as she moves to the Beverly Hilton's event planner to gush about the centerpieces (cowboy hats overflowing with hydrangeas), and finally to Buddy to ask when we should go back to see GJB and Honey.

"Wow," I say to Jake. "You and Savannah have been going to these benefits your whole lives. It's kind of crazy, right?"

Jake leans over the white tablecloth. "Not as crazy as the time you helped deliver that calf." There's a chuckle in his voice. He's talking about one of my farm stories I told him.

"Two calves, actually. The second one was totally a surprise. And that was a different kind of crazy."

"Well, let me lower your expectations about benefit dinners," Jake says close to my ear. "These things are never crazy. Overcooked chicken and boring speeches, yes. Surprise calf deliveries, never."

"You never know, it is the Farmers Union."

"Ha. Get ready for a lot of talk about the stock price of tractor companies."

I touch his knee under the table. "I have a good feeling about tonight. Something exciting will happen. I just know it."

The dinner is fried chicken with mashed potatoes, cream gravy, and green beans. At our table are important men and women from the Farmers Union. They talk about weather reports and seed companies. Even though I follow some of what they're saying, I focus on my plate. I want to do everything perfectly, to be Jake's best date ever.

After dinner, Savannah shows her phone to Jake. "Buddy just texted. We need to go back there as soon as we can. They want to do pictures now."

Jake looks at me. "Coming?"

Addison is already standing, so it's clear I won't be the only non-Bass at the photo session. "Sure." I swallow. "Yeah. I can do that."

Buddy texts directions and we find Jake's parents in another ballroom, where extra tables and sound equipment are stored. Right in the center of the room, surrounded by about twenty VIP fans, is George Jackson Bass himself.

He uses one hand to sign pictures, and he keeps his other arm around Honey. She's wearing a straight beige gown that matches her hair. In her ears are pearl earrings the size of marbles. She grins at every fan and laughs at every joke. I think she might be working harder than GJB, but she's not even sweating. Honey Bass might be my hero.

Savannah and Jake part the crowd to hug their mom. Honey kisses each of them about a dozen times. The line of waiting fans take cell phone pictures of the Bass family. Next, Honey turns to Addison and me and makes a big fuss over each of us.

First, Honey kisses my cheek. I'm not sure how she has any lipstick left at this point. "Poppi, we are absolutely thrilled about you and Jakey. When he said you were coming, I told George, 'I knew that girl was special to him.'"

I say, "Thank you so much for including me tonight," and I can feel Jake's smile shining on us. He holds my waist, like he's stabilizing me. And it feels like the exact right kind of stability.

"Of course!" She squeezes my hands before she moves on to Addison.

I cannot stop smiling. Because no matter what happens between Jake and me, this night will stand out in my personal history as unforgettable.

Even if I move back to Minnesota and marry a farmer and work for the next forty years helping deliver calves. Even if I stay at Eden forever and become the grumpy old cook who burns the lasagna. No matter what, I will never forget how it felt to be in this dress, surrounded by all this glamour—and on Jake's arm.

CHAPTER 56

"I Can Only Imagine"

I had hoped that I could eventually relax into this night. All through dinner, I prayed that sooner or later, I would feel comfortable among these glamorous, sparkling people. But even after they've cleared the plates, I feel zipped up in the itchy skin of someone else. Even with Jake next to me, a little motor of anxiety keeps my heart racing.

I sit very straight at our table and smile at everyone. I smile so much that my cheeks ache. Does this happen to Honey? Does she also worry there's lipstick on her teeth or pecan pie on her chin?

After dessert, the chairman of the Farmers Union steps to the mic, welcomes everyone, and talks about George Jackson's generosity. Next Buddy takes over and tells the crowd how important farming is to GJB. He introduces Honey, then Jake, then Savannah. Each of them stands and waves to the ballroom. The applause goes on and on.

Then GJB takes the stage and plays two crowd favorites, "Heaven Ain't Far from Houston" and "Broken Beverly Hillbilly." When he starts a slow song, "Junior and His Miss," about a young couple, Jake stands, holds out his arm and raises his eyebrows. He wants me to stand too.

I widen my eyes and shake my head. He doesn't really expect me to dance, does he? Couldn't Savannah and Addison go out there and do it? Jake touching me makes my legs feel like cherry Jell-O. What if I collapse in front of all these people?

"Get up now," Jake says between his clenched smile. "Or I will *carry* you to the dance floor."

On wobbly legs and in Nat's too-tight heels, I follow him. Everyone claps when Jake and I step into the bright lights. This must be part of the show.

The floor is parquet and scuffed from thousands of other pairs of boots and heels shuffling right here. Jake rests one hand on my shoulder and the other on my hip. And even with all the eyes and lights and adrenaline, his hand steadies me.

I keep my eyes down, watching Jake's black boots as he steps forward two steps, then back one. By focusing on his feet—and remembering everything I can about dancing with my friends at a country bar by Mankato—I manage to keep up. A couple of minutes later, I glance over and Addison and Savannah are two-stepping next to us. Beads of sweat are on Addison's upper lip. Do I look as nervous as he does? Really, I don't need to wonder because I *feel* that nervous.

Jake took his jacket off at dinner so my fingertips rest on his crisp white shirt, only one layer away from his skin. It's like static electricity everywhere we're touching. He doesn't say anything at first, but when the next song starts, he whispers in my ear. "You're doing so good. Just relax."

"I'm not relaxed?"

"Poppi. You are so tense right now, if I let go of you, you'll fall over."

"Quit teasing me. I'm tense because I'm dancing with the Luke Skywalker of country music. Everyone is checking me out to see if I'm worthy of the monarchy."

"Oh, they're checking you out, all right," he whispers in my ear. Then his hands meet on the small of my back, and he traces circles in time with the music. He sings along, and I lean my head on his chest and listen to the deep vibrations.

Whenever I've listened to him sing—at morning devos or night worship—I've fantasized exactly this. For Jake's voice to feel this intimate, this much like it belongs to me personally. And this is that moment, I can feel it. We're so close to each other. It's different from before. We're connected in a new way.

Jake feels the connection too. I know he does. His strong shoulders hunch around me. He rests his cheek on my head. I feel so safe right here, with him. The Next Right Thing. This is it.

His dad begins another slow song, and the dance floor crowds more. "If Texas isn't in your heart, baby, neither am I," Jake sings along in his baritone voice.

I lean back to look at him. "Do you know what I think you should do right now?"

"Kiss you?"

"I really think you should go up there and sing with your dad."

Jake laughs. It's not his normal, easy laugh, though. "These people didn't pay five hundred dollars a plate to hear *me* sing."

"But they're fans of your dad. He says his fans like to know about him personally. That seems like something they'd be into—George Jackson Bass's son is a singer too."

"First of all, I'm not a singer. Second, it doesn't work that way." Jake stops moving. "Dad's a businessman—he's a professional. He takes these benefits seriously. He's not about to turn this into the Bass Family Jamboree."

"I think you're wrong. Go and ask Buddy if you can. You know that if you can clear it with Buddy, it'll be fine with your dad."

Now Jake totally stops dancing and really does stare at me. Maybe he was humoring me before, but now he's tilting his head and looking at me like I've suggested he start break-dancing. "You're serious?"

"Serious as a heart attack. Come on. I think your dad would like it. Your mom would *love* it."

It's probably the last part, mentioning Honey Bass, that has Jake poking his tongue in his cheek and considering this. "But if he doesn't?"

"If your dad doesn't like it, he'll just say no. You took a risk and it didn't work out. Who cares? What's the worst that can happen?"

"Want to know the worst that can happen? My dad can be pretty condescending. He can get sarcastic and impossible."

"So, he bosses you around. It would be good for you to feel what the rest of us get from you all the time."

"Are you calling me bossy?"

"I'm absolutely calling you bossy," I say, smiling.

"Okay. But then you have to take a risk too."

I'm still grinning. "Anything." I'm sure he'll ask for a kiss.

"You go up there and sing with me."

"Ha! That's a terrible risk. I don't know any of your dad's songs. He *hates* that I don't know any of his songs. Father-and-son moment is one thing. But me up there? Buddy would never allow it." Not to mention I could never do it.

"Sing 'Kumbaya.' I love it when you sing that."

"People did not pay five hundred dollars for fried chicken and me singing 'Kumbaya.'"

"You're a wimp?"

I swallow. "Okay. Go ahead. I'm not a wimp. I will go up there and sing with you."

CHAPTER 57

"All God's Creatures Got a Place in the Choir"

Buddy does not agree to a Jake-and-Poppi duet, but he does check with GJB in between songs to see what he thinks about Jake joining him on "Family Honor, Family Armor." It's a sweet song about a family that gets in a big fight and all the ways they have to forgive each other. Honey loves the idea. And then GJB does too.

When Jake strides to the stage and picks up a guitar and his dad introduces him, it's like Kanye West has shown up. Everyone holds up their cell phones to take pictures of him—the younger version of GJB—harmonizing with his dad.

As Jake and his dad sing, I stand off of the stage and also snap a picture. I want to remember this moment. Jake keeps glancing at his dad. This must be so strange for him. After so many years of being a prop in his dad's show, now he's onstage next to him and really part of it.

The sweet family song, the impromptu duet, and the fact that Jake's voice is as strong as his dad's energizes the crowd. When the Bass men finish, everyone cheers and whistles and stomps their boots. Someone yells, "Encore!" and George Jackson grins at Jake and then at the crowd. Honey is standing near me, and in the lights, her eyes are shining. Even proper, southern Savannah lets out a whoop.

Jake nods a couple of times, and this time his eyes find mine. He winks and I wink back. Never forget this, I want to tell him.

Jake leans over and whispers something to his dad. George Jackson is nodding and he's started to strum the next song. Jake grabs his microphone and says, "Can I please dedicate this next song to my very favorite farmer?" he asks. "She's actually my co-worker. But she's also one of my very favorite people." Someone wolf-whistles, but I can't even look to see who it is because I can't move my eyes from Jake's. "And she's taught this Texas boy a lot about grit. And taking risks."

GJB starts to strum and they sing a cute song called "Planting Cotton at Christmas" about a relationship that doesn't seem to make any sense, "Like sowing those seeds, right here in the snow." The lyrics are about a guy and a girl who are all wrong for each other, but they fall in love, and then they celebrate every year, "still planting cotton at Christmas."

This song—sung by my favorite cowboy—is just about more than I can take. I'm swaying to the music and smiling, and I want to tell Poppi from last Christmas that the world beyond Eagle, Minnesota, is crazy good.

Next Right Thing to the millionth degree, Lord.

Thank You.

CHAPTER 58

"How Great Is Our God?"

Sunday mornings at Eden are quiet. Everyone sleeps in, even the kids. I guess this makes for a weird Sabbath in a place where we worship three times a day. But we do have church. Later on, around one in the afternoon, Pastor Sean from Ascension comes out to lead worship and give us Communion. We have to wait for him to finish up at his church, so Sunday mornings start slowly.

Pete hikes on Sunday mornings, and Bryan makes cinnamon rolls for breakfast. Natalie calls them "sinnamon rolls" because they are so ridiculously delicious. The caramel glaze that he pours over them is like the stuff they wrap around apples at the state fair. It's thick and crackly and melty over the puffy, flaky dough. The rolls are gooey, spicy, buttery softness, and it's impossible to stop at just three.

"This is just like Bryan," Natalie says every Sunday morning. "He cooks for one morning, totally destroys Paleo for me, then goes back into hiding."

Before I eat the horrible, addictive, zillion-calorie breakfast, I always go for a long run. I sprint up to Lakeside and back two times to help offset the sugar high that's coming.

Last night, before we kissed good-bye, Jake said he would meet me at six thirty this morning to run with me. He stayed at the hotel with his parents, but they had to catch an early flight this morning so he's getting back to Eden before sunrise for our run.

I'm stretching when he comes up behind me, groaning.

I turn to see him and note that the stage-presence Jake of last night is gone. Walking up the trail is my favorite scruffy version. He's wearing black running shorts and the long-sleeved Rogue T-shirt, the one from my Night of Crying on the Patio. His hair is all tufts and swirls and his jaw is speckled with whiskers.

"You are brutal, Savot," he says as a greeting. "You keep me up half the night, making me sing and dance for your affection. Then you force me to pound the trails at sunrise." He yawns again. "Brutal, I tell you. I cannot keep up."

I laugh. "No one forced you out here." I'm guessing that Jake slept better than I did. I got back to camp after one and then had so many pictures from the night running through my head, I could not sleep. I turned my pillow over, opened my window, tried lying on my stomach. But my brain was like a computer, downloading scenes from the night. I could not stop playing and replaying the moment of Jake onstage with his dad. This morning my mind is still buzzing with too many thoughts—and not enough sleep.

Jake and I usually don't run together because he likes to do six-minute miles and I like to run at The Speed of Chat. If you're going so fast that you can't talk, then you're going too fast. This morning is no different. Without even stretching, he starts sprinting up to Lakeside.

"Come on," he calls over his shoulder. "Think of those cinnamon rolls."

"This is my very best," I whine. "Talk to me about something. Distract me from my shin splints."

"Shin splints are a myth." Jake is not even out of breath.

"Tell me about what happened last night with your parents. It was good, right? Singing with your dad?"

"It was good," he agrees. "I mean, Dad and I didn't hug it out or anything. But he asked me if I'd like to do it again."

"Oh, I love that. This is the start of something good. This is the start of deeper respect between you two."

"We respect each other," Jake says. But then he's quiet for a bit. "Well, I guess that when we're together, there is some weird competition between us."

"Yeah, I can see that. But that's why you do your own things, right? You in L.A., him in Dallas. You keep your distance. You both focus on what you're good at."

"Yeah. I have my own things. I have college. Dad hated school, but it's always been easy for me. I'll make my own money one day and not rely on him for that."

"You mean that you'll make your own money—as a corporate lawyer? One who tears down camps?" I'm kidding. Only, I'm kind of not.

"Exactly," he deadpans. "I'm hoping to get a job as camp tear-er-downer." He yanks my ponytail. "Ha ha."

"But seriously—Eden. That's your thing. Really different from your dad." Jake keeps running and doesn't answer. "Right?" I finally ask.

"Yep. Eden was my thing too."

"Was?"

He wipes the sweat from his forehead. "C'mon, Poppi."

"What?"

Jake stops running and looks at me. "I'm not having this same conversation again."

"But is that still what you believe? You still believe that? Even after everything this summer?"

He rubs his jaw, studying me. "Come on. I'll play your part and you play mine."

"What are you talking about?"

"Let's go. You have to do this with me. You play my part. I'll play yours."

"I have no idea what you're talking about."

"Here's my best shot at the points you'll make. See if I get them all: Eden closing shows everything stupid about this world. We need more trees, not more cubicles. There is nothing better for a kid than worship under the stars and around the campfire. I can't believe we're taking that away from kids—L.A. kids, who need it the worst. For every soul-sucking second that ten-year-olds spend Snapchatting, they need fifteen hours of hiking and fort building. We have to do everything possible to keep open a place that lets that happen."

I stare at him for a second before I realize that my mouth is hanging open. "You expect me to argue with all that? Because yes. Yes to all those things."

"I meant them," he says. "Now you play me. Fill me in on reality, Jake."

"You tricked me." But I play along because I really liked hearing him say all that. "We've tried. We tried for years to get more kids here. But we can't recruit enough staff or enough campers anymore." My voice has dropped a couple of registers, and Jake is smiling because I really do sound like him. "Poppi, you haven't had to come back every summer and see which kids didn't return and which counselors chose to do something else. You haven't had to make less staff and less money work. Just because something is good doesn't mean it'll last forever. Oh. And yeah, I know Bryan is slimy and worthless now, but he used to be really fantastic. I mean, like really great. Like he used to be so *awesome*."

"All right. Enough," Jake laughs. "You've got me nailed. But I don't really defend Bryan like that, do I?"

"You totally defend Bryan like that. You have some childhood loyalty that blinds you from seeing that he is, literally, the very worst camp director ever. He brought a demolition company to camp—*while* we're still running the summer program."

"But look. He's kind of solving the problem. He's moving on. He must know he's doing a terrible job. Now he's becoming an insurance salesman."

"Thank goodness. But why does he have to sell the place? Wouldn't he want to leave a legacy to show for his hard work the last six years?"

"I can completely understand why he's selling it. It's like breaking up with a girl. You may not want to date her, but you don't want anyone else to either."

"So gross." I wrinkle my nose. "It's like he's claimed Eden as his own. Like he's a dog who peed on it and thinks it's his forever."

Jake busts out laughing. "Oh, I love it when you go all small-town-farm-girl on me. Next, you'll be smacking wasps." He lifts my palm and kisses it. "Okay, I'll always lose at the Eden debate. When I see Eden through your eyes, I see that you're right. Let's chain ourselves to trees to keep it open."

I start to walk down the trail. "And when you see it through yours?"

"I like your eyes a lot," he says. "They're beautiful."

"Do you know what else is beautiful? The six cinnamon rolls I'm about to eat." I sprint the last few strides to beat Jake.

"Yes!" Jake picks me up and carries me to the kitchen. "BEE-YOU-TI-FULL!"

CHAPTER 59

"Hiding Place"

"All right, campers. We have a new game tonight. It's called Operation Interrogation, and all of you could be victorious—*if* you can convince us you're someone else." Natalie is standing on the picnic table and grinning. She passes the bullhorn off to Wolfgang.

Wolfgang's shoulder is smashed right against hers. He looks like a different boy from the one who showed up at Eden two months ago. Different from the one I ate all those s'mores with and led on hikes because he couldn't handle his cabin and he was a hot mess. Now he has a cool confidence: no slouching, no darting eyes, no asking a million questions. Natalie becoming his girlfriend changed everything. She, too, is beaming. Mostly at Wolfie. They are the most lovesick couple I've ever seen.

"You will really like this new game that Natalie and I created!" Wolfgang calls into the bullhorn. "Your job, campers, is to go anywhere you want in all of Eden. You don't have to hide, but you must be with one other person."

The campers are listening carefully, especially the boys. They love strategy games. If they would listen this well when we taught the words to worship songs, we wouldn't still be holding up song cards during Week Nine.

"The counselors will search for you," Natalie continues. "When a counselor finds you, they're going to ask you who you are. Your job is to pretend you are someone famous. You can be the Teenage Mutant Ninja Turtles or My Little Ponies. Whoever. The counselor will question your group. As long as you stay in character, you're safe."

"But! If you are not your character! Even for one word!" Here, Wolfgang furrows his eyebrows and looks very severe. "You will be captured! You are out of the game!"

The kids start talking, grabbing each other's hands, and forming groups. Charlie stands on another picnic table and waves his hands around. "Wait! I have a question. How do we know who the winner is?" He loves to be the champion. Last week during Hide-and-Seek, he slithered through a muddy ditch of lake sludge to make it to base without Sam tagging him.

Natalie grabs the bullhorn and says, "The winning team is the one that stays in character the longest."

"Everyone will stay in character," Hector yells. "It's not that hard of a game."

Natalie glances at Wolfgang with a look that clearly says, "I told you so."

But he winks at her. "Your counselors will try very hard to make you forget your character. If you say or do anything that's you and not your character, then you must come right to the patio and sit here!"

The kids scamper to their spots around the camp while Wolfgang collects the counselors. "Okay, my friends," he says to the staff. "You must make the campers crack. If they say they are Luke Skywalker and Darth Vader, you announce, 'Now we are having ice-cream sundaes!' If they say they want one, they are out. Luke Skywalker doesn't know about ice cream."

"Maybe he does," Aaron says.

"Ah, man. Now I want an ice-cream sundae." Kenny groans. "Why can't we have those at camp? Is ice cream too expensive or something? Because at home, I eat three bowls a day. And then here? Just nothing. Torture."

"Focus, people," Natalie says into her bullhorn. "Charlie is right. This will only work if you can think of hard questions. Otherwise everyone will get bored pretty fast."

"Yeah, they will!" Kenny yells.

This is Kenny's new thing. After anything that anyone says, Kenny yells, "Yeah!" He does this All. The. Time. ("If you want your mail, you have to sing 'The Squirrel Song'!" "Yeah, you do!" "Did you know Jesus loves you more than you can imagine?" "Yeah, He does!" "Come on, everyone! Quiet down! I'm trying to talk!" "Yeah, you are!") At first it was a cheerful refrain to the rowdiness of camp. But now we're all so sick of it.

The campers are in little clusters on the The Hill, near the Trading Post, by the canoe shed, and around the kitchen porch. "Remember!" Natalie yells to them. "Be creative! This will be so much more fun if you pull out all the stops!"

"Yeah, it will be!" Kenny calls.

And we all groan.

CHAPTER 60

"The Famous One"

I nudge Nat as we climb The Hill to interrogate the campers. "Good job on the game. You and Wolfie made this up last night?"

"Last night," she confirms. "We stayed up until sunrise and we talked about everything. Absolutely everything. We were up at Lakeside in that shelter Alpha made and we were just sitting there talking and planning and laughing and telling stories. Wolfgang is the smartest. And he's so cute. All the time, I'm like, *Why did it take me so long to see that?*"

Already the campers are absorbed in their make-believe worlds. The boys have sticks (of course) and are reenacting any one of the Marvel movies. A big group of girls construct crowns from pine needles and twigs.

"I'm so happy for you, Nat. You and Wolfie are my favorite part of this summer." This is not the first time Natalie has told me The Great Love Story of Natalie and Wolfgang. Every conversation we've had since she got back from the canoe trip goes in this same order: How Natalie Felt about Wolfgang Most of the Summer, How That Changed on the Canoe Trip, Everything She Loves about Wolfgang Now.

The last part is Natalie's favorite. She reports every sweet thing he's ever done ("gave me his poncho when it rained," "carried my pack *and his* the whole canoe trip," "toasted six marshmallows exactly like I love them," "made me a daisy chain necklace").

"Come on." I pull her along. "Tell me about it while we interrogate some kids."

"Okay. But listen, Poppi, because this is the best part. He just emailed the paperwork so he can transfer to USC next year."

"He did what?" I stop right in front of a group of girls gathered by the barbecue pits. "For real? Wolfgang isn't going back to Germany?"

"He's not!" She covers her eyes and screeches. "Apparently he had thought about USC before because he is so, so smart and has amazing test scores. Universities love foreign exchange students because it looks really good for their diversity. But after doing his senior year here, he missed Germany."

"So he's staying here for you? You've been together, like, four days!"

"We've been together every second of this summer. We know each other crazy well."

"Wow." I have to let this sink in. "You two might really stay together. You could go to USC for college too."

"I know!" Her hands are in fists, and she's clenching them in front of her face. "It is exactly like a cheesy romantic comedy! I feel like I'm Reese Witherspoon and he's Matthew McConaughey. When Mom comes up for Parents' Lunch, she will love him."

"Interrogate us!" Drama Wren is ahead of us with the girls wearing stick-crowns. She's jumping from foot to foot. "Hurry up! Because we are so going to win this!"

"Well, hello girls from Cabin Truth!" Natalie says in a dramatic voice. "Are the five of you hungry?"

Wren wears a yellow bedsheet over her shoulders. "I'm starving! I haven't eaten anything since leaving Arendelle. I've been way too busy building this snow castle."

"Hey, Manda!" I call to a quiet girl, also wearing a yellow sheet. "It's really hot today, right? Do you feel like coming to the Trading Post? I'll buy you a Fanta."

"No! It's a trick!" Wren screeches. "They know we're from *Frozen* and they're trying to make you forget that our whole country is in an eternal winter. Don't fall for it."

"Every girl for herself!" Natalie yells. "Manda, answer your own interrogation."

"That's a rule?" I ask Natalie.

"It is now."

Manda watches Wren. "No way! It's freezing out!"

"But what about a hike?" I ask Manda. "You're really good at hiking."

"I don't have time to hike," she answers carefully. "I have to convince my sister to free Arendelle from this horrible winter so Christoph can get his ice business back."

Connie throws her arms around my waist. "I'm Olaf and I like warm hugs!" Connie is The Camper Most Likely to Hug Everyone, so this is actually a good role for her.

"Oh, hi, Olaf. How are you doing out here? It looks like you're melting. Are you feeling a little warm?"

"NO!" She doesn't even blink. "I have my own snow cloud right above me!"

I look at Natalie. "Wow. They're good."

Wren steps forward and starts singing "Let It Go" at an ear-splitting volume. Other groups have stopped their own drama fests to watch her.

"No fair!" Michele from The Light calls. "We're doing *Frozen* too."

"Ha!" Emmy yells, pointing at her. "You just broke character! You're out!"

But Wren does not stop singing. Nightly worship hasn't given her a chance to sing her "Let It Go" solo. Clearly, she's been waiting for this.

We leave Wren to her solo and head over to a group of boys who are Stuart, Bob, and Kevin, the Minions. Natalie drops her clipboard and Carter—the boy playing Bob—picks it up. Natalie calls him out for being kind and un-Minion-like. An argument starts over whether he was really being nice or trying to steal classified information.

After an hour, Jake blows his whistle and calls the four remaining teams back to the patio. It's like a middle school cafeteria as everyone yells about who won and can we please play Operation Interrogation every day for the last ten days of camp?

"All right!" Jake yells into the bullhorn. "Counselors, get with your cabin groups. Let's sound off with your cheers. Then we're heading down to the parking lot for a talent show."

"Yeah, we are!" Kenny yells.

"We are?" I call to Jake.

He holds up his watch and shrugs. We've got an hour before worship and nothing else planned. He raises his eyebrows, asking, "What's your idea?"

I shrug back and frown, saying, "Not an impromptu talent show!"

But the campers are already planning their performances. Wren will finally have her chance to sing all of "Let It Go," and she's jumped on Lanie's shoulders to celebrate. It looks like we're doing a talent show.

Jake runs through roll call, stopping every couple of seconds for the cabins to yell the completely unenthusiastic cheers they have done hundreds of times.

"Omega?" he yells.

"Oh-oh-oh-OMEGA!" they mutter back.

"Way?"

"WaaaayyYYYYYYY! OUT!"

"Hold on!" Aaron yells. "Where's Charlie? Hey! Everyone! I need to see Charlie."

"Yeah, you do!" Kenny yells.

"He wasn't playing," Ellie says. "I talked to every group. Charlie wasn't there."

"Who knows where Charlie went?" Jake says into the bullhorn.

"He said it was a stupid game and that he was going to do his own version," Hector calls. His tone is smug. He and Charlie compete like two roosters.

"I saw him down by the lake!" Harriet yells. "I think he's hiding in there."

"In the canoe shed?" I shouldn't panic. Charlie is competitive, but he's not dumb.

"No, he's *in* the lake. He told me that was his plan when we played Hide-and-Seek. He was going to sit in the lake with just his mouth and eyes showing. Every time someone came by, he was going to duck under the water."

The patio is silent as forty-five campers contemplate this as their next hiding place. Maybe Charlie *is* dumb. "No!" I shout. "Everyone understands that's a terrible idea, right? If Charlie is hiding in the lake, he will get in awful trouble."

"All right, everyone." Jake is talking into the bullhorn again. It squeals with feedback and we cover our ears. "Natalie is going to take you down to the parking lot for this talent show." He nods to me with wide eyes—our shorthand for "Get these kids out of here right this second."

"Yeah, she is!" Kenny yells.

"Okay, all you talent show stars! Follow Natalie!" I yell to the group. "And these acts better be spectacular because there's double Trading Post for the group we vote as the favorite."

Natalie and Wolfgang lead the cabins away while I catch up with Jake. "Okay. What's the plan? You're searching the lake? I'll check the trails."

"No. You need to get down to the parking lot. That talent show will be a disaster. We haven't planned anything for it. They need you there. I'll go and find Charlie."

"Jake, he might have drowned. I'm going with you."

"Trust me. I will find Charlie. But the counselors need more than just two directors there, more than just Pete and Nat. Everyone will be out of sorts."

I open my mouth to ask who cares about a stupid talent show. Who cares if all the kids revolt down at the parking lot and refuse to act like Minions or whatever? My camper is missing. I can taste the fear in my throat. He might be hurt. Or worse.

But looking at Jake's face stops me. He looks desperate. "Trust me on this, Poppi. The campers will notice if you're not down there. That will become the drama they tell their parents about tomorrow at Parents' Lunch. I will quietly take care of this. You keep everyone distracted."

"Okay." I take a deep breath. "If you're sure. But I'm trusting you here."

Then Jake does an odd thing. He bows his head to me. "Thank you," he says. His voice sounds like I've just handed him an envelope of money.

"It's fine," I say. "No big deal."

"It's a really big deal, Poppi. You haven't done that before."

I want to argue that I trust him all the time, but I have to run down to the talent show. Plus, I know that Jake is probably right. It is true that I haven't trusted anyone for a very long time.

Aaron and the rest of his cabin mob me, demanding where Charlie is and insisting they scatter to look for him.

"It's fine, guys. Absolutely fine. Jake's taking care of it."

I join the screaming/wrestling/laughing kids at the parking lot. Jake was right. It's mayhem down here. "Okay, everyone," I call. "Natalie and I are the judges. I just upped the reward. *Triple* Trading Post for the group that wins. Do you hear that? The winners will get Trading Post *three* times a day!"

Kenny (of course) yells, "Yeah, they will!"

I look at Natalie, whose wide eyes look exactly like I feel. "Let's do this."

CHAPTER 61

"Pharaoh, Pharaoh"

The whole night is a long exercise in patience that I do not have. Natalie and I yell and scream and dance and introduce acts and laugh and cheer and high-five to distract the kids. It works well enough that we distract ourselves from the fact that we do not hear one word from either Charlie or Jake for over two hours.

Finally, Connie wins the talent show for singing the cutest version of "In Summer." Everyone (except Wren) loves it so much that we cheer until she agrees to sing it again for an encore.

Before the campers are even done clapping—and especially before they can ask where Jake and Charlie are—Natalie and I hustle the whole group down to worship. Aaron pulls the sleeve of my yellow fleece as the kids file past to Alleluia. "I want to go look for him," he whispers.

"Let Jake handle it."

"But what if he was in the lake? What if he drowned?"

I look at Aaron for a long second. "I don't know."

Pete plays the guitar for worship, and Natalie and Aaron fidget on either side of me. Why is Jake taking so long? I've called his cell about fifteen times, but it's off. I tell myself that's a good sign. If there were an emergency—if Jake had to call the police or ambulance—he would have turned on his phone. He would have let me know.

Wouldn't he?

By the time Pete and I do rounds for lights-out, my stomach has soured. It's been too long. Something very bad has happened. I tell Pete and Natalie to keep everything calm at base camp so I can go search on my own. I begin rehearsing the phone calls—to the police, to Mike and Eva, to Charlie's parents. And I pray and pray and pray the same words over and over: *Please, Lord. Please, Lord. Please . . .* Every time I breathe this out, I think of that promise I heard at Flowerhead. "I will take care of you." *Okay, Lord. Take care of me by taking care of Charlie. Bring him to me.*

I'm halfway up Lakeside—far enough from camp that the kids probably can't hear me—when I start to scream, "CHARRR-LIIIEEEEE! JAAAAAKE!" I shine my flashlight around, the beam like a spotlight on the black curtain of the forest. "CHARRR-LIIIEEEEE! JAAAAAKE!"

It's as silent as the day I hiked Flowerhead. Nothing—only the sound of my own fear. Where is that feeling of Next Right Thing and being taken care of? How do I know God is taking care of anything? Why did I let Jake go on his own for this? I shouldn't have trusted. I should have gone straight down to the lake by myself. I would have found Charlie. I would have—

"POPPIIII!" echoes back through the woods. "WE ARE COMING!" It's Jake.

And he said "we."

Ten seconds later, I hear quick, loud footsteps on the trail. Jake comes first; he's doing his thing where he sucks on his lips until they disappear. Behind him is Charlie, and his eyes are huge. He looks five years younger.

I hug them both. "Oh, thank You, LORD! There you are. What happened?" I step back to look at Charlie. "WHERE HAVE YOU BEEN? For the past four hours?"

"Charlie spent Operation Interrogation in the lake." Jake nudges Charlie, who is staring at my flashlight beam on his shoes.

"I said I was sorry for that." Charlie looks up at me. "Sorry to you too, Poppi. I was waiting under the water until the whole camp came down to the lake. Then I was going to jump out and scare everyone."

"I could see the ripples, so I knew he was in there," Jake says to me. "Finally, when Charlie wouldn't come to the surface, I had to jump in."

"You didn't have to." Charlie looks over at Jake. "I was hiding, not drowning."

"So, what happened?" I ask. "Why are you up here now?"

"By the time we both showered and changed into dry clothes, everyone was down at worship. So, the two of us went on a hike to talk about why he's going home tomorrow."

Charlie takes a deep breath and sniffs. "I said I was sorry." His voice is thin and high-pitched with tears.

"I am too, buddy." Jake touches his shoulder, but Charlie shrugs it off and starts down the trail. He sniffs every couple of seconds. He's crying so hard, I'm worried he'll trip on the trail.

"You all right?" Jake asks as we follow him.

I nod. "I'm all right. Are you?"

"I am." Jake grabs my hand and squeezes it. "All right then."

"All right." I squeeze it back. I take a deep breath. "Everything will be all right."

CHAPTER 62

"Put Your Hand in the Hand"

Tomorrow is the Parents' Lunch and I'm too nervous to sleep. Eden does Parents' Lunch late enough in the summer that the families can see what their kids have done at camp, but not so early that the kids miss them and want to go home. This year the timing is not so great since we are all so focused on the barbecue.

After trying to sleep in about twenty different positions—completely flat on top of my sleeping bag; head buried under my pillow, which smells like rancid campfire and dirty hair; and facing the wall and trying not hear Nat's snoring—I finally pull on my yellow fleece and sneak outside to the picnic tables.

It's better out here. Our room was stuffy with stale air, and all my energy from the escapade with Charlie is still buzzing in my brain. Out here I can write thank-you notes to parents that I'll hand out tomorrow. Maybe a handwritten note will encourage them to come to the barbecue, register their kids for next summer, and give a big donation.

The moon is so bright, I don't need a light. I've finished ten thank-you notes when I start to yawn. I can hear our resident raccoon in the trash cans. I hope Pete took the dinner trash down to the dumpster.

"Hey. You're up too?"

I jump and yelp.

"Shhh." Jake comes up behind me. He's wearing pajama pants and a navy UCLA sweatshirt. "You're going to wake everyone up."

"You scared the living daylights out of me. What are you doing out here?"

"Same thing you are. I couldn't sleep. Big night. I tried to study, but I can't focus after everything that happened."

I hand him a stack of white folded cards. "Good. You can help write notes to parents telling them they are fabulous for sending their kids to Eden."

"I hate writing thank-you notes." He takes the pile from me anyway. "I haven't written a thank-you note in years. My mom's still waiting for me to send them for my graduation presents."

"I gave up writing them last year too. Half of Eagle, Minnesota, keeps asking me if I got their flowers after Mom's funeral."

"See how perfect we are together?" He sits next to me on the bench. "We both blow off thank-you notes."

I laugh. "That probably makes us not perfect together. One of us needs to write them."

"I'll write them for you after you go to sleep. Talk to me right now."

"That's a good deal for me." I push away the stack of cards. "Okay, tell me what you're studying."

"That's seriously the very most boring conversation I can imagine. Thank-you notes are more interesting than that."

"Really? Try me."

"Real estate law and tax codes. It's horrible. It's like an exercise in your tolerance for the truly meaningless."

"Why are you taking this class again?"

He raises his eyebrows. "Why are we having this conversation again?"

We stare at each other for a few moments like that, both of us grinning and not saying the same things we've said to each other so many times. Why law? Why Eden? Why money? Why ministry? Why a life outside? Why a life inside? Why work you don't love? Why loneliness? Why this instead of that?

Then, suddenly, I think of the Next Right Thing to say. I blurt out, "You could not go back to college next semester. You could stay here with me instead."

"What?"

"Take a semester off from college and live here. Help me do Rehab Eden. You and I can work on the maintenance projects and run the retreats. It would be so much fun." In this moment, after the big day, after trusting Jake, this plan makes absolute perfect sense.

"Where is this coming from?" He studies me. "Is this because of Wolfgang and Natalie?"

"No. It's because of you." I put my hands on his shoulders. "Can't you see it? You don't have to follow some ancient plan you made up a long time ago to make lots of money. You can edit your own life. You can take a semester off. We could create something really amazing here. We have good ideas. We work really well together."

He opens his mouth, his forehead creased. "But I've got a whole life at college, Poppi. It's taken a lot of work to get there."

"Just one semester off. Just take off until Christmas. Come on. Imagine it. It could be like a sabbatical." But even as I'm saying it, I can feel that my gaze is too heavy on him. He's squirming.

"Poppi, I . . ." He smiles. "I really like you."

"And?" I ask.

He wraps his arms around me. Then, very softly into my hair, he says, "Enough for tonight, okay?"

CHAPTER 63

"Children of the Heavenly Father"

Parents' Lunch is a bit of a disaster, and now I'm worried the barbecue will be too. Next summer—if there is a next summer—I'm doing Parents' Lunch much earlier in the summer, before the counselors are so tired of camp. Because by Week Ten, we're all snapping at one another like a family at the end of a very long road trip.

One bright spot is that Harriet's mom skipped her brother's soccer game to come. Dr. Ramos is a short woman with a fancy purse and long, curly hair. Although she tells me her sons are "soccer prodigies" and she brags about them in front of Harriet, I can forgive her because she is here. And that is so important to Harriet. While Dr. Ramos chats with me, Harriet leans against her mom and eats three plates of chips with Catie.

Next, I'm trapped in a long conversation with Sam's dad. He's been on the "Save Eden" Facebook page and is upset that Eden might really close. "How did this happen? This camp is a family tradition for us. Sam wanted to work here one day. Is there anything we can do?"

"Come to the barbecue!" I say, sounding like I just thought of this. I hope my voice chimes with spontaneous fun—and not the weariness of worry. "We're doing a dunk tank, an auction, lots of games. It will be the perfect way to support Eden! It's July thirtieth."

He rubs his mustache. "No can do that day. We'll be in Cabo. It's the last weekend for my wife and me to get away while Sam is at camp."

"Hmmm." I pause. "Well. If you'd like to help Eden, maybe you could just write a check?"

He stares at me. I might have forgotten my manners here. Maybe I'm not allowed to just ask for money?

"Let me explain what she needs," Aaron says, wiping his mouth. "If we don't raise a whole bucketload of money in the next week, everything here will be flattened. Poppi needs you to hand over some serious funds in the next, like, three days."

"Three days?" Sam's dad asks. "The sale will go through that fast? Wow. That's a quick turnaround." He takes a bite of his hamburger. A blob of mustard hangs in his mustache. "Sounds like a done deal then."

"It's not a done deal." I slam my palm on the table. "It's not even close to a done deal. We will absolutely raise the money at the barbecue. The Association will not sell."

"Oh, absolutely." Kenny rolls his eyes. "Come on, Poppi. No one believes that except you. Even if we do raise the money, those churches aren't going to say no to five million bucks. Open your eyes. They will sell, but they're not going to admit that to *you*."

I give Sam's dad a tight smile. He is suddenly riding shotgun on our awkward family trip. Then I glare at Kenny and Aaron. "Look, we're all tired. And I know it's hard to stay positive when we don't know what will happen to Eden next week. But if we have faith, we *can* raise the money—"

"Bulldozers," Kenny says. "That's what's happening next week."

"Hey!" I snap. "I'm doing my best here."

"Just saying. This place is kind of a lost cause," Aaron agrees. And he doesn't even look upset. Just tired.

"Yeah, it is," Kenny says, nodding.

CHAPTER 64

"Seek Ye First"

Trying to find someone to play music at this barbecue will be the end of me," I tell Natalie and Mike. "I have called every band in L.A. I've even called the bands that those bands know."

Tonight Nat and I are in the office with the Brownes, pulling together last-minute barbecue details. I'm scheduling Saturday's deliveries (two bounce houses, three snow-cone machines, extra chairs, and all the donated meat and potato salad). Mike is at the desk, setting up an app that lets people bid on silent auction items from their cell phones.

"Clearly Jake's dad needs to just show up and play." Natalie is stretched out on the floor, painting a huge sign that says, "SAVE CAMP EDEN!" To transform the office into the barbecue headquarters, we've had to shove everything into the corners. Now the junk is ceiling high around the perimeter.

"There's absolutely no way he's going to miss being in Dallas for Savannah's big recital," I say. "It's enough of a scandal that Jake isn't going."

"That's dumb. We need him here way more than he needs to sit in some auditorium in Dallas." She scoots on her belly down to the next *E*. "If we had him here, it would be slam-dunk thirty thousand. What good is it to have the kid of a celebrity on our staff if he doesn't show up for the last hurrah?"

"Not the last hurrah," Mike says. "I really don't believe it will be." He looks at Eva. "We both think the money will come through." She nods and squeezes his shoulder.

I like to watch Mike and Eva together. They still flirt with each other, even though they have two kids and are busy with their jobs. Eva writes Bible studies and Mike writes textbooks. He's working on a biology one right now, which is funny because I always think that he looks exactly like my sophomore bio teacher, Mr. Gatton.

"What about Jake?" Mike asks. "Maybe he could sing? I've always thought he's got a great voice."

"I already asked him," I say. "He's going to be too busy helping with the games and keeping the night moving along."

Eva leans over to Mike, her phone playing a YouTube video. "Hey. Check this out." She holds it out to him. "These guys built a dunk tank with plywood. Do you think you could make this happen?"

He takes her phone but then sets it down. "Before we talk about that, there's something we want to tell you girls about Bryan." He glances at Eva. "STUF is paying Bryan a commission. If the deal goes through, he will get 3 percent of the sale price—the amount that the selling realtor would have made."

"What?" I look at Natalie. "Bryan is getting, like, $150,000? Are you for real?"

"We just heard yesterday. And we're as angry about it as you are." Mike scrubs his hands down his face. "I suspected he had some motivation to sell, but this is so much money."

"But this is really good news!" Natalie jumps up. "This proves that Eden never should have been for sale. This proves that Bryan just wanted the commission. Eden wasn't sick—he's sick!"

"What does it prove?" Mike asks.

"Eden was only for sale because Bryan is a greedy scumbag, not because it needed to be sold. The Association never wanted to sell in the first place. Now they don't have to!"

She looks at me. I turn to Mike and Eva. "Right?"

Natalie is jumping up and down. "Now that everyone is clear about why Eden ended up in the hands of STUF, we can cancel the whole deal. Camp as usual! Poppi can be the winter retreat director!"

"Oh, I really wish that was the case." Mike shakes his head. "Maybe that's the reason we first got the offer from STUF. But now two of the churches like the idea of selling. Five million dollars has them thinking about Eden differently. Suddenly they believe that there's not enough community interest in Eden. They are calling us an outdated ministry. They want out."

This doesn't sound good. "But what if we prove it's sustainable?" I ask, thinking about what Aaron said. Maybe he's right. "If we make the money at the barbecue, if we get the campers, they won't sell, right?"

"I promise." Mike nods. "We've taken it to a vote. Everyone agrees that if Eden just needs fresh enthusiasm, this barbecue will get us back on track."

I let out my breath. "Okay. That's great."

"But Poppi, if we can't reach the goals, you have to be ready to sell. You have to find something else."

CHAPTER 65

"Rise and Shine"

The next morning, I wake up very, very early to the sound of one bird squawking right outside my window. Even before I open my eyes, the whole heavy weight of the day rolls over me. Deliveries start at eight. We need to make lemonade for three hundred people. Have the signs that the kids painted dried? Did Mike and Jake finish building the dunk tank?

Thirty thousand dollars, Lord. One hundred campers. With that prayer, a picture appears in my mind. It's an image of exactly what I need to do right now.

I jump out of bed and throw on shorts and my yellow fleece. "Natalie! Wake up!" I pull off her sleeping bag. "Jake! Pete!" I yell across the staff lounge. "Get up!"

"What's going on?" Pete yells back. His voice is a half-asleep groan.

"Meet me on the patio!" I call, pulling my hair into a ponytail. "We're having a predawn meeting."

Natalie covers her face with her sleeping bag and screeches about it being too early and too cold and that she's too tired.

But a couple of minutes later, she's up The Hill at the cabins with me, tiptoeing in to wake up the counselors and whispering to them that they need to get down to the patio right away.

Ten minutes later, the pajama-clad staff is gathered on the slab, yawning and stretching and complaining. The sun is rising, and golden light glows around the edges of the patio.

I climb onto a picnic table and look at my staff. "Please listen, everyone. I know it's been the longest week ever. I get that none of you want to be up this early. I see that you're kind of done with camp." I can't help but glance at Aaron and Kenny. Their hair is sticking up and they are both watching me carefully. Kenny does not yell, "Yeah, we are!" Instead, he is scowling.

"Why are we up?" Beth asks. She pulls her hoodie around herself and yawns. Everyone—even sweet Beth—looks angry to be out here.

"We are up because this morning, we all need to see the sun rise together. Because I need to tell all of you the very hardest and best lesson I have learned. I need each and every one of you to realize that life keeps moving forward. One sunrise at a time, we have absolutely no control over it."

Everyone is glaring at me. No one is in the mood for lessons this early in the morning—or this late in the summer. If they haven't learned it by now, they have no interest in cramming it on the second-to-last morning of camp. They all kind of hate me.

"You woke us up to tell us that the sun rises?" Aaron's voice bites with sarcasm.

"Look. I know I'm talking crazy. But today is going to be an insanely long day. I have no idea what will happen at the end of it. Either Eden will make it or we won't. But no matter what, I know that whatever happens, God has something good coming for us. I just want all of you to know that I believe in hope."

I see Jake furrowing his brow at me. This was my worst idea ever. I suddenly want to crawl off this table and just go back to bed. But that would be even stranger. I have to finish this.

"This is it for us all together. Today will be the end. Tomorrow morning, we'll wake up and have to get the campers ready to go home. Then, by tomorrow afternoon, all of you will be leaving. I don't want that to happen without being able to tell you that this has been the best summer of my life. This is the summer I really learned about trust, about God, about hope."

Someone is sniffling. We all look around and see it's Ellie. Her nose is bright red and black spiderwebs of smeared mascara frame her eyes. Her thick brown hair, which has been in a messy bun every day of this summer, hangs loose around her face. "This is stupid, Poppi. Why do you have to wake us up to make us cry?" But she's grinning at me.

"I'm sorry," I say. "I had to. And I also have to pray with all of you. Just one last time."

Ellie lets out a crescendo of sobs. "Oh, Poppi!"

"I'm sorry. But we've all prayed over so many things over the last ten weeks. We've prayed over hundreds of meals and worships and sick campers and campouts. If we don't take time this morning, we might not get a chance to do it again."

"Oh, man." Jake inhales sharply. "You are killing us, Savot. Unfair, orchestrated tears, that's what this is."

"No," I say. "This is me telling all of you thank you. Because you are all my favorites."

"Yeah, we are!" Wolfgang yells. He's wearing a sweatshirt that's a bit too small, so when he pumps his fists, his belly shows. Apparently he's adopted Kenny's habit now too.

"Just know, everything that has happened this summer—all those weird s'mores and awful corn dogs and cabin fights and Lay-and-Prays and Hide-and-Seek and wasp stings and hikes and worships and really bad skits—all of that meant something." I can't say all this without choking on my own tears.

"STO-O-O-O-P!" Natalie wails in a half-fake, half-real way. Jake rubs her back and she leans her head on his shoulder.

I laugh. "I don't know what tomorrow's sunrise will bring, but I do know that everything that all of you did this summer has meant a lot. All of your work counts for so much."

"*Y* to the *E* to the *S*!" Natalie yells, even though she's still wailing. "It totally does."

"I've never worked this hard in my life," Kenny says. Then he adds, "So, yeah, it all counted!"

"All right then," I say. "Let's all pray together. Just shout out your prayers. Whatever's on your heart." Why couldn't I pray with Eva, but I can lead this whole group? Maybe this is progress? Actually, I know it's progress. Everything I'm saying—all this that I have to get out—is faith.

It's quiet for a long time. So awkward. Everyone glances around at the others in their pajamas. Aaron yawns loudly. Ellie sits down on the concrete.

Finally, Natalie yells, "Thanks, God, for Poppi. We love her!"

Everyone cheers and Jake whistles.

"Praise You, Lord, for Natalie!" Wolfgang yells. "And for Camp Eden. The best camp in America! And Germany!" He holds up Natalie's hand like she's a prizefighter. "And Natalie is the most beautiful girl in both also."

More cheers—plus a couple of wolf whistles from the guys. Natalie keeps sniffling, but she's also smiling.

"For my friends here," Ellie says, getting into the spirit. "And my campers. I love them so much."

"For Bryan," Natalie says. "Help him right now, God. With whatever. Just help him." Jake pats her hair.

"For Natalie!" Wolfgang repeats. "The most beautiful girl!" We all laugh.

It's quiet for a few moments. "Help us with tonight, God," Beth says in her soft voice. "Help us make thirty thousand dollars and get one hundred campers so Eden doesn't close. We need Your help, Lord."

"Yeah, we do!" Kenny yells.

Emmy looks around. "This has been my best summer too. Ever. I love you so much, Poppi." She looks at Jake. "You were great as the director too. But nothing like Poppi."

"I know. Nothing like Poppi." He comes over, slides an arm around me, and kisses the crown of my head. The whole group explodes clapping. It's all too much. I'm laughing-crying too.

"I KNEW IT!" Beth yells. "I knew you two liked each other!"

"Thanks, God." Aaron looks at the sky, and I think he might cry too. "Even though I'm so sick of camp I could puke, I've changed. I always learn a lot at camp, but this summer was different. This summer I feel like I really grew up."

"You were right, Poppi," Nat says. "This really was the best summer in the whole history of this crazy place. We did it. We were Team Eden."

"Write all this stuff down," I say. "Write down all your favorite memories of Eden—as counselors or campers. Have your kids do the same thing. We'll set up a big pin board and hang them all up. They'll inspire everyone tonight."

"Hey!" Ryan is standing up on The Hill, watching us. His cabin mates are crowded behind him, also in their pjs. "I hope you guys are making us breakfast!"

CHAPTER 66

"We Can Change the World"

The barbecue starts at five o'clock, and by four thirty, the patio is decorated with pictures of Eden over the past sixty years, artwork by the campers, and the board with the counselors' testimonials. In less than hour, almost three hundred people—Eden alums, representatives from the Association churches, and the families and friends of campers—will be here.

We end up with no music. I tried to use my phone to record the kids singing, but it wasn't at the right volume so it sounds terrible. Jake's convinced me that the games will be so loud, music would just be a distraction.

The barbecue's biggest attraction is Jake and Mike's dunking tank. They built a seven-foot by seven-foot plywood tub. The campers will throw Velcro darts at a felt board. When someone gets a bull's-eye, the counselor who is getting "dunked" has to dive into the tub. The plywood can't hold water so I filled it with paper shreds instead.

I found zillions of paper shreds and scraps when I was poking around Bryan's office, looking for Styrofoam peanuts. The floor around his industrial-strength shredder was littered with torn-up paper. The shredder was so full, I don't think it had been emptied in years. Eva and I carried armloads of paper to the tank so the counselors have enough padding to jump in when they're "dunked."

The caterers show up with the food at five o'clock, right around the same time the church vans pull into the parking lot. Suddenly everything is happening at once. The campers and staff and their parents and Association members are all scampering around the patio. Even Bryan is helping, which I didn't expect. But it's really nice because the line of hungry people snakes all the way to the parking lot.

"What do you make of Bryan being out here?" I whisper to Nat as we fill lemonade cups.

"I guess he figures we won't make it," Natalie whispers back. "He might as well be nice to us since he's getting his $150,000 anyway."

"Then I guess he'll be wrong," I whisper, waving to Chloe and Dan, who are waiting in the back of the line. They're wearing cute matching Eden shirts. "Look who's here!" I poke Natalie. "Let's go say hi."

When everyone is done eating, each of the counselors takes a turn at the microphone to tell about their history at Eden. The crowd loves the stories. Wolfgang entertains the group by giving a highlight from every week this summer. I asked him to not mention The Hike of the Lost Boys or the Wedgie Wars that his cabin loves to have.

There's a crowd around the pin board too. "Look," I whisper to Jake. "Everyone keeps reading those testimonials."

"People love them." He nods to the registration table, where Eva Browne is helping parents fill out paperwork for next summer. "Last time I was over there, we had over one hundred campers registered for next summer."

"We're going to do it." I squeeze his arm. "We have enough kids for another summer. And people are donating lots. It's going to be a yes. I *know* it's going to be a yes."

"I don't know if it's enough money, though," Jake says. "Everyone is playing the games and bidding on auction items, but no one's making huge donations." He points to Mike's table, where he's accepting checks. "We haven't gotten the kind of big gifts I thought we would."

"It's still early," I point out. "People who are making big donations will give them at the very end. Jake, I'm serious. I think this is it. God is totally saying yes. Can't you feel the excitement?"

"We need to make sure everyone *keeps* feeling the excitement. We can't risk anyone leaving without giving. We have to keep the energy high the whole time."

A group of girls who were at Chloe's party flash me a thumbs-up. I'm not sure if that's for the fund-raiser or for being with Jake. "What else can we do?"

He's quiet for a second. "I'll take the next spot on the mic. I'll tell my story."

"What are you going to say?"

He smiles. "I don't know."

"You don't know?" I laugh. "Then don't go over to the microphone and talk to three hundred people."

He moves me out of the way. "Don't tell me what to do."

Natalie is announcing her list of Ten Reasons Eden Rocks the Planet. The crowd is laughing as she finishes, "And the number one reason is because . . ." She turns to see Jake. "This guy right here has played his guitar for over fifty thousand campfires."

Jake squints at her. "Fifty thousand?"

"Whatever," Natalie shrugs. "I'm bad at math. A *lot* of campfires."

He takes the microphone. "I'm Jake. I've been at Eden for ten years. And these have been the very best summers of my life."

The crowd is quiet—even the dunking booth game has paused. Something about Jake's confidence makes people realize he's about to say something interesting. The wind blows over a trash can with a thud, but no one moves.

"I truly believe that Eden changed my life. Or that God changed my life through Eden. When I was a kid, my parents were crazy busy. My sister and I spent a lot of time with nannies. I got a cell phone when I turned ten. I really, really wanted to learn everything about the world. And I didn't care what my parents told me was right and wrong."

This is Jake, exactly. Yes, he has to discover everything for himself. I can imagine a whole different scenario for him if his parents hadn't found Eden.

"But then, I came to Eden. It was such a tight community, and the counselors were the coolest people I'd met. They weren't my parents; they were the people I wanted to be like. These incredible Christians loved me and filled in the gaps of my life. They were exactly the people who I needed to tell me about Jesus. In exactly this place. They changed everything for me."

"Yeah, they did!" Kenny calls. Everyone looks from Jake to Kenny, and he waves at the crowd.

"The counselors were just as cool as our staff this summer." Jake smiles at our hodge-podge counselors. "When my parents sent me to Eden, they had no idea that a little distance would bring me so close to God."

The kids cheer and the parents clap. Across the patio, Chloe catches my eye and winks. I wink back because I know exactly what she's thinking. This was the conversation we had. Jake—like this. Loyal and sweet and passionate. I think I love Chloe, even though I just met her this summer. I know I love Jake.

"I've come back every summer, trying to be as cool and honest and on-fire as the counselors were that first summer." In the glow of the late-afternoon sun, Jake's eyes are bright. "And even though I can never even come close, serving at camp is like fulfilling a debt of honor for everything they did for me."

Unbelievable. Jake Bass is crying. Even if we don't make our thirty thousand dollars, I'll consider tonight a miracle.

"If you believe Eden should be a place where kids learn about their Lord, then keep it open. Sign your kid up for next summer. Make a donation. And above all"—he looks at me—"pray for us."

CHAPTER 67

"For Those Tears I Died"

The night goes long. Every single staff member (except Bryan) takes a turn telling stories and making lemonade toasts. Wolfgang has a natural gift for the toasts. He's quick-witted and the crowd loves his jokes. ("To the girls of Alpha for building a fort that can't be torn down!" "To Ms. Wren, who will become all of these: an actress, a writer, a singer, and a poet!" "To Bryan, who has created cinnamon rolls so good, his recipe needs to be trademarked!")

The crowd—especially those from Chloe and Dan's era—cheers like crazy about Bryan's cinnamon rolls. They "clink" their plastic cups against his and he grins.

Natalie turns to me, crossing her eyes and sticking out her tongue. "Do they even know that he bled Eden dry and then sold the corpse to STUF for hundreds of thousands of dollars?"

"Looks like not," I say. "And I'm guessing they never will."

Just as the church vans are pulling out of the parking lot, Aaron grabs Ellie and yells, "Now for the square dancing!" The campers start cheering and screaming. Kenny yells, "Yeah, it is!"

I look over at Jake and shrug. He rolls his eyes and nods. I guess we're not enforcing any lights-out time tonight. Might as well have one last all-camp square dance.

By midnight, everyone is even tired of dancing. The kids are yawning and happy to go up to their cabins. The patio is still trashed, but that's tomorrow's problem. Tonight's question is whether or not we got the money. Mike has been in the office for an hour, adding up the donations. He knows the answer.

When I'm coming down The Hill from putting down the kids, I stop by the spot in the parking lot where I stood on Day One. As I look out at the canoe shack, the inky lake, and the silhouette of pine trees, I inhale deeply.

Every time I've passed this spot over the summer, I've felt a sparkle of that premonition I had when I first got here from Minnesota. I've wondered what that moment meant. Is this really supposed to be my home?

But this time when I look at Eden, it's very different. I notice each individual tree, the trail marker signs, the canoes, the oars, the patch of dead grass. Tonight, a different kind of chill passes inside me. No sparkle. Instead, it's the bone-deep chill of real fear.

Jake was scared that no one was making big donations. I noticed that too. Every time I checked with Mike, his lips were in a thin, tight line. He and I have prayed over the numbers so many times, talked about what a sustainable amount was, discussed who might come and how much they would donate. If we were even close, he would have been celebrating. If we had made it, Mike would have already told me.

As I stare at this camp, I feel the truth more than I actually understand it—Eden will close.

"I trusted you," I say, even though I don't even know who I'm talking to. Bryan for bringing me here? Mike and Eva for telling me to hope? Jake? *Who* did I trust?

God, of course. I trusted God that somehow He would work this out. It was like a bargain—I had faith in Him, and in exchange

He was supposed to give me what I wanted. Isn't that what has happened to Wolfgang and Natalie and—in a weird way—even Bryan? They're getting their happy ending. I'm probably not.

Here, I kneel on the ground. I sit on the backs of my heels, press my nose to my knees, and cry hard. Too many images come too fast, as I see everything that will be lost. Future campers. My retreat job. Jake and me. The trees and trails and every tree and cabin. The office and the junk in there. No more campfires or worship songs or first best friends. No more summers with Natalie or Beth. No more paradise.

Why, Lord? Why don't You love me enough to give me this?

"I believe in hope," I hear myself saying to the group this morning. Wait. Was that really this morning? That seems like five years ago.

But that was me, telling all of them that I trust God.

Do I? Because either I do or I don't. Either I believe that God loves me enough to save me, knows me well enough to understand what I really need, and is taking perfect care of me . . .

Or I don't believe that at all.

There's no gray area here. If I do believe that God is taking perfect care of me, then His answer to this prayer might be no. And also that He still loves me.

I stand up and look down to the patio. Jake is standing near the "SAVE EDEN" sign, rubbing his eyes. If the answer to Eden is no, then so is the answer to the possibility of Jake and me as a couple.

Without Eden, we are done.

CHAPTER 68

"I Love You"

Finally, I do make it down The Hill. I sit down beside him at the picnic table.

"There you are." Jake looks at me. "We need to talk."

"I'm not going to like this, am I?"

"I just checked in with Mike. Seventeen thousand. We didn't make it." There are no tears in his eyes, but he's holding his jaw very firm, like he's clenching in the emotion.

Suddenly, the air feels too cold. I start to shiver. Vaguely I remember doing the same thing when Mom was in her last days. Sad news chills me. My insides are shuddering, like my ribs can't contain them.

"This is the answer then," I whisper. "God is saying no to Eden. That's it."

"No, don't oversimplify this, Poppi. I have an idea."

"Not oversimplifying. Jake, I've been here before. Sometimes a no really is just a no."

"Listen to me! I would just go with my idea and take care of it, but I know you. You would want to hear the whole story."

"Okay." My teeth chatter, but Jake doesn't put his arm around me. He is looking at me with so much intensity, I feel like he's trying to will me to like whatever his plan is.

"I'm calling my dad right now to ask for the last thirteen thousand dollars. That'll make it an even thirty. It's still the night of the barbecue, so it'll still count. He'd do it—for me and Savannah. And he'll keep doing it every summer, if that's what Eden needs."

"You know that won't convince the Association. The point was that Eden could prove we're still relevant. We were proving tonight that our community values us. Your family underwriting us isn't doing that."

"The goal was thirty thousand dollars." Jake's tone is the bossy one he gets when he thinks I'm being silly. "Who cares if it's my dad who gives the money or someone else?"

"Your family isn't sustainable support. You weren't planning to come back next summer. Savannah isn't even back this summer. Eden is part of your family's past, not their future."

I stare at the trees and wait for the sour taste of anger at God. I wait for the bite of lost trust. But I don't feel it. Instead, I'm very still, almost peaceful. "Jake, I meant what I said this morning at sunrise. Hope means knowing God is still taking care of us."

"Poppi. Think clearly about what you're saying. Where will you go if Eden closes? I mean, you don't have anywhere else."

"So that's what this is about. It's not Eden that you want to save. It's me."

He takes my hand. "You're tired. Don't make this into a fight."

"Jake, I don't need saving. I will work at Christ Camp. I don't need you to keep Eden open as my halfway house. I can be the retreat director there."

"Christ Camp is two thousand miles away from me. And you're not even excited about that job. Who goes to Minnesota for retreats in the winter?"

"Minnesotans, that's who." I look around at the patio, cluttered with the dunk tank and the lollipop pull and the ring toss. Another chill moves down my spine. "We asked Him the question, now we have to trust there's a longer view then this."

"I have another plan. Come to L.A. with me."

"What are you talking about?" My voice is a whisper. I sort of expected Jake to want to underwrite Eden. But this idea is new.

He pulls me close, into his warmth. "Poppi, I want to be with you. You could try a semester of college. You're better now. You could get a degree like Pete is, in forest management. When you graduate, you could work at a California camp as the executive director. My family will help you with anything you need."

Isn't this what I wanted? For Jake and me to end this summer like Natalie and Wolfie? I try to imagine me in L.A. I could try community college, and I could work at Cove or someplace. Or how easy would it be to take Jake up on his offer for financial help? But that would also be pretty awful. "I would be your charity case."

"No, Poppi." His eyes are so vulnerable. "*I* would be *your* charity case. I need you close to me."

"Jake." I drop my head to his shoulder. "We're too lopsided already."

"What are you talking about?"

"Us." I look up at him. "We fall into this same place every time, into this rhythm of me wanting to be saved and you wanting to do the saving. L.A. is your world. I would be following you around."

"Poppi." He takes my face in his hands. "You're part of me—my hopeful, crazy, idealistic, beautiful part. The part of me that's been missing."

My breath stops. Everything is happening so fast—the good news, the bad. Two steps forward, three back. My body can't adjust. I'm shivering and crying and feverish. "I'm sorry, Jake. I don't like L.A. It isn't right for me. I'll go to Christ."

CHAPTER 69

"God of This City"

As excited as the campers and counselors were for the fundraiser, they're equally dejected today when we announce that Eden didn't raise the money. Everyone's enthusiasm sours into a tedious busyness. Tired and irritable, we all start packing. But it's the most awkward packing ever because it's not just good-bye to one another, it's good-bye to this little world. For everyone and forever.

As I help the kids, my feet feel like they weigh two tons. The end of camp is always hard. Every summer there are tears, millions of hugs, good-bye songs, the signing of T-shirts, and the constant refrain, "I'll see you next summer!" Because our staff and kids can't say that this year, we are all just constantly crying. Seriously, it's all so depressing.

Finally, it's noon and just about time for the parents to come. The scene on the patio as we all wait for them is chaotic. Kenny's boys found Sharpies in the camp office and they're tattooing each other with the words "Eden Forever!" The old Michael W. Smith song "Friends Are Friends Forever" plays from an iPad. Pete has to hold a paper bag for Wren because she's afraid she's hyperventilating.

Beth gathers her girls together for a picture and they all lose it. They're crying so hard, they're leaning on one another and can't look at the camera Eva is holding.

Natalie stands next to me as we watch the girls from Omega yelling their cabin cheer over and over, sobbing more each time.

I look at her. "The parents won't be here for twenty whole minutes. We have to do something about this."

"Agreed. What?"

"Jake!" I call.

He looks up from the Omega girls, who are trying to convince him to get his guitar so they can square-dance one last time.

"Help us gather everyone over here!"

The group seems exhausted from their own emotion and more than happy to form a circle around Jake, Nat, Pete, and me. Someone turns off Michael W. Smith. The patio is almost quiet.

"All right," I say. "Let's play a game. Find a partner and ask each other one thing they've learned this summer. Be ready to share your answer with the group."

The crowd is a mass scramble of partnering up for One. Last. Time.

"Okay, stop!" I call to them. "Best thing you've learned this summer. Go!"

As the teams report their partners' replies, the answers range from simple ("Connie said she learned how to make the perfect doughboy") to mushy ("Maddie said she learned that Eden is the best place in the world, and that she has the best friends in the world right here") to truly rewarding ("Harriet learned God loves her") to sentimental ("Hector learned that Eden was the last good thing ever").

Then the kids start talking about how Eden won't be here and the tears start back up. I look at Natalie with wide eyes. Seven more minutes.

"Here's the deal," Natalie says. "It wasn't about whether or not this barbecue worked. It never was. Poppi has taught me this, in six million different ways this summer, it's always about the bigger thing God is doing. We tried our best for Eden. We worked together. Remember the hope, everyone."

"Something better is coming!" Pete yells.

"Yeah, it is!" Kenny yells. And for once, I'm glad for his affirmation.

"Because there is always hope," I say. I'm suddenly desperate for all of them to know this message, for God to seal it in their souls, so they don't try to learn it the hard way. If your parents split up! If your mom dies! It you fail out of school! If you have no place else to go! No matter what happens, have hope!

But the parking lot is filling with minivans. It's over. If this group hasn't learned this message from our Bible studies, our worships, then I can't teach them now.

They're in God's hands.

CHAPTER 70

"The Lord Bless and Keep You"

Natalie sighs as we start to clean the patio. "And then there were three. I've always wanted to be one of the last ones left on a reality show so I could say that into the camera."

I laugh. "Why does that not surprise me?" Natalie and Jake leave today, and we're all on autopilot. We have so much packing to do that we have no choice but to keep moving forward.

It seems silly that we're cleaning up from the barbecue when Eden will be a pile of rubble in about a week. But it feels more wrong to just leave the barbecue destruction on the patio. Like we're sore losers. Or really just throwing Eden away.

"All right, Girl Scout. We've got a whole lot of mess here. Do you want to save any of this?" Natalie holds up a stack of the testimonials the counselors wrote yesterday.

"Recycle all of it. I don't have any space in my car to save anything." I look at the huge dunking tank. "How should I tear this down?"

"I'll get you some trash bags. Just throw the paper in there and I'll take them to recycling. Jake said he would use a cart to haul away anything too heavy. He'll take the plywood."

Jake is supposed to be leaving by noon. His classes start on Monday, and he has to get moved into his dorm before that. We've been avoiding each other because what can we say at this point? Good-bye . . . forever! Hope life works out for you!

"I'll tear it down as much as I can." I pull away one side of the plywood tub, and the other three sides bang to the ground. The paper spills out lazily, like even it is exhausted from trying to save Eden. I grab an armload of paper filler and stuff it into the trash bag Nat holds.

"Did you shred all this paper just for the dunking booth?" she asks.

"No, I found it in that big Zamboni of a shredder in Bryan's office. It was the only filler I could find in the office."

"Speaking of filler in the office," she says, "has Bryan left?"

"Nope," I say. "And his office is still full. He's got a lot of work to do."

"No problem for him. He's got a bonus as motivation to get it done." She tosses a bag of paper aside.

I look at the ripped-up paper scraps and shreds I'm stuffing into the black trash bag. Some of the torn pieces are large enough that I can read what's printed on them. I thought they were old camp policy forms, but most of the paper has numbers on it. The numbers are big. Lots of zeroes.

"Do you know what this is?" I hold up a torn piece with part of a yellow-and-green emblem on it.

"Hey, that's the logo for Sunny Savings." Natalie squints at it. "I can tell by the edges of the sun—they're neon green. It's where I have my account. It's the cutest place. The tellers wear sun T-shirts and these bright green shorts to match."

"These are bank statements? But Eden uses First United Bank."

"Are they statements?" Natalie looks at the pieces in her hands. "I have no clue. I just know they're from Sunny."

"Who tears up bank statements? That's so weird."

"I rip up my statement every month too. It's dumb that they even send it. I mean, everything about your account is on the app."

Natalie picks up another clump that isn't completely shredded. "This one says it's a withdrawal receipt."

"Wow," I say. "Look at this. It's for nine thousand dollars. I wonder what that's for."

"You could ask Bryan. Except he'll probably passively-aggressively ignore you, avoid your question, and then leave. It'll be the exact right ending to his exactly wrong reign here."

I feel a slight nudge, deep inside my brain. Suddenly these numbers seem really important. "I'm probably still desperate, but maybe this means something. I'm going to check them out."

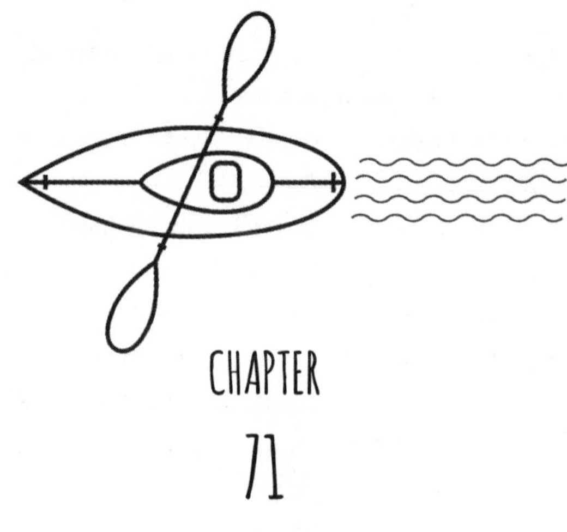

CHAPTER 71

"Give Thanks"

"What are you looking for?"

I jump up and bang my knee on the open filing cabinet drawer. Natalie stands at the office door, wearing oversize gold sunglasses and holding a matching rose gold purse.

"Nat! Are you leaving already?"

"Already? I'm late, like always. I told my parents I was leaving here by one." She looks at her cell. "It's two thirty now."

"Two thirty?" That means Bryan will be back any minute. "Where's Jake?"

"Stalling, if you ask me. He really needed to leave by noon to get his dorm assignment before the residence office closed. But he's still in there packing. He even tolerated a long, rambling walk down memory lane with me. We stood in every cabin, and I told him my best and worst moments."

I smile. "Sorry I missed that."

"Me too. I even looked for you." She cranes her neck to see into the open filing cabinet drawers. "What are you doing?"

"Trying to find out where these bank statements are from. It's a waste of time, I'm sure. I should be packing."

"The Sunny Savings one? It's superstrange, right? You said Eden doesn't even have an account there."

"It's nothing, I'm sure." I walk outside and Natalie follows. "I just have this unsettled feeling."

"Maybe you'll discover the secret and save Eden." Then she turns to me and puts her hands on my shoulders. "You're in luck. I'm all good-byed out. You're dodging the biggest sobfest of your life."

"Darn." I smile.

"Don't worry. You still get the slew of unsolicited love advice."

"Not unsolicited. You're actually leaving this summer with a boyfriend. Your advice is valuable."

"Poppi, take a page out of the German Playbook of Love. Tell Jake exactly how miserable you are to move to Christ Camp. Tell him how you will one day come back to him." She shakes my shoulders. "And then do that, Poppi. You belong with Jake."

"Oh, Nat. You know it's much more complicated than all that."

"This is me, Queen Complicate-It-All. I'm telling you it doesn't have to be. Eden is over and gone. Be one of the lasting good things to come from it."

I hug her. "I love you, Nat. Promise to visit me in Minnesota? You'll love Christ."

"Minnesota? You mean the motherland of the entire Target corporation? And home to the largest mall in the United States? Um, *ye-ah*. Count on me before Christmas. I'll show up on your doorstep with my AmEx, ready for major retail therapy because both you and Eden have disappeared from my life."

"Oh, good." I hug her again. "I'm holding you to that."

CHAPTER 72

"Lord, I Lift Your Name on High"

There are no answers on Eden's laptop. The spreadsheet I've looked at so many times this summer has the exact numbers I've seen before—the big gift from George Jackson Bass, the YouCanShare donations, the money from the barbecue, and the camper registration fees. I know all these deposits. I worried over these amounts all summer. These aren't the huge numbers that are on the Sunny Savings shreds. These match up perfectly with the balances on the First United Bank website.

Where is the Sunny Savings account? Is it Eden's? And if it is, why have I never seen it?

I tiptoe to Bryan's office door and try it. Locked, of course. I pull my keys from my pocket. My master key that's supposed to unlock any door at camp doesn't turn.

Somewhere else. There has to be a key to this door somewhere else—besides in Bryan's pocket, of course.

I take out my cell and call Natalie. It rings three times before she answers. "Hey," I breathe. "Quick question for you."

"Poppi? What's going on?"

"Where's the key to Bryan's office?"

"Oooh. Did you figure something out with Sunny Savings?"

"Not yet. But I'm trying,"

"I'm not sure about the key. You could ask Jake."

"He's all the way over in his cabin. I only have one minute before Bryan comes back."

"There are two keys in the main desk drawer. Try those. If they don't work, you'll have to ask Jake."

I run to the desk. "I promise to call you soon," I say. "Love you."

The second key works, and within ten seconds, I'm pushing Bryan's door open. The place is packing chaos. Every inch of floor space is covered with boxes—one with his baseballs, another with desk supplies, another filled with fat manila folders.

Panting, I rush to that one. Bryan left the lights on, so I'm guessing he'll be right back. I pull heavy folders out of the box, but none of them are about Eden's finances. Architectural plans for his house in Michigan, lists of contacts, receipts from eBay auctions, notes about the STUF deal. I hear a noise and turn toward the door.

And then, bingo. There's the box right there. It's sitting on his black desk chair, and it's labeled, "Statements."

I toss off the lid and find a pile of papers from Sunny Savings. With Bryan's name on them. These are the numbers I was looking for—on an account summary dated last week, there's a record for a balance of $260,000. I take a picture of it with my phone.

What am I doing? Stealing? Maybe the money is legitimate and I'm taking pictures of Bryan's personal property. He could have inherited the money. But then why would he shred the other statements? Maybe Natalie is right. Maybe he manages his account electronically and these statements are redundant. Maybe he's innocent.

Yeah, right. That shredder is too nice. No one invests in a ginormous shredder unless they're serious about covering something up. Bryan is too careful, too paranoid, too sneaky, too shifty, too bitter. I believe this quarter of a million dollars is Eden's money.

I have to prove it, though. I can't paste the Sunny Savings shreds and pieces back together before the real estate closing tomorrow morning. The statements in this box are only balances. I have to find a record of transfers from Eden's First United accounts into Bryan's Sunny Savings account.

Pushing the lid back onto the statements box, I look around for anything else. I thread my way through the boxes. Just as I'm reaching to pull off the lid off the largest one, the office door opens.

I look up to see Bryan marching toward me. "What are you doing in here?"

CHAPTER 73

"One, Two, Three, the Devil's After Me!"

I back away from him. "What do you mean?"

Bryan grabs my arm. "Why are you in my office?" he growls. "How did you get in here?"

"There's a key in the desk. I needed—something."

His fingers are digging into the flesh just below my sleeve. "Nothing in here belongs to you."

I yank my arm and it slips from his fingers. "I needed something for the closing tomorrow. Eva asked me to grab some past records." I'm terrible at lying. Someone as slimy as Bryan will see right through me.

His eyes dart to the box of bank statements. The lid is on. He won't know about the picture on my phone. "Get out of my stuff," he snarls.

I scoot through the door, adrenaline pumping as I run straight to my cabin. I rub my arm where it throbs from Bryan's grip as I yank out my laptop.

"Jake!" I can hear him packing in his room. "Get out here right now!"

He comes into the staff lounge, holding a stack of shirts. On top is the pale blue alligator shirt he was wearing the first day I met him. "What are you doing?"

"Saving Eden," I say.

He sits next to me on the stained orange couch. "What are you talking about?"

As I open Eden's account on the First United Bank site, I fill Jake in on what's going on. "We need to go through every withdrawal from the summer. We have to find one suspicious withdrawal. Just one. We can take that to the Association with the picture on my phone to prove that Bryan's been stealing money."

"How do we know what's suspicious?" He leans over to study the computer. "We can't remember every legitimate withdrawal from the past three months."

"We'll remember the big ones."

"I've never even heard of a Sunny Savings account. When I've handled the books, it's always been First United."

"Exactly. Because Sunny Savings is Bryan's personal account."

"You really think he's been pilfering money from the Association's special offerings into a whole separate account? That would be insane."

"It would be just like him," I say.

Between the two of us, we do manage to account for every single withdrawal. But after an hour of checking, nothing seems out of line. "I'm sorry, Poppi," he says. "No proof here that Bryan has taken anything."

There is proof somewhere. All the little questions from the summer are swirling together to make sense. His watch and signed baseballs. The timeline of building his house. The mysterious repairs he did over the winter. "But what about the winter finances? Bryan handles Eden's books the other nine months of the year, right?"

"That's true." Jake looks at me. "I've never seen the other months. They're not on these spreadsheets. Remember? The computers crashed this winter. We have no financials from those months."

"But we're logged into Eden's account now. First United has the whole year on their website. We can check the past few months for something strange."

I double-click on April. The page opens. I gasp. "Look at this!" I yell. "Look look look!" Listed there are some of the typical $30- and $40-dollar withdrawals. But that's not all. There are account transfers for $734, $3,020, $4,300. "What could those be for?"

"I don't know." Jake's voice is breathless. "Hold on. Check March."

The withdrawals are even higher there—several for over $5,000, one for $9,060. "Look at February!" Jake yells. "These are crazy."

"This is it," I whisper. "This was the problem all along." I look at Jake. "Bryan."

Jake's mouth hangs open. "He did it in withdrawals of different amounts so no one would get suspicious. It looks like he really spread them out." Jake grabs the laptop from me, and he's scrolling back through months of Eden's accounts. "You know what? I've never seen the books for any months except for summer."

"And you never checked the bank's website?"

"Why would I? It's hard enough to keep up with Eden's finances in the summer. When would I have time to look at past months?" He's shaking his head. "But now I feel like such an idiot. Eden has terrible finances because Bryan has embezzled $260,000."

"Why didn't Mike or anyone from the Association check the accounts?"

"I guess they just trusted him."

"We can prove this to Mike." I hold up the Sunny Savings picture on my phone. "We've got evidence of the withdrawals from the First United website. And the proof of the Sunny Savings account balance. That's enough."

"That is absolutely enough!" Jake stands. "Let's get over to the Brownes' house."

CHAPTER 74

"More Precious Than Silver"

Mike and Eva Browne live only a few minutes from camp. While Jake drives to their house, we piece together what this might mean. "Eden will stay open. I could live here and work as the retreat director!" I'm bouncing up and down, feeling very much like I'm Natalie after a morning of coffee. "I don't have to go to Minnesota. Maybe God is still saying yes to Eden!"

We ring the doorbell at the Brownes' house, and Mike lets us in. He sees the laptop in my hand and starts by saying, "Poppi, I'm sorry. There's really nothing I can do about tomorrow morning. There's no way they're going to change their minds."

"Hear us out," Jake says. "Because I think they might."

I'm already heading into their living room. "We have proof, Mike. Bryan has been stealing from Eden."

We sit on the couch with Eva and Mike on either side of us and present the evidence: an account with a quarter of a million dollars in Bryan's name and large withdrawals from Eden's account during months Bryan had solo access to the accounts. When we lay it all out like this, it lines up as perfect sense. Of course, this has been the problem the whole time. Bryan.

Mike looks over at Eva, blinking. "You've been right about Bryan." His voice sounds sad. "Look at this. Look what he's been doing for years. Right under our noses."

"Eden was making it," I say, my voice high with excitement. "The donations, the camper tuition, the low expenses. It was self-sufficient. It was thriving."

"Call an Association meeting!" Eva yells.

"Eden doesn't have to sell, does it?" Jake asks.

"No." Mike smiles. "Eden does not have to sell."

It's almost eleven by the time the Association members gather at the Brownes' house. It becomes kind of an impromptu party as Eva pulls out chips and salsa and sodas. Beth is up too. She's dying to text the news to all the counselors, but her dad makes her wait until we know something for sure.

The Association members seem to be in shock. Harvey, a grandpa type in his sixties, keeps asking for the timeline of everything. And he's full of questions. When did Bryan start this? Was he asking for special offerings to use the money for himself? Harvey's been around the longest, so it's hardest for him to believe it. The other members were elected in the last couple of years—after Bryan had started this. Maybe it's easier for them.

Mike starts talking to the Association. "We will have to have an audit, of course. But if we can prove that $260,000 belongs to the camp, we could use that as the foundation for the next several summers—no more special offerings. Eden will be healthier than it's ever been."

I'm bouncing on my heels. I add, "With over one hundred campers registered, we're all ready for next summer. I can use some of the funds to travel to colleges and recruit more staff. Eden will host retreats in the winter, and the barbecue can become an annual event. Over Christmas and Thanksgiving we'll rent the camp out to families for reunions."

“But we still don’t have an executive director,” Chris points out. He’s in his twenties and a youth director at a church in Altadena. He’s one of the members who wanted to sell Eden.

Harvey, who was the director before Bryan, raises his hand. “I could step in for a while. Until we find someone else.”

“Actually . . .” Mike stops pacing to look across the room at Eva. “I think we would be happy to take over that role.”

“We need to talk about what we would do with the house. And the girls would have to drive farther to school,” Eva says, but she’s grinning.

“YES!” Beth screams from the steps where she’s been listening. “Yes to living at Eden full time!”

Eva laughs. “I think that’s a yes from the Browne family.”

CHAPTER 75

"Friends Are Friends Forever"

Jake sleeps on the couch and I sleep in the other bed in Beth's room. Actually, we barely sleep at all. We're too full of plans about what this means for Eden. We FaceTime Nat and the other counselors. Jake keeps reminding us that we don't know for sure what's happening, but his is a lost cause. The whole night is a blitz of phone calls and texts and screeching. Natalie complains she always leaves just when something exciting happens.

After Mike eats breakfast, he calls the nonprofit attorney who represents Eden. His name is Nate and he listens while Mike explains everything to him. Nate calls Hilary Steinmal, and she calls STUF's legal counsel. While the attorneys are battling out whether the sale is legal, Mike notifies the police and tells them to meet us at Eden. They say they'll have a detective there by Monday.

Beth makes Jake and me (really Jake, of course) very crispy bacon, and we all sit around the table and listen to her parents on their phones, updating the other Association members.

Jake sips his third cup of coffee. "I want to ask Bryan what he was thinking. Was he also stealing from Eden all those years when I was a kid? Is he a kleptomaniac? Or did he just get greedy?"

Beth pokes at her Frosted Flakes. "Maybe it was just too tempting? He had no accountability for so many years. And he always struck me as kind of an insecure guy."

We sit quietly for a moment, listening to Mike in the next room on the phone with Nate. I kick Jake under the table. "In the end, the lawyers will be the ones who save Eden, huh?"

"There won't be an end for a very long time," he says. "Bryan's going to have to return the money. I wonder if he was using that account as his down payment for his new house. He'll probably have to declare bankruptcy."

"Do you think he'll go to jail?" Beth asks. Her little sister, Marie, is five and listening closely to everything we're saying. I think she's trying to figure out if she's moving to Eden.

"No. I'm sure they'll strike some kind of deal with him—maybe he gives them all the money back and they don't press charges." Jake takes another piece of bacon. "But he's pretty busted."

Marie asks Beth to go upstairs with her to help her get dressed. Jake takes my hand. "Come outside with me to talk for a second. I really do need to get back to camp and finish packing."

We pass through the living room, and Eva, who is sitting next to Mike on the couch, is nodding dramatically and smiling.

I smile back and mouth, "YAY!"

I follow Jake out onto the porch. He sits down and pulls me next to him. "And look at that. You just got the job as Eden's retreat director."

"I think you might be right."

"Are you happy?"

"With Mike and Eva as my bosses and the Browne girls as my co-workers? It's all pretty amazing."

"Almost perfect, huh?" He kisses the top of my head. His voice is sad. Because we both know the other half of that "almost."

"Want me to go back with you to pack up?" I ask.

"No, you stay here. Help them figure out everything with the Association. You have so much to talk to them about now."

"Okay," I say. Because, really, what else can I do? We both know this is good-bye. There will not be a last-minute discovery that saves us. From the moment we met, through all the moments together this summer, we knew we would go our separate ways in the end. I was an idiot to imagine anything else.

He tilts my chin up to him. "Things are about to get crazy for both of us. Don't forget everything. Don't forget how much I don't want to leave you. Don't forget that you can call me anytime. Don't forget how much I'm going to miss you."

"All right. And you don't forget . . ." I say the only thing I can think of. "We believe in hope."

Jake looks at me with his certain mix of pity and affection. It's the look he always gets when I believe in something impossible. "Okay."

He stands and walks to his Hummer, only looking back to wave once at me. It's that little wave that makes my tears start. Because that wave—more than the words or the kiss—reminds me that I might really never see him again.

CHAPTER 76

"Give Me Oil in My Lamp"

From: natsthename@freespace.com

To: poppisavot@eden.com

Date: December 20

Subj: We Are Going To Minnesota in Six Days!!

Poppi!

Attached are so many details you need to know about our trip. Please stay calm about the itinerary. I can already hear you complaining about three days at Mall of America, but when you see the attached store directory, you'll understand that we will need at least that long to really do it justice. If you want to stay home with your Aunt Lily ONE DAY, you can, but don't pick Wednesday because that's Sporting Goods Day, and my Christmas gift for you is a new fleece. That's not yellow.

My other Christmas gift to you is that I will probably just sleep at the airport because—OHMYGOODNESS—do people really get up this early? When you get to LAX, you'll find me wrapped in my blankets by our gate, and then just roll my body down the hall and onto the plane. And no comments about my luggage because sweaters and snow boots just take a lot of space, okay?

Wolfie is crazy jealous we're going to Minnesota. And I'm like, it will be all snow, and then he tells me so many little-known facts. (The farmland in southern Minnesota is the most lush in the United States. And—more importantly—Target tests all their products at their flagship store at the Nicollet Mall.) This will be my official pilgrimage to see Everything Target.

BTW . . . just so you're prepared for our trip, please know that I have been schooling Wolfgang about stuff too and I'm currently living in '70s TV shows. I found all these old *Scooby Doo* episodes on Netflix and I'm making him watch them. I've convinced him they're important American pop culture, but really I just like the part at the end where the villain goes, "And I would've gotten away with it, if it wasn't for you meddling kids!" Totally Bryan. Don't you think?

Thanks for forwarding along his apology. SO WEIRD he's going to the same church as you and the Brownes. When Pastor Sean preaches on the Ten Commandments, does everyone look at Bryan for the Seventh? KIDDING!

Also, I haven't heard from Jake all week. Where is he? I've done it all, dominated his Facebook wall, harassed him on Snapchat, stalker-level texted, and even called to actually speak to him, like they did in the olden days. Nada.

If you ask me (you didn't, but whatever), he is taking too many classes. You called it, sister. The guy is obsessed with getting into law school at some crazy early age—like he's trying to set an actual record.

Okay! Text me that you got this. I cannot wait to hug your neck and meet the whole Savot clan.

EEEEEK!

Nat

CHAPTER 77

"Everlasting God"

I click away from the email and smile. The trip home is exactly what I need. In the Cities, we'll stay with Aunt Lily, and I think she'll like Natalie. At least, she'll be entertained by Natalie.

In Eagle, we'll stay with my Uncle Ed, who will not know what to make of Natalie. We'll see my dad, and I'll drive Natalie by the old farmhouse. Taking her along will feel like when they bring those Comfort Dogs to a disaster area. Natalie is like the golden retriever of emotions. Everyone needs a Natalie to turn hard things into inside jokes.

Except for anything about Wolfgang—she does not joke about him. She's going to USC next year and she—seriously—has their entire future planned.

We don't talk about Jake much. As I've pointed out to Nat, if I were in L.A. right now, I would spend all day waiting for him. Exactly like I told him—we would be lopsided. This worked out so much better. Jake's doing his dream, I'm doing mine.

Being at Eden without Jake can be so hard. Every day I think about what he would say if he were here. When I'm eating crispy bacon and drinking the (evil) coffee, I imagine him sitting next to me, telling me the plan for the day.

Better not to think about that. Better to focus on Rehab Eden. Winter here is quiet and peaceful. Eva and I work together on retreat plans and recruiting trips and camp projects. In the afternoons, Beth and Marie come home from school, and I help them with their homework. We're kind of a little family.

Most of all, it's like a new season for God and me. Eva and I are working through a Bible study on grief. I think about what I said to the staff on that last day. Over and over I think about it . . . every time I pass the patio or that spot where I first knew I belonged at Eden.

I believe in hope. And our God is the God of all hope.

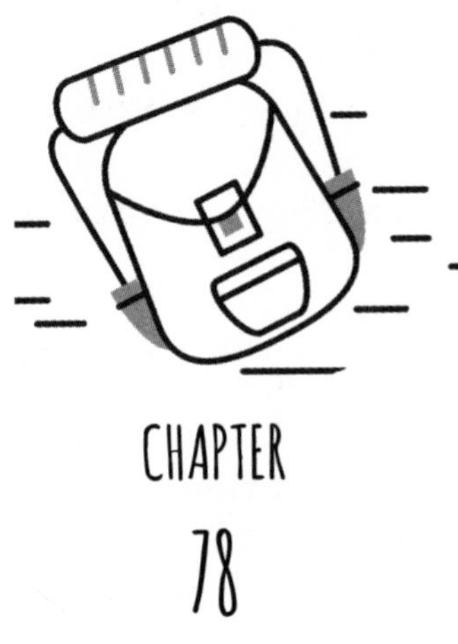

CHAPTER 78

"Everlasting Love"

"Eighty people. Are you ready for this?" Eva looks at me from her computer. "We'll have every bunk full."

"It'll be fun. I want to test the new beds. Nothing like filling them up to see if they're comfortable."

"I guess. It's just so—new. The winters have always been quiet at Eden. We used to always come to hike during the holidays. I'm having trouble getting used to the idea of sixty people here for Christmas. That's a lot of ham!"

"It'll be fine. So fun to have a family reunion here."

"So fun," she agrees.

Eva and I have so many plans for the Erickson family. A bonfire one night. Doughboys another. S'mores (with peanut butter cups, of course). Maybe even a game of Operation Interrogation.

"I'm going up to the cabins to make sure everything is perfect for them."

Eva nods. "Good. See if we forgot anything at all. One hour left."

As I sweep pine needles from the patio where the Erickson family will hold worship, I think about Jake. I wonder what he's told his family about us. Will they ask about me when he goes home for Christmas? Maybe they're so used to him cycling through girlfriends that they realize I was just another summer fling. For all I know, he's making Christmas plans with another girl right now.

"Hi."

I look up. My rake drops to the ground. "What are you doing here?"

Jake smiles. "Watching you."

His voice sounds so strong and real. But I don't believe it. Surely he's a figment of my imagination. "Are you really here?"

He closes the distance between us and lifts me off the ground. "Are you really this beautiful?" He sets me down, wraps his arms around me, and kisses me like I've wanted him to for four months.

I clap my hands. "You haven't been answering texts because you're spending Christmas *here*?"

"I'm not here for Christmas."

"You're not?"

"I'm here to apply for a job. Anything you got—maintenance man, cabin cleaner, grouchy cook?"

"Hold on. What are you talking about?"

He sits down in a patch of sunlight. "I'm taking that semester off." A sunray streams onto his face, and he looks as tired as I've ever seen him. Actually, he doesn't look much like himself at all. He's thinner—the skin hangs on his face and has a grayish glow. His shoulders are hunched. His eyes are bloodshot.

"What happened?"

"I made a mistake, Poppi. I prayed about my decision to leave—and it felt wrong. I should've known not to go back in August." He shakes his head. "But it seemed completely irresponsible to not follow through with college."

"What felt irresponsible? UCLA and all the classes?" I'm having trouble understanding everything he's saying. I'm having trouble believing I'm talking to him. "But I asked you to stay here. I asked you to take a semester off, way back when you had the flu."

"I should have listened to you." He rubs his eyes. "I don't know. I'm trying to figure all this out. All I know right now is that I'm not happy. And I want to be happy. I hated school this semester. All the time, I want to be at Eden. With you."

"Stop. I need to know the facts. Did you drop out of college?"

"I'm taking a one-semester leave. To figure stuff out. When I looked at my life, I always thought that I was successful in spite of my summers at Eden. I looked at them as a break from real life. I thought Eden looked good on college applications and that school was real life."

"Right . . ."

"But you rubbed off on me. I started to see that success could be a lot of different paths. And this whole semester, I've been thinking about that. What if I tried something totally different? What about a sabbatical this semester? I could spend a few months here, working outside with you, and then help out during the summer."

"Really? This is so incredibly weird." I squeeze his shoulders. "So incredibly good."

"And then it just clicked. It doesn't have to be as hard as I was making it. You're at Eden, I could be here too. Why not give it a try? There's a ton to do before summer." He gazes at me. "And if you'll have my help, this is what I'd be happy doing."

I gaze back at him. "Before you say that, you need to know, there are some tough times going on at Eden too."

"What are you talking about?"

"If you want a job here, you have to understand that the days are long."

"Okay?"

"We get up early and start with a run. None of these pansy nine-minute miles. I'm doing eights now."

He grins. "Finally."

"Other tough parts about Eden—we eat outside, under the trees, in the sunshine. It's usually as hot as seventy degrees or as cold as sixty."

"Brutal."

"And then more work. If you promise to work hard, you can set your desk next to mine—"

"No way." He buries his head in my shoulder. "My work will be outside. I'm not staring at a computer under fluorescent lights ever again."

"Okay, outside for you then." I tap his nose. "But you have to come up for dinner. Homemade every night. And then more work—walks around the lake, sometimes we light a campfire for late-night meetings. And then there's your salary. The pay here is pretty low."

He wraps his arms tightly around me. "I would say this position pays off perfectly," he whispers in my ear.

"You're hired," I whisper back.

The End.